For Gale, the sister
I never knew I needed

THE LAST RIDER

MIST RIDERS
BOOK SIX

Stella Fitzsimons

BUTTERFLY ELECTRIC PRESS

THE LAST RIDER

The Chronicles of Luna Mae

Chapter 1

"Impossible," I told Winter. "There's no chance I can extract drinking water from my own cell energy. That's not a thing. Stop messing."

He pulled my back against his chest as we lay in bed. "It most certainly is a thing," he insisted. "And I promise I'm not messing with you. You only need to have a little faith."

Right.

He took my hands. "Good," he said. "Keep your hands sealed, just like this, and let your core latch onto the humidity in the air."

I squeezed my hands together. Nothing. I sighed. "You're not funny."

He turned my head to peer into my eyes. "The trick is to bypass the outward energy burst, then force moisture to your skin. Mix that with a hyper fluid elemental source and... *Shazam!* You'll have water. It will literally flow from your fingers."

"Have you ever done this?"

Darkness crept up his face. "It's a mist rider thing."

"So, if I'm getting this right, if I am ever stuck in a desert, I'll just be able to suck my thumb, *like this*, and I'll never go thirsty."

I winked.

"Stop that," he said, swallowing hard. "You'll need some elemental source, even if it is only a few drops of morning dew, or the last drops of water in a flask, but basically, in theory, yes."

I laughed. "Sometimes you're all theories and no fun."

He reached under the sheets to attack my midsection with his fingers.

"Stop," I protested as I squirmed away. "You know I hate tickling."

"Then don't be a brat."

Uh, no. It's too fun being a brat.

We kissed. I never wanted this simple, sensual state of happiness to end. And I never wanted to put clothes on again. For three days, we'd stayed in bed, ordering food delivery, catnapping and making love.

"How much longer do we have?" I said.

Winter shrugged. "Not long. I can try to prolong my mortality if that's what you want."

Yes, please! Mortal Winter was the most fun.

"I'll take as much as you can give," I said, hopeful.

A mischievous light played in his eyes.

"All men have the same mind," I said, maybe blushing a little.

He squeezed my hands again, pushing my palms flush together. Water sprayed from my fingers like a tiny fountain, then stopped abruptly.

Holy fu--!

The doorbell rang.

Winter furrowed his brow. "Kirsi."

I slipped into loose shorts and a t-shirt and headed for the door. Kirsi's grim expression warned of bad news.

She looked over my apartment. "It's great that you guys are getting it on like rabbits, but maybe check your phones every now and again."

My eyes darted to my phone on the floor. Dead. I'd figured the world could take a backseat for once.

"What manner of mayhem do you bring to us?" Winter said, pulling on an Aztec t-shirt I bought him at the bookstore.

"The Society of Immortal Sisterhood is under attack," she said. "Our central enclave was ransacked last night. We fear our coffeehouses could be next."

The sisterhood ran several bookstore-cafés around the world.

Winter raised an eyebrow. "Who? And for what possible reason?"

Kirsi hesitated. "It's just a hunch, but we think maybe it's a necromantic sect coming after the Seventh Council Seal."

Necromancers? If Horror was behind this, I swear, I'd skin him alive.

Kirsi was the official guard of the Seal, but she didn't exactly carry it in her purse. Last time I checked, the Seal was safely tucked away in the magistrate court vaults along with other potentially hazardous magical artifacts.

"Why would they think the Seal would be with the Sisterhood?"

Winter looked away. He knew something and hadn't bothered to share it with me. *What else is new?*

Kirsi exhaled noisily. "Düsternis asked me to hide the Seal."

"Wait, the Grand Magistrate asked you to remove the Seal from the court? There's no way that's allowed. It makes no sense."

The magic of the Seal was instrumental in safeguarding the council from supernatural intruders and augmenting the council's access to powerful ley line energy. Removing it from the grounds would make the magistrates more vulnerable. Every council and every order in the magic realm had at least one seal bonded to them, some more powerful than others. The Seventh Council Seal was one of the most powerful.

Kirsi struggled to get the next words out. "Düsternis added cyphers written in the Eternal language to the script at the core of the Seal. When spoken, they can banish Eternals."

Wow. I had no words. "Again, that can't be sanctioned."

"Of course not," Kirsi said. "The council thought it a necessary contingency to put in place in case Horror came for us. But if the Eternals were to find out their archaic symbology was being used as a weapon by the council, the consequences would be dire."

Yeah, Eternals would see this as a provocation. No doubt about that. They were a faction of hyper charged sourpusses who hated sharing. A rift between Eternals and the Seventh Council would lay waste to half the magic world.

I struggled to comprehend. "So, the Seal is with the Sisterhood?"

"No."

"Where then?"

Winter sneered. "She won't tell you. She can't. She must guard that secret with her life."

I glared at him. "You better shut it. I can see you're clearly keeping a closet full of secrets from me yourself. I'll deal with you later."

Kirsi was amused until she received my glare.

"Are you entirely sure the Seal is safe wherever you've hidden it?" I said.

"It is, but all bets are off if an Eternal goes after it."

Shit. "And what if it's Horror himself?"

Their silence confirmed what I already knew in my gut. Horror was suspect number one. So much for stepping back and giving me space.

What are you up to now, Daddy from hell?

I asked the obvious. "And we think he'll use it to banish any Eternal who might wish to stand in his way?"

Kirsi shrugged. "Who knows what's in a maniac's mind? He might want access to the exact combination of the banishing symbols, or he might want to protect himself from Düsternis, or use the Seal for some still darker purpose. There's no way to know what shade of crazy he desires."

"Either way, we're fucked."

They both regarded me with blank expressions.

"Sneaky bastard," I said. "It explains why I couldn't connect to his essence or locate him when I tried the other day. He's locked me out."

"The only thing we can do now is defend the Sisters and our coffeehouses," Kirsi said. "It won't be easy."

"Count us in," Winter said.

Kirsi arched an eyebrow. "In your condition? I don't think so."

"Kirsi, I might not be a magistrate anymore, but I'm still your friend."

"Yeah, an all too *mortal* friend."

"Mortal or not, I have access to a significant amount of power, not to mention I can still kick ass with my good old bare hands."

Kirsi hardened. "I will not be responsible for your death."

She was right. He was the strongest man I knew, but being mortal made him forever vulnerable. All mortals hung by a thread, but most of them didn't have deathless gods as enemies. Powerful entities were lined up to vanquish Winter. Everything was fine and dandy as long as we hid out in our little love nest, but the moment he stepped outside it, he'd be in perpetual peril. Hell, he could even die in a car crash or slip on wet pavement.

I cupped his shoulder. "Switch back. Reboot your immortality."

"That's not how it works. My core isn't there yet."

"That settles it," Kirsi said.

Winter looked pissed. "Does it?"

"Yes, you thick-brained man," she said. "You're sitting this one out."

Winter's eyes flashed with frustration, but he said nothing.

"Are you going back to the coffee shop?" I asked Kirsi.

"No, I'm off to alert Herja."

Herja was co-founder of the Sisterhood, along with Sigrún, and she was among the high order of Valkyries who possessed the rarest supernatural powers. The Sisters trusted her, even deferred to her. When Ölrún died in the Night-wood battle against Horror's necromantic forces, Herja had blamed herself. Soon afterwards, she retreated to her land in the old Valkyrie realm to cleanse her aura and mourn the passing of a beloved friend.

"I thought maybe you'd go with me, Luna," Kirsi continued. "Herja is unreachable by design. We'll need all the magic we can muster to penetrate her wards and subdue her pets."

Uh... pets? What now?

Winter stood with a pained grimace.

Kirsi blinked. "Where do you think you're going?"

"I am her shadow and therefore am forever by her side," he said.

"You may be her shadow, but you're not now a Shadow Warrior."

"Come on, *Kirs*," I said, "at least give it up for his play on words. If we're just going to Herja's fortified dwelling, there's no harm in bringing along a little arm candy."

Kirsi hissed. "Okay, that's gross. The only lovesick dove I want to see is one roasting on the tip of my spear. And if you think no harm can come from breaking into Herja's retreat, you still have much to learn, mist rider."

Chapter 2

THE BATTERED SIGN HANGING from a giant skeletal tree creaked in the howling wind. The words, carved unevenly into the splintered green wood, had chipped away at their edges but were still legible: Time wasted is no time at all.

Just beyond the tree, a translucent boundary of wards guarded a wintery landscape. Red and yellow cottages spread across the land. Behind the homes, snow-covered fir trees led back to a frozen pond emanating an arctic mist. The Valkyries had claimed this enchanted piece of land in Lapland centuries ago and made it their home.

"Will Herja sense we're here?" I said.

"Not likely," Kirsi said. "She's absorbed herself in a ritual of introspection for months. Her instincts have completely surrendered to a meditative state of consciousness."

"Then how will we breach that enormous ward fence?"

Kirsi chuckled. "Nothing in life is easy. I'd be more worried about what lies behind it, to be honest."

The cute Scandinavian style farmhouses and icy winter woods appeared as wholesome and safe as a Christmas card.

Whatever danger it was that Kirsi alluded to was not visible to the naked eye.

Kirsi approached the fence, sword in hand.

I threw a side glance at Winter. "Any insight would be appreciated."

He shrugged. "I'm not a Valkyrie whisperer."

The fence flickered, changing colors multiple times as it did. I couldn't latch onto the magic that propelled the wards. There was nothing familiar about their formation.

"Can you deactivate them, Kirsi?" Winter said.

"Herja was among the first Valkyries. I am no match for her powers."

"Maybe if we all joined forces..." I suggested.

Kirsi shook her head. "That's messy. It could take days to locate and defuse all her traps. Our best bet is that a few of her companions will feel the disturbance."

"What disturbance?" I said.

And what companions for that matter?

Kirsi rammed her sword through the fence. The wards thundered and roared so loud we had to cover our ears. The sky above us turned dark purple. A viscous, black liquid spilled out of the fence like tar. I jumped back.

A huge and furry creature exploded through the fence. Standing at least seven feet tall at its shoulders and bearing thick, imposing horns, two camel-like humps and a furry midnight-blue hide that covered its entire body, including the eyes, it snorted as it came to a sudden halt.

The creature exhaled fire as its jaws snapped open revealing two rows of sharp yellow teeth.

I inhaled its foul scent as I tried to swallow.

The blue beast glided to us slowly like a giant buffalo-camel on wheels.

"Don't hurt it," Kirsi said.

The beast charged.

Don't hurt it? Really? It's about to gore us all to hell.

I swerved out of the beast's way just in time, then planted myself in front of Winter to protect him.

He moved me aside and ran at the beast, locking his hands on its horns.

Oh shit.

I quickly formed a lasso of raw energy and hurled it at the beast, trapping its back legs. The beast's body vibrated with energy of its own, quickly dissolving my energy lasso.

The beast snarled and knocked Winter back. Winter's feet slid, his face straining, before he dug in and regained the upper hand.

Kirsi jumped on the beast's back, grabbing the stringy mane.

Oh, yeah, I forgot. Both of them are idiots.

The beast shook Kirsi off its back and snorted. I reacted instinctively, pressing my hands together. A fountain of water spilled out, drenching the beast and extinguishing the fire pouring out of its nostrils before it hit Winter's chest.

The beast wailed as if the water were hot oil.

The fence's tar-like discharge came to life, spreading out on the ground in every direction like a burning moat. The beast retreated to the fence.

"Now!" Kirsi yelled out as a wedge opened in the ward fence to allow the creature reentry.

We dashed as one, then clutched to the beast's fur to pull ourselves through the seam to the other side of the ward wall. I felt the surge of the wards on my skin as I slid through them, infused with a power both living and ancient—almost divine.

We hit the ground and tumbled onto our feet, sprinting in the direction of the first row of cottages. The cottages receded away from us, back toward the forest like a cruel mirage.

The blue beast charged after us, its heavy hoofs striking the ground with hellish thuds. I sensed the snow all around us puff up, forming shivering mounds like waves made of Jell-O.

Things drilled their way through the waves, springing to the surface. I focused on the moving farmhouses ahead. Whatever monstrosities Herja kept as pets, I didn't want to know. My breath came out in clumps of steam that froze immediately.

"Herja!" Kirsi shouted. "This is urgent!"

Out of the corner of my eye, I saw a blood-red snake uncoil to a length of thirty... forty feet, painting the snow a deep crimson as it slithered our way.

Holy hell, Kirsi's warning was an understatement. Herja didn't play.

The cottages stopped moving. The front door in one of them swung open. A magical shower of cotton threads rained down on the house like dispersed dandelion seeds, shrouding it in a soft white light, a stark contrast to the mess of fangs and horns all around us.

Herja stepped outside. Tall, imposing, with chestnut-brown hair and a strong, toned body with centuries of murderous muscle memory, Herja had that otherworldly feel about her that only the fiercest of ancients possessed.

"There better be dire cause for all this fuss, sister," Herja said.

"This wouldn't happen if you shared a key with one of your sisters."

Herja frowned. "This is my solitary retreat, not a social salon for bored and gossiping Valkyries."

Kirsi sighed. "Believe me, if there was another way…"

Herja glanced at Winter and me. "And them? Why did you have to bring your whole caravan?"

"I didn't want to die alone. They make good chew toys for your beasts."

Not funny, Kirs. (Okay, maybe a smidge.)

Herja huffed. "I suppose I have to invite you in."

Everything went quiet. The creatures vanished back into the snow, all except for the humped blue buffalo who keeled over and began snoring.

Nice trick.

We followed Herja inside to a cozy living room with flower pattern wallpaper, a vaulted ceiling and a crackling fireplace in a corner.

Herja's eyebrows came together. "So... what mischief is afoot?"

"Our enclave was ransacked," Kirsi said.

Herja didn't miss a beat. "Your council's Seal?"

Kirsi nodded. "Most likely."

"I recall warning you not to get involved," Herja said.

Kirsi bowed her head. "If I had refused, the task would have fallen on some other magistrate. I trust no one more than us."

I sat down gently on the couch, trying to avoid drawing attention. Herja intimidated me. Winter stood by the fireplace. His eyes locked onto mine, clearly regretting the decision to come along.

"Now's not a good time," Herja said, almost as if talking to herself. "I'm not finished here."

"We need you, Herja," Kirsi said. "You are our greatest strategist."

Herja paced the room. "You couldn't have come to me with news of a wedding or a rare Loki sighting. No, my sisters always bring news of war."

"Isn't war what Valkyries do best?" I said, instantly regretting it.

Winter quickly glanced out the window.

Coward.

Herja's inquisitive eyes landed on me. "We are more than moths to the flame, barely born witch," she said. "War comes in with the tide, wave after wave. We merely have the courage to face it." She paused for a moment. "I know of a place where the Seal can be protected."

"What place?" I said, not really expecting an answer.

"Curiosity can be molten metal, Luna Mae. Once cooled, you might find yourself chained to a heavy burden."

Well, when you put it that way.

"Normally, I shouldn't know where the Seventh Council Seal is kept, but these are desperate times," I said.

Herja studied me. "Desperation never validates. Prophecies are not etched in stone. All things are fluid, adaptable. But when one succumbs to things foretold, destinies harden, free will loses its grip, and only then does it become impossible to veer away from the predicted path."

So Herja knew about Horror and me. *Thanks, Kirs.* I understood her intention. Horror wanted the Seal. If I stood in his way, the first step in the prophesied rift between us would transform from a possibility into a fact.

Herja's stare intensified. "Once you know, you know," she went on. "You will have to fight for the Seal with your life. Are you ready for that battle?"

"I'm never ready for battle, but when there is no choice..."

Winter walked to me. "There is always choice, I agree with Herja."

I shrugged. "You're both protecting me. I don't need it."

Herja grinned for the first time. "I had heard that you are as brave as you are naïve. Did witch school ever teach you of Ideon Andron?"

I nodded. "Not witch school. San Diego State. Ideon Andron is a cave on the highest mountain in Crete where Zeus was raised according to the myth."

"It is no more a myth than any of us. Zeus's mother hid him in the cave to protect him from his father. A group of demons shielded Zeus so his father would not sense him. Lucky for us, those very same demons owe me a favor."

I stared at her, not sure how to respond. In a single sentence she had informed me that the story of Zeus was based on real events and that she hung out with demons.

"I thought the Ideon cave was off limits," Kirsi said. "Didn't the Great Eternal Magistrate himself block all entrances to the hidden chambers?"

"He did after the Fire Giants tried to take residence in the cave. The Eternal Magistrate could not allow them access to such potent enchantment. That's where the *favor owed* comes in," Herja said.

"And should we really be consorting with demons when so much is at stake?" Winter said. "In case you've forgotten, a demon's favorite pastime is manipulation."

Herja's face slipped into a stoic state. "I forget nothing. That's why I meditate. It becomes unbearable. You must trust me on this, Shadow Winter. We are to fight fire with fire. Unless you lot have a single other idea."

Winter looked to Kirsi. "It's your head, and ultimately your call."

Kirsi looked like she wanted to bury her head. "I trust Herja's mind over any other. Let's do it. Whatever keeps the Seal from Horror."

"I'm finally getting my trip to Greece," I said. "I was thinking more bikinis and martinis than demons and caves, however."

Herja slipped on a black cloak, pulling the hood over her hair. "Let Kirsi and me deal with that." She stopped in front of me. "The Seal was not your secret, and it is not your fight, but now you must stay the course. Killing your father won't be easy, but your deciding to kill him may prove even harder."

Herja's words dizzied me, but I managed to steady myself. "Perhaps, but compared to letting the world fall, it won't be hard at all."

Kirsi clucked. "Sometimes it's good to be an orphan."

Chapter 3

My head still churned with everything that Herja had said to us two days ago and all that her words implied. Valkyries were hardened warriors with a single-minded purpose. They could be killing machines or they could serve peace. Whatever the time required. I had no such ability to override my many contradicting impulses. I was shaped in a human world and carried a host of desires, principles and thought processes. When the time came, I had no idea if I could bring myself to take my father's life, assuming I could even find a method to do that. Right now, it felt like an impossibility.

A silver sedan swerved into a visitor parking spot in the lot across from my apartment. The driver's door opened and Lily stepped out, holding a pink bakery box.

She spotted me in the open window and waved. "I come bearing gifts!"

The grand opening for her mother's bakery was not until next week, but the baking was already in full force as Lucia tested all her recipes.

"You're late," I told Lily as I opened my door and she handed me the box.

"Lucia insisted I stop by the shop to get many fresh pastries for her darling little Sophie. Trust me, you'll forgive my tardiness."

I set the box on the table and opened it. My mouth watered instantly: chocolate croissants, blueberry pie slices, éclairs, cream cheese Danishes, walnut brownies and fresh fruit tarts taunted me with their scrumptious perfection.

"I have no idea what to eat first," I said.

Lily grinned, grabbing a pie slice. "I do," she said with her mouth full.

I decided on a chocolate éclair.

"How's everything?" I said. "Your text sounded urgent."

Lily plopped down on the sofa. "It felt that way when I texted. I'm calmer now, more rational."

I stopped chewing. "Lily, what's going on?"

Her eyes flashed irritation. "I was at Emmet's last night. Guess who showed up."

"No one you were happy to see, so..."

"Cue wedding march," she said with an eye roll.

Oh shit.

"What did Cyrus want?"

"I have no idea. Emmet keeps his worlds separate. All I know is that after Cyrus left, Emmet was quite pissed."

"Okay, there's no way you left it at that."

"Hello, have you met me? I tried to get him to tell me

something, but he would not budge. He said it was better for me not to know. I just hate all the secrecy, and that Cyrus dude... Sophie, I've no idea what you saw in him. He screams *toxic* and it's like he has Emmet on a string."

Tell me about it.

The bathroom door swung open. Winter strutted out in shorts and a t-shirt, his hair wet. I'd completely forgotten he was in the shower. My brain was lagging since the meeting with Herja.

"What's this about Cyrus?" he said.

Lily stared at him wide-eyed. "He's just *extra*," she said.

"Clearly," Winter said. "What tedious deed has he done now?"

"That's between Emmet and Cyrus," I said. "Not our deal."

He smiled for Lily. "If that mutt ever troubles you, come find me."

Lily welcomed his words.

Before she responded, I squeezed Winter's hand and pulled him close. "Are you off on your errand?"

He nodded, reluctantly, then grabbed his keys. "Yes, I am. Enjoy yourselves."

We waited for the door to close behind him.

"That lacked subtlety," Lily said. "Is he staying here now? Are you two *together* together? I bet he's no fan of Cyrus."

"It's complicated," I said, "but we're working through it."

"Yep, he's jealous. Wait... Does he have superpowers, too?

Is he like Emmet and you? Cause that could be some real fireworks... if they clashed."

Okay, I guess we're having this conversation.

"He's not a shifter or a witch, but yeah, he's part of our world, he can do stuff."

"I bet he can," she said, smacking her lips together.

"Uh," I said, trying not to shake my head at her. I didn't want to tell her Winter was immortal. The mere mention of immortality would lead to the discovery that Winter and I had the potential to live forever, but Lily and Emmet did not. That would result in her dreading her own mortality and the fleeting lives of everyone she loved. No basic should have to carry such existential angst along with every other burden of life. "He's basically a super athlete," I said. "Very strong. Very fast. All that."

"A ha."

"What do you mean, *a ha*?"

"I mean, you definitely have a type. Have you ever dated a regular guy?"

"Of course, I have."

"You sure about that?"

"I thought we were talking about your problems, not mine."

She batted her eyelashes at me. "You're right. I really need to know what hold Cyrus has on Emmet."

I was well rid of Cyrus, but while Lily was with Emmet, she was stuck with the pack Alpha. I owed her answers, whether Emmet approved or not.

"What has Emmet told you?"

"He said Cyrus is a shifter. That's all he'll say."

"Okay, that's right, he's a shifter, but he's also the Alpha of the San Diego pack. That means every shifter in the county answers to him. Alphas are no fun. They tend to be pricks as they are by nature autocratic, but Cyrus, oh boy, he comes off like a total dictator. *Extra* was right."

"His arrogance is palpable," she said. "This sucks for Emmet."

"It totally does."

"So, Emmet has to deal with Cyrus for the rest of his life?"

"For as long as he's in San Diego County, yes."

She pouted. "I can't be dating a guy who's subservient to another guy. There is zero mojo in that."

I sighed. "That's something you have to discuss with Emmet. Understand that there are things he won't be able to share with you. Ever. But you have to make it clear to him where you stand and how much you can take. He needs to know you won't break if he tells you there's a battle he has to fight. And there will be battles, Lil, trust me on that."

"I don't know what I want. Maybe I'd rather pretend nothing has changed, that the world's the same, that supercharged monsters are not real."

I'll drink to that.

I hugged her. "I one-hundred percent wish that were the case."

Lily closed her eyes. "I'm falling for him, Soph, but he has this whole other life I'll never be a part of. It bugs me."

"It's like dating a fireman or a cop," I said. "There are mortal dangers. Or a soldier... remember poor Lindsey from Freshman year?"

"That's what you want to say to me right now? I'm like that girl we know whose boyfriend was killed in Afghanistan?"

Not smooth.

"That came out harsh," I said, "but I'm just saying you can decide if this is something you want to sign up for, because it's a lot."

"Maybe if I could be supernatural too, I wouldn't mind as much. Like you."

"Lily, I mind. I get worried sick about him. And not just Jonas, but Emmet, too, and others."

She looked at me with a dark determination. "Wait, is there actually a way I could get magic powers?"

"No, silly Lily. It's genetic. There is no magic potion or spell that can turn a basic into a magic."

She frowned. "A *basic*?"

"It's just a word, our slang."

"So, I'm a *basic*? Is that all I am to you guys?"

"It's just a word to describe the visible world, Lil, don't get hung up on it."

"I'm not," she said, slightly irritated. "Offended a little, but I get it. The whole thing is so goddamn complex. I feel like Alice in that hole, Soph."

"Welcome to the club."

Lily grabbed a brownie from the box. "But Emmet has the best eyes and I like kissing his—"

"Lily!"

"What? I do," she said. "I'm all in because I'm danger girl when it comes to men anyway, and when I like a guy... I'm fixated. The devil himself couldn't chase me off my man, okay? You feel me?"

I laughed. The world might be ending but Lily could still make me laugh. "Yeah, I know, Lil. You are as stubborn as any man or ox. And the hottest of messes."

Lily furrowed her brow. "I like that last part... because it's true."

"Cyrus is like the Sun. He'll always show up, just don't pay him any attention and don't be around him long enough to get burned."

"You've been working on that one," she said.

"Yeah, it's good, right? I had to find a way of dealing with him to prevent me from launching him into the moon every time I see him."

"Or... you could just launch him into the moon..."

"Lily, we're better than that. I think."

"If you say so."

"I want to repeat what I was saying before. You should carefully consider the risks and try not to be stubborn and make the best decision. You were not born into this.

You don't have to be a part of it."

"But he's so yummy."

Okay, she's done being serious.

Winter opened the front door. He flashed guilt, like a teen boy caught admiring the wrong website. He must have been out there listening.

He stared at me. "They want you at that appointment, too."

"Oh, they do. Okay, then, let's go, I guess." I turned to Lily. "Continue the conversation over coffee?"

Lily chewed on the last piece of her brownie. "I see lying is not one of your powers. Sure, hit me up... after said appointment."

As soon as she was out the door, I glared at Winter. "You're so awkward. What have you learned?"

"Kirsi's returned from Crete. She wants us to meet her at the coffeehouse."

Chapter 4

THE STONE STEPS LEADING to the cellar above were so narrow I wondered how Winter managed to squeeze himself through. Once upon a time, the troglodytes had built an elaborate network of tunnels underneath San Diego that extended all the way to the Mexican border. One of those tunnels led straight to the Sisterhood's coffeehouse basement.

The large cellar was stocked with bottles of wine, brandy and sherry, sacks of cocoa and coffee beans, flour and sugar, as well as cheese wheels and sausage logs. Housed in a cute three-story, colonial style building with white awnings, the coffeehouse overlooked Breakwater Way Beach.

Winter and I climbed up to the cellar through a narrow trapdoor. I pulled pieces of spider web from my hair and face.

Arsha sprang toward me to give me a tight hug.

Carter grinned, sprawled out on an old, velvet couch with polished wood armrests.

"Can Shadows come out and play?" I teased Arsha.

She shrugged. "When they have special privileges, they can."

"That's right, you're the shiny new celebrity of the Umbra Order."

"Maybe not that, but I do have some pull with the management."

Carter scoffed. "They gave her time off to prepare for her next trial. If she fails, little Miss Celebrity will be kicked out by said *management*."

The management being the fabled Shadow Master, who had been running the Shadow Warrior crew for more than a thousand years. Since he had assumed control, the Umbra Order had been taking slow, painstaking steps away from cultish exclusion and toward more inclusion. The Shadow Master also happened to be Winter's close friend and mentor.

"Arsha's going to ace the trial and break that gender barrier," I said. "That's happening, Carter. And the Shadow Warriors will be stronger for it."

"Yeah. Yes, of course," he conceded. "I know."

I took a chair at the table. "So, where's Kirsi?"

"She'll be here," Carter said. "She better be, or I was lured to the Valkyrie's lair under false pretenses."

I could see Carter wanting to say more, likely an inappropriate innuendo, but Winter's rigid presence caused him to swallow his usual overtures.

"Tell us what is known," Winter said, sitting next to me.

"Herja and Kirsi have secured the council's Seal," Arsha said. "They have also warned that an attack at the coffeehouse is imminent."

A chill ran down my spine. I heeded the words of Chaos that the war for the five realms was at hand. Was this the first spark?

"Does the venerable Shadow Master offer any insights concerning the attacks?" I asked Arsha.

"Nothing I can share."

"Well, *he's* part of the whole insufferable chain of command, right?" I said, referring to Winter. "And he's your superior. I'll just cover my ears and you can Shadow whisper it to him."

Arsha grinned. "If I do that, it's as good as telling you. I will not doom your promising relationship by enticing Winter to break binding oaths."

Oh, boy.

Kirsi came running down the stairs. She took a stern look at Winter and froze in her tracks. "I thought we agreed this was not your fight until your cell regeneration does its thing."

Winter said nothing.

I glanced at Kirsi. "Then why did you text him to meet you here?"

"Text who? Winter?"

Carter raised his hand. "I texted the magistrate. He asked me to let him know when the fair Valkyrie returned."

Kirsi shook her head. "Just because you manipulated the frisky squire, doesn't mean it will work on me, Winter. You know the exit."

Winter stepped to Kirsi, his blue eyes like polar ice. "You can't expect me to idly sit back while everyone is risking their necks."

Kirsi looked to me. "Speak to him."

If she thought I could command Winter, she had forgotten his nature.

Winter sat back down next to me. "Tell me what you discovered, then I'll go. You have my word."

Kirsi relaxed and took a seat across from us.

"The Seal is buried in the depths of the Ideon Andron in Greece," she said. "The Kouretes, the demons who guard the cave, have vowed to shield its essence from all Eternals." She paused, hesitating.

"Isn't that good news?" Arsha offered.

"The Kouretes informed us all debts owed to the Valkyries have now been paid in full. We can't expect more from them."

Winter frowned. "We should have never trusted those duplicitous demons in the first place."

Kirsi sighed. "Relax, the Kouretes will honor a debt paid. We moved on to visit the Oracle at the temple of Apollo."

First Zeus, then demons, now the Oracle of Delphi. Was she traveling along ley lines or through time?

Kirsi noticed my sense of awe. "Shed your human

doubts," she scolded. "The people of our world were never myths. Man made them such."

"The Oracle's most definitely real," Carter said, "but count me out on knowing the future. That's usually a curse."

He sounded like he knew firsthand. His bloodline traced back to Greece.

"Agreed, but it might be our only advantage," I said. "What did the mighty Oracle have to say?"

Kirsi leaned forward, elbows on the table. "The fabric of time is cracking. The great war the Oracle has foretold since before the Greco-Persian wars and the Achaemenid Empire, is upon us. The spokes in the wheel of history are forming as we speak."

I struggled to comprehend the immensity of her words.

"Did the Oracle foresee any possible path to keep the wheel from turning?" Winter said.

"She did," Kirsi said, hesitant. "Luna must kill Horror before he sets his plans in motion. Like Penelope said."

Two seers, the same prophecy. A shot of pain cut through my heart. My lungs emptied. I had to kill Horror before battle. I had to kill him in cold blood. The fate of the world depended on me murdering my father.

"Such bullshit," I managed to say. "A prophecy made before I was born, a prophecy made without knowing who I am at all."

Kirsi sat back. She licked her lips.

"Speak your mind," I said.

"The Oracle foresaw your reluctance as well. She questioned your allegiance, Luna. There is a third way this could play out."

"I'm all ears."

"One, you kill Horror and you avert the war. Two, you hesitate and the world falls."

Kirsi paused and stared at me.

"And behind curtain number three?" Carter said.

"The third way... you join Horror and the greater world falls, but you are left standing to rule over what remains."

"Huh," I said. "I knew you were going to say that and it's complete nonsense. You can get that out of your heads. Your old heads may not get it, but I'm a product of this century. I don't kneel to superstition, demon feuds and doomsday prophecies. I will write my own story, thank you very much."

My audience looked concerned.

Winter covered my hand with his. "It's not superstition. Imagine the prophecy as a predictive model. Everything repeats. Scenarios unfold. There are known entities and but a few ways to oppose great power. It wasn't precisely you that was prophesied. It was a possible you, a necessary you, a hopeful you. The Oracle sees patterns align. You were never guaranteed to appear in the world, but you were needed, and the world always waits for what's needed. She sees scenarios that could quite possibly unfold and when you add an endless amount of time, most things will happen. A child with the capacity to control the Dark Eternal would also have the power to rule the five realms. These three ways are the most likely outcomes should one like you ever come into existence and now, here you are before our very eyes."

The man I loved thought I could only be a coward, a killer or the dark ruler of a fallen world. So much for my storybook romance.

I sighed. "I hate all three."

"I wish there was another way," Winter said.

Kirsi furrowed her brow. "We're running out of time."

"I guess we know what I'm going to do already," I said. "Something dreadful, but I want all of you right here by my side, so we can become despicable together."

"Sounds like a plan," Carter said. "I hope it makes me an anti-hero. Women are intrigued by an anti-hero."

"I am faithful to the rider," Arsha said, "now and forever. I will defend you until my final breath."

Their pledge of undying allegiance made the pit in my stomach tighten.

I relented and considered Winter. "Kirsi told us what happened in Crete. You need to go rest and heal while we're preparing for the necro army."

"Actually, there's one more thing," Kirsi said.

Of course, there is.

"The Oracle requests your presence, Luna. There are things she will only reveal to you. She will send for you when the moment is right."

"Now we're waiting for a moment? I thought we were quickly running out of moments."

Kirsi shrugged. "The Oracle speaks when the Oracle speaks. I doubt it will be long."

I was about to be snide when the ground beneath our feet shook.

Dark magic crawled inside the cellar walls, strong, putrid, concentrated. I'd never felt such a swelling of dark magic before.

"They're in the tunnels," Kirsi said.

"They know about the tunnels?" Arsha said, terror in her eyes. "How did we not sense them sooner?"

Kirsi's face grew rigid. "There's no place left to hide."

I grabbed Winter. "Get upstairs, leave this place. Now."

Kirsi threw him a set of keys. "Take my bike."

Winter let the keys drop at his feet. He clenched his teeth. If we wanted him safe, we'd have to physically remove him.

There was no time for that.

The trapdoor on the floor exploded. Black tendrils of smoke spilled out and crawled across the floor like slithering vipers of death.

The cold sting of destiny was upon us. I stepped back to draw power into my hands. I could feel it. The fabric of time. The wheel of history. Everything cracking. Everything turning.

Chapter 5

THE DARK POWER COLLAPSED my defenses and invaded my bloodstream like an army of fire ants, setting my body ablaze. My insides churned and my lungs tightened. I summoned every shred of power to push back against the overwhelming necromantic current.

"We can't fight them in this tight space," Kirsi said, struggling to speak. "They are too many, they'll overrun us."

"Where are the Sisters?" I said.

"Defending their shops," Kirsi said.

No reinforcements. *Brilliant.*

Arsha drew her sword and chanted an ancient Shadow incantation. Winter didn't join her. His Shadow magic had clearly taken a hit when rendered temporarily mortal. His face hardened into a lifeless mask.

Kirsi motioned to a nearby shelf. Winter lunged over to dig out two swords from a flour sack. He spun and tossed me a sword. It landed heavy in my hand, magic pulsing through its hilt.

There was no escape. We would have to stand our ground.

My throat dried. My skull throbbed from the crushing strain of fending off the necromantic power. I spun up a shaky force field to shield us from the initial onslaught. It would not hold for long against such sinister magic.

Winter heaved the heavy oak table over the gaping hole in the floor where the trapdoor used to be. Seconds later, the table flew up and smashed against the ceiling.

Two necromancers emerged from the hole, wrapped in long black cloaks, hoods drawn over their heads, and oozing sinister magic. A scarlet light shone through their eyes. Their distorted faces hardened, glowing with the promise of fresh blood.

They prodded at my shield with surges of necromancy, but I held firm. My ability to sustain a force field under heavy attack had bolstered with combat experience.

The necromancers stepped forward. Their hands were shrouded with dark tendrils of smoke.

Burly beasts sprang from the earth behind them. They had pointy heads, stubby ears and short, bushy tails. Their ashen faces were striped with silver. They resembled misshapen and oversized badgers, a whole mob of them.

Copious amounts of dense dark magic erupted from the necromancers like long, suffocating tentacles, piercing my shield. The shield vibrated against the stream of necromantic power, mending itself quickly.

The beasts bolted forward, foaming at the mouth, flooding the cellar with a foul stench.

Carter zipped past me, wielding a sword in one hand and a dagger in the other. The beasts hissed as his sword plunged and his face shook with strain.

The necromancers flowed to the back of the cellar. A muffled cacophony resounded through the tunnels below, signaling the presence of scores of foul entities lurking beneath our feet.

Our foes would use the advantage of numbers to block any escape routes, and then pummel us from all sides with the hyper relentless badger beasts and the infernal dark sorcery of the necromancers.

A jolt of energy burst out of me and blasted the first line of badgers, sweeping them up off their feet. Bones crunched as they collided with the ceiling.

The whimpering creatures scurried down into the hole to escape in the tunnels.

The necromancers moved about behind me, trying to determine how to breach my shield.

A high-pitched scream sounded off like an explosion and the second line of badgers stalked forward like a single organism, foam spilling from their mouths, as if commanded by a single brain.

More and more creatures climbed into the cellar until it was packed full of them. They seemed to pop out of nowhere, and no matter how many we cut down, they were immediately reinforced by a new wave.

My friends battled the beasts. Swords sizzled as they found

flesh. Blades swiped at throats. The beasts rallied forward, storming past us with their mass and momentum.

I flung open my arms to let my magic swell. A blinding white light burst through the cellar. The badgers squealed in agony. The thick stream of necro magic was temporarily stymied. The luminosity was so bright it hurt. The blinded beasts stumbled back into the hole from whence they came.

The current of dark magic dug back in and surged.

A hard punch hammered into my back. I gasped. My chest tightened and a scorching heat invaded my energy core. I tumbled onto my knees. The world blurred. Everything shook.

The necromancers had broken through my shield. I gasped for air and collapsed hard to the floor. I tried to right myself, but my limbs felt like they were filled with lead.

Winter lifted me to my feet. I leaned into his embrace. His eyes met mine, concerned but reassuring. The panic slowly dissipated; the familiarity of his gaze restored my determination.

I spun away. The necromancers glistened with heinous energy. I gripped the enchanted sword in my hand. Dark magic coiled around me.

Enough.

I advanced quickly, spinning my blade at a dizzying speed, beheading the first beast to challenge my path, then fell to my knees to twirl back and slice clean through another beast's torso.

Mist magic wrapped around my body, whipping me into a frenzied whirlwind that aided me in swiftly disposing another ungodly creature and giving me time to mend my shield, then shock back the necromancers with a pulverizing pulse of my power.

I had to hold them off long enough for the others to chase away the wretched badger mutants. I threw myself in front of the necromancers, struggling to keep my magic firmly in check.

A mournful shriek echoed throughout the cellar. The creatures stood still, their eyes blank as if receiving instructions. They suddenly scaled the walls like their paws were suction cups.

They were connected, like a hive mind, to something or someone, almost palpable, like a frequency or voice in their heads leading them to certain deaths. Whatever had control must be below in the tunnels. I needed to find that beacon and eliminate it, or this savage battle would never end.

As if sensing my thoughts, the horde closed in, blocking my view of the necromancers. I turned on my heels and dashed for the gaping hole in the floor. I glimpsed Carter's stunned face before I dived into the darkness.

I tumbled down into the depths of the cool earth. My glowing fingers cast a dim light on the walls around me that were lined with stacks of yellow bones. An icy draft bit into my skin as I kept plummeting further down.

Why am I alone in here? And why am I still falling?

The realization landed like a punch to the gut. I remembered idle talk of time portals infiltrating enchanted tunnels and secret passages, sucking in anyone who entered.

Oh, come on! I thought they were messing.

My magic anchored itself within the portal, slowing my descent. I floated onto a surface, trying to orient myself.

The time portal shimmered through the gaps of the bones around me, flashing purple spears of light into the tunnel. The clashing of blades and the roars of the beasts echoed from above, as if a dream or memory.

Shrill cackling echoed through the subterranean corridors. Glowing ruby-red eyes illuminated the shadows at the far end of the tunnel. The rustling of claws against the bone walls grew in intensity. It felt like hundreds of invisible demonic badgers closed in around me.

The source of the controlling power hid deep within the time portal. I could sense it, pulling and prodding at me. A sinister presence emanated from within. It was primal, feral, fierce, roaring in my ears as it attempted to breach the protective walls of my mist core and corrupt my very essence with something malevolent.

The dark entity communicated with the necromancers and, through them, controlled the hordes of beasts the portal spewed out.

I took a cautious step. A massive column of inky darkness erupted from the portal, smashing into me and throwing me back. My entire frame shuddered from the force of the blow as I was lifted off my feet.

I crashed back onto the floor. My skin felt like it had been jolted by a thousand volts of electricity. I heard my name screamed out—maybe it was Winter, maybe it was Carter, maybe a voice in my head—but all I could do was focus on the ominous force trying to swallow me whole.

In my weakened state, the enchanted sword became extremely heavy as I hoisted it high. It trembled in my faltering grip.

A necromancer glided through the air, his eyes burning like two distant suns, the last vestiges of his humanity gone. He was gaunt and tall, a scarecrow of decaying bones and withering flesh stitched together with threads of dark magic.

The dark sorcerer raised a skeletal hand. A ripple of energy rattled the walls of the underground passage. I stumbled back, my vision flickering with flashes of light.

His slithering voice echoed inside my mind: "Yield to *He Who is the Dark* for none shall traverse the fissure of eternal night."

I clenched my fists, steeling myself against the temptation to lunge at the necromancer and strangle him with my bare hands.

The midnight-black void became an abyss of confusion, an ocean of sinister energy. I could feel the presence of a foreign consciousness trying to overtake me, trying to drag me into the depths of the portal.

Fight this, Luna. Break free.

I planted my feet firmly on the ground and pushed through the fog in my mind, the dark energy palpable and seething in the air. I felt a great weight pressing against my chest, growing heavier by the breath.

I gritted my teeth, summoning my mist magic. It felt like all my muscles being torn open at once. My eyes rolled back as I unleashed the swelling power out of me like a cannon blast. The portal quaked. The crushing pressure on me was so immense I thought I might black out.

The necromancer's eyes widened in confusion, and his face distorted into a mask of rage. I should confirm his doubts and send his head to Horror in a nice Valentino hat box.

My veins ran wild, boiling with the same ancient magic that coursed through the necromancer's veins. My core reacted to the great power radiating from the time portal. Primordial magic and recognition from within my cells emitted a deafening internal hum.

Two can play at this game. Time to get salty!

I pulled in more energy, every ounce I could, until it built into a cataclysmic crescendo, bathing the trifling necromancer in its brutal potency.

The infernal sorcerer convulsed as if I injected a deadly dose of mist venom into his bloodstream.

"The mission... must be accomplished," he sputtered out.

"*Nah*... it mustn't. This city is defended. The Sisterhood yet stands. Tell my psycho father that."

I raised my hands, sculpting the energy that had ensnared him into an unraveling rope. I grabbed the end of the rope and pulled hard.

The necromancer's eyes bulged out of their sockets and a screeching wail escaped his throat. Tremors wracked his body as my venom burned through his veins and arteries.

A silver light emanated from his flesh before his body imploded into a thousand pieces that scattered wispily like confetti from a cannon.

I deflated like a balloon and dropped to all fours, wheezing for breath. The clammy air around me thickened and sapped all energy from my body.

A violent boom detonated behind me. I pivoted, barely able to lift my neck, to discover a horde of demon badgers sprinting my way, before they suddenly froze in suspended motion—some with gaping mouths, some skidding across the ground, some in mid leap—then they were all sucked back into the shimmering walls from which they sprang.

The entire time portal, the fissure of eternal night, condensed down into a spinning sphere of light and vanished into a small black hole. The hole itself disappeared with a low *pop!*

The powerful grip on me finally loosened and my vision cleared. Winter stood before me, his shirt sleeve dripping blood which pooled on the ground. I had been so transfixed I hadn't heard him approach.

A few steps behind Winter, Kirsi was studying me with

narrowed eyes. Carter stood next to her, concerned, but his sword at the ready. Arsha was there, too, mostly unreadable, but maybe I saw a glimmer of compassion.

What quotient of viciousness had they seen in me? Had I shown them something too gleefully murderous from my gallery of grotesque faces?

Of course, they were worried. *Join the club.* I had lost touch with reality in that portal, and it scared me.

I wiped away sweat from my forehead. If this was Horror, this hive mind necromancer puppet master, and if he was the one after the Seventh Council Seal, did it mean he no longer cared whether I lived or died? Had I become expendable to him, to *He Who is the Dark,* or whatever he's calling himself now? The decency in me, whatever I still possessed, found it hard to believe he would risk my life like this, not yet anyway.

Then again, delusions were my brand.

My legs quivered as I rose to my feet. Winter collapsed to the ground into a pool of his own blood.

Chapter 6

I PACED BACK AND forth in the waiting room. My neck was slick with sweat as my sneakers squeaked against the discolored tile floor. Blood, dried mud and vile gunk caked my jeans and sweater. I'd barely had the presence of mind to wipe my face clean before jumping into the back of the ambulance.

Carter looked haggard physically but composed. I could not fathom how he held himself together like that.

The clock ticked so slow. Every minute was its own eternity. How much longer would we have to wait?

The image of Winter collapsing in the tunnel flashed before my eyes. "What the hell's keeping them?" I muttered.

"Luna, they're stitching him up," Carter said, pushing back his blond, wavy hair. "He's in the best hands."

"He's too mortal now. What if..."

"Stop that. He'll make it. Even mortals survive flesh wounds."

"Yeah, but not a hundred of them."

"Good," Carter said through a sigh, "because he had more

like ten wounds. It's Winter we're talking about. He'll make it. He's a fucking bull."

"So much of his blood spilled out. It was everywhere. He's never been mortal before. His body might not know how to heal like humans. Why aren't they telling us anything?"

"Luna, you're just driving yourself crazy. You need to stay focused. There's more at stake than just the three of us."

To me, right now, there's only him. Let the rest be damned.

I shook my head, rage boiling within. "What was I thinking? I should have never left his side."

"If you hadn't, we'd still be in that cellar where Winter would have been wounded much worse and have no medical attention."

I don't want the truth right now. I want to hate myself.

Hospital waiting areas are like holding cells, the air stagnant, where time stretches out refusing to pass. Arsha had rushed off to inform the Shadow Master, and Kirsi stayed behind to set up an emergency zoom call with the Sisters. I slumped in a stiff plastic chair and wallowed.

I looked to Carter. "Does he even have health insurance?"

Carter's face twisted trying to control his laughter. His lips twitched and his eyes narrowed as he finally let out a chuckle. I followed suit, my laugh coming out in uneven gasps.

"You idiot," I said. "Don't laugh."

"You're laughing."

"Because you're absurd."

"Ah, and absurdity is the first truth," he said. "Winter has his wallet, and he has a black card. Not even the American health care system can fuck with a black card."

I rolled my eyes. "Don't underestimate the Medical Industrial Complex."

A nurse walked over to us. "Mr. Sandell is out of surgery. The doctor will meet with you shortly."

My heart raced as Carter asked with great concern, "Is he okay?"

The nurse hesitated, her expression unreadable. "The doctor will explain everything."

"Please, madam, give us something," Carter implored. "His wife is desperate with worry."

Wife? Nice touch.

The nurse studied me for what felt like an eternity.

Ah, I get it. She expected a leggy runway model to be his woman.

I placed my hand on my flat belly. "Please, Miss. We just found out we're expecting."

Carter threw me a glare. I might have pushed his wife bit too far.

"If you could find the good will..." His gaze fell to her name tag. "Nurse Matthews, I would be forever indebted."

Nurse Matthews smiled and leaned in closer, her voice hushed. "The patient came through the operation without any complications," she said with a spark of optimism. "The doctor is hopeful of a full recovery."

Carter grinned from ear to ear, elated. "How can I ever

repay your kindness?"

Oh, I'm sure she'll think of something.

The nurse blushed before departing.

"You're shameless," I told Carter.

"You use what you got," he said with a smug grin. "Now we know."

This guy.

"Thank you," I said. "But one thing's for sure. Winter can never engage in any battle till his immortality is fully restored."

A gravelly snicker filled the air.

"I heard that Frosty lost his magic hat and now he's melting all over the ICU. Why must children's stories be so frightful?"

My heart skipped. I spun around, adrenaline pumping. There he was, Chaos, standing just a few feet from me. His hands were tucked casually away in the pockets of his khaki pants, a snug teal t-shirt hugged his ripped torso, and his hair had been trimmed into an off-putting crew cut. The scruffy stubble on his face gave him a rugged energy, and I couldn't deny the feeling of relief stirring in my stomach.

"Don't worry, he will live to annoy us another day," he added.

"What is this look?" I said. "Did you join 21 Jump Street? Are you undercover?"

"A man can't keep the same look for a thousand years. I have to rotate the products from time to time."

"Aha. Is there a point to your rambling?"

He shook his head. "Sister, you can never let an Immortal get this close without sensing them. Prince Charmless gets a paper cut and all systems go offline? And what if I was Horror instead? What then? Get your blood pathways back online, moon kitten. Stay with the program, yeah?"

"Is that supposed to be brotherly love?" I asked, my patience thinning. "What's the real reason you came out of your hole?"

He stepped closer. His musky scent overwhelmed my senses. He looked down at me with his piercing dark eyes. "We need to talk."

The unease on his face could only mean one thing. My mother.

"There's a cafeteria," I said.

He scoffed. "*A hospital cafeteria?* I think not. Perhaps a warded portal where Horror can't listen in? A far better option, don't you think?"

"Always so dramatic," I muttered. "You can just ward the cafeteria."

Chaos considered me with a familiar condescension. "Sure, and why don't I just ward the entire planet and travel back in time to rescue all your lame companions flailing in the tunnel?"

Did the arrogant bastard know everything? My mind was an open book to him. He was right, I had to do a better job safeguarding my thoughts.

"Fine," I said. "We'll do it your way."

I glanced at Carter.

He nodded. "I'll wait on the doctor."

"Thanks, Carter. If they let you in to see Winter, tell him I... just tell him I'll be back shortly."

"I'll tell him you went to the restroom."

I followed Chaos to the elevator. Once inside, he wrapped his arms around me, holding me tight against his chest. Blue smoke swirled, snaking up our legs.

The world dissolved in a blur of blue flashes, the force of the telekinetic transport tugging at my clothes and hair. We spun faster and faster until my head felt like it was going to explode.

Then as fast as it began, it all stopped. The blue smoke diffused and we found ourselves standing in a clearing surrounded by tall trees, their thick trunks a deep purple black. A crystal-clear pond reflected the strange constellations above. A faint white mist drifted through the air and the chirping of crickets was the only sound I could hear.

As promised, we had journeyed through a portal to an enchanted realm, encircled by strong wards. Chaos was hyper cautious when it came to Horror. It felt like paranoia, but I couldn't help but respect his unwavering vigilance.

Chaos engaged his third eye vision to search for any sign of Horror.

"All is good in the hood, my reckless sibling," he said with a wink. "This is my favorite hideaway. You like?"

"Yeah, I suppose. It's peaceful."

"I shagged Cleopatra for the first time right about there," he said as proud as men are about such things.

"Dude, for real? Don't be so crude."

He tried to look sheepish, but that was not one of his powers.

"Fine, Cleopatra was a nice pull," I admitted.

"Right?"

"But never bring me to another one of your little love nests or love shacks or any place of conquest whatsoever again. Deal?"

"Uh, that eliminates all of my places."

"You're so gross," I said. "Okay, speak. What's up?"

"*Tsk tsk*, always the buzzkill. Why must you forever put fun at the bottom of your list? You are so perfectly matched with that human icicle."

I walked about the clearing to let nature soothe my soul. The moonlight cascaded through the trees, illuminating a babbling brook snaking through the clearing into the woods. I felt my energy invigorate.

"I think you have a serene side that you hide from everyone," I said. "All that bravado conceals whatever's vulnerable inside. You can fool the world, but you don't fool me."

Shockingly, he had no response.

"Did you ward the land yourself?"

"Little by little," he said. "I made a study of wards through the centuries, bits of primal magic gathered here and there along the way. None of the magic I used came from Horror. This way Papa can't discern the patterns."

I found it even more unsettling that Chaos was Horror's offspring than the fact that I was Horror's child. Their energies could not be more foreign to each other. *As different as chalk and cheese,* as Gram used to say.

But here my brother stood, in all his gloom and glory—living proof that life can be completely fucked up, completely random, completely lacking in rhyme or reason.

"Is this about my mother?"

Chaos shifted his weight to avert my gaze. "It would appear that Time does not wish to grant me an audience."

Ugh. "You couldn't have told me that at the hospital?"

"Hold your mist horse, eh? We may not have spoken, but I managed to send her a message, and today I got her reply."

Fear and anticipation bubbled up inside me. "And..."

A hint of relief curled his lips. "She'll meet with you."

His words sent a shockwave through me. "But not you?"

The hopeful glint in his eyes faded. "Jury's out on that."

He turned away so I could not read his face. After all these years, was he still in love with my mother? In the history of complicated romances, theirs must have been the most complicated. His silence made it clear that the torch he carried for her had not gone out.

"So, what's next?" I said.

"We wait. She will reach out with details."

Eagerness and anxiety collided in my stomach. If I could

meet my mother, I could finally look her in the eyes and ask why she stayed with Horror, what she felt about giving me up, and if she ever once had any regrets about the whole thing.

"If we can persuade Time to side with us, it'd give us a necessary advantage," I said. "Horror doesn't have the crystal shield anymore, but we'd have Time, and by your accounts, she is a crystal shield in and of herself."

Chaos tilted his head and stared down at me.

"What?"

"You're hoping she'll say you don't have to kill him."

"Would that be a bad thing?"

Chaos shrugged. "It would be the prime example of a *bad thing* in all the realms and in all of time. We dodged a bullet, *no*, we dodged an extinction event when we snatched back the crystal shield from him and destroyed it."

"Yeah, it's destroyed now."

Chaos paced back and forth. "You must understand, Luna, the Shield of Time would have been far too dangerous even in the right hands. That much power corrupts, even one who is a shield in her own right. A shield like that when wielded is destined to break apart life as we know it."

All these men talk about is destiny.

I crossed my arms. "My mother already controls time, and have you ever seen her make a single plan to use the Shield of Time? You can't cry *destiny* and think that's an excuse for all manners of ill intent, even murder."

Chaos stopped pacing. "Your mother doesn't only control time, she also controls the Horae."

My eyebrows lifted as I processed those words. The goddesses known as the Horae were revered in ancient Greek mythology for their influence over the natural world and the passage of time. They were said to possess the power to bring forth the changing seasons and to reset balance and harmony in the universe. It was their crystal tears that Horror had gathered in order to forge the Shield of Time.

"Come on, you're telling me my mother was essential in the creation of the Shield? Really? She just bestowed the precious crystal tears to Horror?"

"I cannot say. The woman I knew had only the best interests of all beings at heart, which was rather annoying, honestly. Here's what I'm saying, we have to beat Horror to the punch. We have to get to her first, Luna."

I panicked. "He can't gain access to the Horae."

And what of the remaining crystal tears I had given to Horpheus for safekeeping after shattering the Shield into a thousand fragments? The Great Chanter had declared that no Eternal, not even the most powerful among them, could crack the barriers of the Deep Down and sense the crystal tears. But there was no end to Horror's resourcefulness.

"We must protect the Horae at all costs," I said. "We can't wait for her to send details. We have to make our way to Time without delay."

His eyes narrowed. "And how, my calamitous sibling, do

you propose we do that? Punch through her time domain like Marty and Doc in our silver DeLorean?"

"You watch a lot of movies."

"Only the good ones," he said. "They help to fill up the hours. Every day is a cruel eternity for an Immortal."

"Huh, okay. We have to do this, brother. The safety of all must come before the request of any one individual, even my all-powerful mother."

The bastard laughed heartily. His laughter stopped cold, and I felt a chill sweep over me. "No one can infiltrate her ever-shifting realm—not even the shit movie science of Doc Brown could do this. The moment she senses a threat, the realm jumps to a new timescape. All we can do is wait."

"And what happens if Time decides to take her time?"

"What happens, my little puff, is we're all fucked."

Chapter 7

THE SUN HAD BEGUN to set by the time I returned to the hospital. The distant clouds were painted a soft orange. Chaos had vanished in a swirl of dust, leaving me standing alone on the cracked sidewalk.

A stillness overcame me. The implications of our conversation weighed heavy on my heart as I cut across the parking lot to the hospital entrance.

My head spun with premonitions. A dark storm was brewing. A great fury would descend upon the city. *Whatever that means.*

Thoughts of Time and the Horae played tricks and ran loops in my mind. My mother and her unfathomable power. Darius and his wicked schemes. Her involvement. I shuddered at the thought of the destruction that could have been unleashed had Horror of all people not stepped in to assist in bringing Darius down.

What was Time's ultimate goal? I needed to hear it from her.

Dread clogged the air like a thick fog. Every noise faded

into a distant hum, and I could feel my heartbeat drumming in my chest.

A shrill sound, like a cacophony of angry bees, buzzed in my ears. My skull pounded with a splitting headache. My eyes blurred with the pressure that built behind them.

Shit. Horror was trying to make contact.

I filled my lungs then exhaled, trying to calm myself. I had prepared for this moment. Winter had always said cooler heads prevail. Hell, even Chaos, the biggest skeptic in history, would have told me that.

I peeled back my defenses, granting Horror access to a space in my mind isolated from all the thoughts I kept concealed under lock and key. I searched for indications of an aggressive intrusion. His presence in my head was like an icy grip that wrapped around my brain.

"Daughter, why do you evade me?" Horror thundered in my mind with that deep, raspy voice he used to chastise me.

Ha, Chaos's wards had worked. Horror had not been able to break through and follow us into my brother's enchanted retreat.

Take that, Dad from hell.

"I have kept my promise. I stayed out of your head to give you time to ponder," he continued, "but I have monitored your etheric essence, to make sure your life force thrived, until an hour ago when you restricted your bloodpath wavelength." He paused, trying to remain calm. "Perhaps you'd like to put your old dad's mind at ease and tell me where you've been."

He did his best not to sound pissed. So much for our little farce where he was going to be a hands-off dad and I was going to pretend to buy it.

"I've been right here, trying to calm down with some meditation tricks," I said. "Maybe I achieved some higher state of consciousness, I don't know. I kind of blacked out. Maybe you're losing your touch."

His voice simmered with restrained menace. "So, you're an accidental Zen master and not an intentional consort of those who wish me harm."

"I am neither of those things or any other paranoid concoction in your head. Winter is lying in a hospital bed. My place is here."

"Ah, what mischief has your inferior mate encountered?"

"Nice try," I said. "You are once again the reason he fights for his life. I am too tired to play your word games, Father."

"*Me?* You think I caused him harm? Dear child, I've been off on a lark, enjoying a rejuvenating spa holiday in the Himalayas."

"That sounds made up," I said.

"Perhaps, but it is not. Your bloodpath dropping offline cut short a quite restorative salt bath and beckoned me here to investigate."

"Sure, the guy who ruthlessly dispatched a whole legion of vile creatures through a time portal in order to steal the Seventh Council Seal for his own scheming megalomania, and with no concern for his daughter's wellbeing, is now the world's most conscientious dad."

He was silent for a while. "What happened?" he said in the end, sounding concerned.

Give him his Oscar. I took a deep breath. "The necromancers. Please, you know what happened. I'm tired."

"What about the necromancers?"

"Oh my god!" I said. "Fine. You decided you wanted the Seventh Council Seal, as always for your tedious aspirations to wreak havoc, and banishing other Eternals was on your list." I paused, letting my words sink in before continuing. "And so, we waged battle with the necromancers and demons you sent to hunt and kill anyone who stood in the way—which would always include me, your daughter, the mist rider. Ring a fucking bell?"

"First, swearing does not convey strength, quite the opposite. I would not be doing my job as a father if I let that pass," he said. "Second, that is an utterly ridiculous plan, and I am not ridiculous. You can't be killed. The whole enterprise you say I authored was a pointless folly."

The ground under my feet trembled. An oppressive thrust of energy swept over me. I had tried his patience.

"That folly has Winter fighting for his life," I said.

"You're emotional," Horror said. "Your mind is cluttered. All your intermingling with humans has made you soggy with sentiment."

"Go back to your salt bath, please."

"I did sense trouble earlier," he said. "Normally I would have intervened, but I made you a solemn promise."

Something was not right. He sounded *sincere*.

"What is this? Are you still trying to convince me you didn't send the necromancers? Don't bother."

"Falsely accuse me and you'll be playing right into the perpetrator's hands," he said. "Driving a rift between us was almost certainly the very purpose of the attack."

I shook my head. "You're confusing me. I'm not trying to hear all your word soup right now. Do what you're good at. Disappear."

"You gave me an ultimatum, Luna. If I meddled in your life in any way, you would never come to me of your own free will. I remained at a distance."

"Wow, what strength!" I snapped back. "Have you forgotten the first time you put me in peril at Nightwood? Without a second thought."

He stayed silent for a moment.

"I'm not to blame for everything that happens to you. Even I can make errors in judgment, but I'm here now," he said almost tenderly. "I offer you aid—the aid of a necessary ally if you mean to retaliate against those who wish you harm."

"An ally," I said, laughing quietly. "Why? You want me to put my guard down to make it easier for you to dispose of me when the time is right?"

"If we combine our forces, my doubting daughter, we will

instill fear in the heart of all creatures great and small. And with that fear will come desperate souls, ready to save themselves and betray those who put your boyfriend in mortal peril."

My chest tightened as the Oracle's words rang in my ears: *One, you kill Horror and you avert the war. Two, you hesitate and the world falls. Three, you join Horror and the greater world falls, but you are left standing to rule over what remains.*

"I can't even with you right now," I muttered.

"You are yet delicate, even though you are capable of unfathomable destruction. I make a solemn pledge to shield you and your little playthings from harm. On my honor, I will safeguard you from any future suffering."

Until such time...

I had no doubt he meant every word, but somewhere between breaths there was an unheard whisper that surely clarified that his pledge lasted only as long as it benefitted the great and mighty Horror.

"How do I say this politely?" I said. "I'd rather die. Leave my thoughts and my friends alone."

An eerie stillness hung in the air. Horror remained silent, but I could feel his etheric essence bearing down on me. "Explain once more," he said finally, "how is it that you came to be part of the Seal's guard? What promises have you made the Immortal councils, daughter?"

There it is. The real Slim Shady.

I purposely smiled like I had secrets, because why not?

"Never mind all that," he redirected, his stern tone softening. "What matters now is that I am aware of a new enemy targeting you. I claim the right of a father. I cannot stand idly by and watch any longer."

Every nerve in my body tensed. "Did I dream this whole conversation? What part of *stay out of my business* did you not hear?"

I felt his frustration growing. "I thought you would listen to reason," he said.

"Say that again with your best Nazi voice."

He exhaled and his voice trailed off. "Impossible child!"

"You know, Daddy, it's been a long day. Thanks for checking in."

He got loud. "Think, Luna. If I wanted to seize the Seal and use it for my own gain, would I challenge a mist rider? Would I rely on clearly incompetent agents to do my bidding?"

"I don't have your toxic Eternal playbook, so I haven't a clue."

He moaned. "The Seventh Council Seal is immensely powerful, yes—it can be used to alter the balance of powers, allowing one to summon vicious forces from nature and the solar system itself, and it provides access to arcane knowledge long forgotten, but, dear girl, I can do all of that without it. You mentioned the Seal can banish Eternals. That's something I did not know. If true, would not any Eternal quite justifiably covet the Seal?"

Fuck. Was he truly unaware that Düsternis had incorporated cyphers crafted in the Eternal language into the core of the Seal? Did I stick my foot in my mouth by revealing that, or was he manipulating me?

I weighed my options. If I turned down his offer, he would just go behind my back regardless. Maybe I could ask him to prove his loyalty by performing a difficult task for me. Doing even that would mean I unleashed him and would have little to no control over his actions. I would have to accept whatever method or madness he devised. Why was I even considering such things? Did I really not believe he was the one who enlisted the necromancers and demons?

No matter what, the path ahead would be grueling.

I decided to roll the dice. "Very well," I said. "If what you say is accurate, I'd have you do something for me."

"Interesting," he said. "What foul errand did you have in mind?"

"Track down whoever cracked open a time portal beneath San Diego."

"Ah, you want me to be your muscle," he said. "Okay, boss."

"But here's the catch," I said. "You have to bring them to me. Unharmed."

"Come on, dove, where's the fun in that? How *unharmed*?"

Oh my god. Toxic alpha alert.

"Almost completely unharmed," I said. "Don't be a psycho."

Horror considered my request for a few moments. "I shall see to it," he proclaimed. "This is a difficult task. If a being can control time portals, they can also cover their etheric tracks, but I shall do the impossible as a gesture of my goodwill."

Yeah, that's you, the goodwill ambassador.

"One last thing, my petal," he said. "How does all this connect to your disappearance from the basic world for an entire hour?"

Time is a flat circle. We're back at square one.

"I'm at the hospital, father. It's where I've been and it's where I'll be. I am, as you say, *soggy with sentiment* for those I love."

"With sentiment, yes, but also with deception," he said, disappointed. "You lie to your own father, but I forgive you."

"Really? *You forgive me?* Excuse me, but trust must be earned, especially by you who sent your elite vanguard of Eternal Warriors to kill Winter during the battle at Nightwood. How do I forgive that?"

"Forgiveness is liberation," Horror said unconvincingly. "We both know that accusation was you changing the subject from the fact that you teleported to a protected place, most likely in an effort to keep me out. But let's not keep track of our duplicities. I'll carry out the assignment you gave me, but then we will choose honesty between us."

Let me count the reasons that can't happen.

"Just carry out the assignment," I said. "Baby steps."

He exhaled. "Listen, my princess. You may think me a heartless despot, but I will always be your father. Sometimes it takes a firm hand."

Apparently, to men like my father generosity must always be expressed in the form of a threat. This new dynamic he was trying to make happen bewildered me. The whole world was spinning out of control, and yet my absentee father was trying to grow into his caveman parental skills.

"Luna," he said, wistfully. "Destiny moves slow, but it's always coming."

Chapter 8

I TRUDGED MY WAY through the hospital, uncertain who had ordered the attack that nearly killed Winter. If nothing else, Horror had succeeded in planting a seed of doubt, triggering my paranoia. Not only was everyone now a suspect, but I felt crushed by the weight of the ancient prophecy, a prophecy of which I was sure my father was well aware. How could I trust a word that came out of his mouth?

Taking a big breath, I knocked on the door of Winter's room and pushed it open.

His blue eyes glowed with a bright coral fluorescence, otherworldly and welcoming. I wanted to fall into his ocean and stay there forever. He was resting on a pile of pillows, paler than normal and flashing me a warm smile. His exhaustion was palpable, but his etheric essence still radiated like a strong force field. I could feel it all the way to my core.

"Hey, big guy," I said, trying to stay upbeat. I felt a pang that I hadn't told him I loved him enough and saying it now, after he came so close to dying, would sound forced.

"Hey there," he said wearily.

"I just want to look at you," I said, my eyes scanning even the tiniest details of his face to make sure he was truly okay.

His eyebrows came together in a frown. "Wasn't I out a long time? Why do you still look like you've been to hell and back? I can't believe they let you in here like that. Look in a mirror. You need to go home and change."

Ah, right. There was grime and gore slathered all over me. Almost forgot about that. When Carter spoke to Winter, he must have skipped the part where Chaos literally yanked me out of the waiting room.

Might as well. Winter didn't need to worry about anything else right now.

"No time for that," I said. "I just grabbed a bite to eat and hydrated."

He peered into my eyes. He knew I was lying.

"You're not a stress eater," he said.

"No, not usually, but then you recklessly put yourself in harm's way, despite being sickly with mortality, and you dare scold me?"

"I just think you should go home," he said firmly. "Rest."

I shook my head. "I'm not going anywhere until I speak to the doctor."

He sighed. "I get that you're worried, but I have it from here."

I sat on the bed beside him. My body ached for his touch despite the doubts swirling in my mind. I placed my hand on his forearm.

"Why did you let yourself become mortal? It's so cruel," I said, despair creeping into my voice. "The thought that I might have lost you was unbearable."

He shifted closer and placed his hand on mine. "Forget all that," he said and pulled me into a gentle embrace.

I let out a sigh and whispered into his chest, "Never again. Promise."

There was a playful sparkle in his gaze. "I'd face a thousand deaths to be with you, Luna. The fear of losing the one you cherish is stronger than any other fear. And promises, they're as frail as humans. Only love is immortal."

"Are you on a lot of drugs right now?" I said, drunk on his words but knowing something must have made him so… delightful.

He laughed. "Big time. Drugs are more effective when you're mortal."

Not fair. I want some of those drugs, too!

Despite his charm, my stomach grinded. I scrambled to find the right words, while he effortlessly spewed beautiful, heartfelt sentiments and… *wait.*

"Hold on a second," I said. "Did you deliberately choose to stay mortal as some kind of romantic gesture? At a time like this?"

"Did it work?" he said, winking. "Relax, I'm only teasing, Luna. There are complex ramifications to any decision Immortals make. You know that. I'm not trying to be a martyr."

I could hardly believe my ears. "You idiot, I'm right, aren't

I? You've *chosen* to stay mortal, haven't you? I mean, the original plan was to reboot your etheric essence and clear your head and all that, but then you decided to take the long road back to immortality. And for what? Just to get me into bed?"

He looked away. *Busted.*

"Luna, we both needed it. You know this. Your hungry libido was fracturing your energy. You are a young being."

Wow... just wow.

"So, you what? Gave me a sympathy lay? When you give yourself to someone, it's charity work then? You feed the sex starved? Such a noble act," I said, briefly considering zapping him with a little energy. "History must be filled with lucky women you saved by fucking them. This is so cool. I never met a saint before."

Winter grabbed my arms to make me look at him. Even in this reduced state, his physical power was staggering.

"Listen," he said. "The physically and emotionally taxing process of bathing in the cathartic waters of the eternal springs is no joke. It's an excruciating ritual that left me exposed in many ways. There was a great chance I could have lost my most fragile early memories. Memories are all I have. No, I didn't endure all that to satisfy a sexual desire, even if that singular experience with you turned out to be a most welcome byproduct."

"Geez," I said, "I've never been referred to as a byproduct before. Please, excuse me if I blush."

"This is an explanation, not a flirtation."

"You describe our relationship like you're selling vacuum cleaners at a trade show."

"I want you to understand," he said. "After discovering that Chazona was responsible for the deaths of Helen and Christian, I found myself slipping into a crushing darkness, and I had to act before I lost all sense of myself. You think you've seen me at my worst, but you have no idea what lurks beneath the veneer of my subconscious. Only by clinging to humanity have I managed to stave off the terror lurking in the darkness."

I could feel the weight of his words. He believed a beast lived within him, a beast who could devour the world. Almost everyone I knew had cautioned me about him. Celia, Penelope, Darius, even Horror—each of them had told me Winter was bad news, yet no one had explained why.

"Winter, perception is reality," I said. "You've survived so much pain and tragedy. There's always going to be damage buried deep within, but you're a good man. Even if you slip and lose yourself, you'll always find your way back. Trust yourself—I do. I trust you with my life. I mean, look at me. This day has been tough. One day and my nerves are shot. If someone cut me off in traffic later, I might melt their car. Nobody's perfect."

He pulled me in to hold my head on his chest. "Luna, I saw things, down in the tunnels. An interdimensional time warp erupted, spewing out a necromaster, a mindbender. I saw you swept up in a vortex, a dark energy swirled around you like an inferno, and then there was an incredible explosion. From where I stood, it appeared you had made the master of the dead implode through the sheer force of your will."

"Yeah," I said, quietly. "It was gnarly. I don't know how I did that. It was mist energy, I somehow fed it into his core. It corrupted him, his bones, his bloodstream, everything. It worked like toxic explosives, I guess." As the words came out of my mouth, I knew they sounded strange.

Winter lifted my head to size me up. "I've only ever heard of Eternals practicing the dark arts of total body corruption."

"Dark arts are not a good thing, huh?" I said, growing tired. All I wanted was to fall asleep in his arms.

He shrugged. "It's not good, bad or ugly. There's no humanistic valuation at play here. The question is whether you'll be able to handle such a dangerous level of telepathic power should you use it again."

"Well, I come from a very old line of Eternals, so maybe I won't burn down the world with it." I let out a deep breath. "Hearing myself talk makes me wish I was anyone but who I am."

"It doesn't work that way. No one is born an Eternal."

"Then Horror must have gifted me with this power. He's been doing that. This was probably one of his manipulative gifts, because, you know, he loves me so much."

He felt discomfort and repositioned himself in bed.

"Better hope not. What he can grant, he can also take away, and Horror will do it when you need them most."

I had so many questions, but before I could ask anything, my phone buzzed. Faion's name flashed across the screen. "Hold that thought," I told Winter as I answered the call. "Hey Faion, what's up?"

The line stayed quiet. Eventually, his voice came across short of breath, tinged with panic. "*Where've you been? The most terrible thing has happened.*"

I braced myself. "What happened?" I said, not wanting to know.

"*Horpheus was attacked.*" Faion's voice sounded thin and cracked. "*It's not good. The mage healers won't say it, but they look defeated.*"

I felt sick. All my thoughts collided. Horpheus was more insulated, more protected than any being. What power could have penetrated the godlike shell of magic around him?

"That's not possible," I said. "Horpheus is untouchable."

Faion's voice wavered. I knew he was hiding tears on the other end of the line. "*Catch up, Luna. The dude's dying, for real. There are entities in this world capable of all manners of mayhem and doom. Ancient evil, you feel me?*"

I stole a glance at Winter. His face was as pale as a mask of death, most likely a reflection of the fear on my own face.

"I'll put you on speaker," I said. "Winter needs to hear all of this."

"Horpheus was attacked at his crib. The crystal tears were snatched," Faion said. *"They were being kept in his enchanted vault. No one outside the Board of Supernatural Orders even knew he had a vault."*

My bastard father, he played me yet again.

"Are you in the Deep Down?" I asked Faion.

"Yeah, just got here with my Gran."

"I'll be there soon."

I hung up. My mind blazed with anger.

Winter's body tensed. His eyes were heavy. All of this was too much excitement for a partially mortal man in recovery.

"Horror must have read my mind," I said. "There's no other explanation. He popped into my head on my way here. He acted all innocent and paternal, like he had nothing to do with the attack of the necromancers. I thought I had formed an impenetrable thought barrier, but I must have been wrong."

Winter took my hand. "You're not responsible for what Horror does."

"He raided my mind," I said, disheartened. "He stalled me with lies so that he could scavenge through my thoughts. It's the only way he could know I gave Horpheus the crystal tears of the Horae. He wants to do it all again. He wants to forge another Shield of Time."

"Luna, did you know Horpheus's enchanted vault existed?"

I shook my head. "I didn't."

"Then it wasn't you," Winter said calmly. "More likely it was a member of the Board of Supernatural Orders who tipped Horror off. Someone very close to the Great Chanter."

I glared at him wearily. "Maybe, but the result's the same. Horror can make a brand-new shield of terror. I must go, Winter."

"Yes, you must. I'm fine, Luna, really. I may be mortal for now, but I still recover quicker than most basics. The doctors stopped the internal bleeding, and I feel almost no pain."

Such a heroic liar. My lovely Shadow.

"If that's true, you're a big faker," I said with a surge of love in my heart. It always felt wrong to leave his side, but even more so when he was hurt.

He mustered up a mischievous grin. "Well, I do love watching you fret over me, but, really, I'm feeling better already."

This time, I'll pretend it's true.

Chapter 9

As I crossed the enchanted gate, a cool gust rippled through the air, causing me to shiver and clutch my jacket around me. Faion and his grandmother, the legendary diviner Celia Trice, were already waiting for me, anticipation etched all over their faces.

The trip to the Deep Down had been fraught with apprehension over Horpheus's fate and dread about Horror's intentions should he manage to piece back together the Shield of Time. Every footstep felt like plunging into an icy abyss rather than a journey home.

Faion looked haggard—worry lines creased his forehead. As soon as he spotted me, his expression softened, and a smile tugged at the corner of his mouth.

Celia's penetrating eyes lacked their usual spark. Her thick locks were threaded with more streaks of silver and gray than I remembered, and her posture was bent. Time and events seemed to have taken a substantial toll on her since the last time we were together. Yet, despite it all, her presence still commanded respect and her etheric essence radiated around her, making me feel insignificant next to her power and wisdom.

She flashed me an unsuccessful smile as I inched closer. Her gaze betrayed a deep sorrow, like her spirit had been eternally broken.

"Miss Celia," I said, clasping her hands in mine. "It's so good to see you again. How's Horpheus doing?"

She shook her head. "He doesn't have much time left, dear child."

"It doesn't make sense," I said.

Celia glanced up at the silver stars painted on the dome ceiling. "This was not foreseen in any of the prophecies," she said. "The time-weave is fraying more quickly than we ever thought it could."

A new fear overcame me. Everything seemed to be running away from me like a night train barreling toward a deadly cliff.

"We must hurry," Celia urged. "Horpheus has requested your presence."

My jaw dropped. "He's asked for me? That has to be a mistake."

"That's what I said, but we're both wrong," Faion said. "You're the only person he asked to see."

Celia's warm eyes sparked. "It's true, Luna. I think he's clinging to this world solely to speak with you one last time."

The realization hit me like a ton of bricks—Horpheus must have known who and what I was since the first time he set his eyes on me. Whatever he had to say would be of great importance.

We stepped through an iridescent portal into a kaleidoscopic transport passageway. Our images bounced off the mirrored walls, multiplying us in dizzying arrays as rooms, corridors and lights whizzed by in a blur. My eyes widened with every passing reflection. The Deep Down looked nothing like I remembered it. Every detail, from the subtly shifting geometrical patterns on the walls to the dazzling carpets to the altered shapes and sizes of the buildings, was unlike anything I had seen before.

Despite my shock, it wasn't unexpected. The Deep Down was a vast, complex maze capable of rearranging its pathways and restructuring its layout when threatened by intruders. Descending into its depths was akin to delving into a Minoan labyrinth of ever-morphing walls. Without knowledge of the arcane and ritualistic principles that drove its architecture, outsiders had little hope of navigating their way in or out. It made sense that the assault on Horpheus had activated the realm's defensive mode and triggered a complete configuration shift.

Three warrior mages materialized from the shadows as we stepped out of the moving passageway. Their armor glimmered as they bowed their heads before striding ahead to form a military escort.

The further we descended, the more stark the atmosphere became. The streets appeared abandoned, the only signs of life coming from the soft flickering of candles in windowsills.

We passed through a succession of stone arcs and climbed down several flights of stairs until, finally, we traversed down the long, humid hallway that led to the chambers of the Great Chanter. Above us, the smoke from burning wicks clung to the ceiling, and the smell of incense invaded my nostrils.

The warrior mages stayed back, their eyes fixated on us as they maintained a reverent distance.

I hesitated to enter, fearing the state in which I might find Horpheus. The thought of causing him further distress weighed heavily on my heart.

Celia's reassuring hand landed lightly on the back of my arm. "You must walk through this door, Luna Mae. Your time with Horpheus may be the only thing that can protect the realm of magic from imminent doom."

I gathered up my courage and crossed the threshold. My steps echoed on the marble floor. The room pulsated with an eerie stillness. Ancient, ornate tapestries of fabled mages and witches adorned the walls. A lone moonbeam streamed down through an intricately carved oculus in the ceiling, illuminating the hulking four-poster bed at the center of the chamber.

Horpheus lay there motionless, his breathing labored and shallow. The mage healer tending to him bowed before leaving the room.

I found myself alone in the presence of the Great Chanter.

Horpheus stirred and his hand weakly reached for me. I inhaled sharply as I edged closer. His eyes were shut and his body frail, yet I could feel his spirit emanating off him in etheric waves.

He opened his eyes slowly with a look of recognition and urgency.

I grasped onto his frail hand. Tears instantly welled in my eyes.

"You made it," Horpheus said, struggling to keep his voice steady.

"Of course. There's no place I'd rather be."

"You must be told," he said, barely audible. He heaved and wheezed with each breath.

"You should be resting. I can call the mage healer back in..."

He latched onto my hand. "I've lived long, mist rider. Longer than any soul should ever live. I am not afraid to cross over. This cannot wait."

The tears spilled onto my cheeks. "Tell me."

"The prophecy," he uttered ominously.

"The prophecy about killing Horror, my father?"

"Aye, but that is only the beginning of what's foretold. You see, the mist rider who slays Horror shall ascend the throne."

"What throne?"

He struggled to swallow before he spoke. "The Eternal

throne in the Eternal Halls, a place detached from all other realms."

"No... I don't want that. I don't want any throne and I won't be removed from my world." The idea of having to watch over all I knew from a distant, unemotional place was unbearable. I said it again, "No."

"It's too late for that, young rider. Your choices are written."

"There has to be another way. Tell me how to stop Horror without taking his life," I pleaded. "How much time do I have? How long will it take him to reforge that damned shield?"

Horpheus coughed violently when he tried to speak.

"Please, let me get the healer..."

He grabbed my shirt, struggling to hold his head up. "Listen. Hear me," he said. I let him rest against my shoulder to keep his head from falling. "Not Horror alone. The others. You must worry about the others. All of them."

All the Eternals? How the hell could I take on all of them? Their combined power was unstoppable—their strength and their rage could explode the Sun. Since I was a child, whenever I thought of them, I could feel their staggering presence looming over everything.

Horpheus gagged, then cleared his throat. He sat up, having found a second wind.

"When they realize a mist rider is the prophesied child, the one who will annihilate the strongest among them, they will know that the etheric transference from killing Horror will be immeasurable and grant you enough power to rule over them. They will not allow that to happen. They will banish or slay you without hesitation to retain control."

I shook my head in disbelief. His words were ridiculous. I felt none of that potential. Not that long ago, I was just Sophie, a recent graduate of San Diego State.

Go Aztecs!

Horpheus struggled to take in his next breath. "The Eternals will deploy their own rider." His eyes suddenly glazed over, as if he were in a trance. "Beware the one who rides the night, Luna."

Um, that sounds like good advice.

"Another beast for me to vanquish?" I said.

His voice echoed now as his strange words filled my ears. "When shadows stir... the night rider wakes... his cloak flutters in the wind like raven wings. You can feel him, cold on your skin, dark as death, breath of ice... destroyer... shadow swallower, predator of light. The night creatures follow him... entranced by his energy... none can look away as he draws near. I know not what will come to pass, Sophie of Astoria, but be prepared. All that is coming will soon be here."

I gasped, feverishly trying to process the incomprehensible words that flew by in his almost possessed mutterings.

"Great Chanter, how will I stop such an apparition?"

His eyes remained open, but he could no longer see. He

was slowly slipping away from the problems of this world and the living.

I rose to call for the healer mage. Horpheus could no longer help. Instead, the Great Chanter had left me an impossible task with no direction, no hope, not even a single magical chant.

Chapter 10

I plodded up the stairs to my apartment, wishing I could take out my anger on someone or something. My hands buzzed with the urge to blast back all the evil of the world. Chaos had told me not to underestimate Horror. Emotions were making me hesitate. I had to overcome my human sentiments. Like Horror himself said, destiny might move slow, but it's always coming.

A nagging feeling of being followed persisted as I made my way back from the Deep Down, first riding on a ley line, then on foot. A vague, primal energy seemed to enshroud me. My mind spiraled into paranoia. With each shuffling step, I felt a presence at my shoulder. Casting a glance behind me, I thought I caught a glimpse of a shape lurking in the shadows—a tall, perhaps hooded figure with eyes sparking like glowing rubies in the deepening twilight.

I felt somehow changed, a coldness settling deep within. The sight of Horpheus, the benevolent magic leader I had revered my entire life, lying helpless on his deathbed, gasping out dire warnings of dangers approaching, had not only soured my mood—it had also overridden any sense of self-preservation as I headed for a full-blown collision with my father. I knew now, beyond the shadow of a doubt, that I had to kill him, and by doing so, I'd be offering up my own neck to the Eternals.

That's what I get for saving your eternal asses?

Horror had obliterated the truce between us when he infiltrated my mind to extract the information needed to breach the Deep Down. He challenged me directly and, by attacking Horpheus, declared open war.

Did I really expect more from him? The selfish bastard cared about one thing only—being a step ahead at any cost.

Standing outside my door, I felt as if I teetered on the brink of a precipice. The call of the void resonated in my veins, pulsing with each heartbeat and every breath I took. The manic impulse to find Horror and force him to come clean was maddening. The idea of inflicting pain on him made my head giddy.

This is not who I am.

No, but it was who I needed to become.

Who else is going to sign up for this shit anyway?

There was a pool of one who could have the slightest chance to pull it off. And, once again, I was alone in that pool.

The raw energy I felt coursing through my cells was electrifying. Power bubbled up inside me—an overwhelming force which I now realized I had kept restrained my entire life, but the relentless pressure of the past few days made it harder to keep it caged. Every muscle in my body tightened until they ached. I fought to control all my dark gifts. The longer that fight went on, the closer to madness I ventured.

I jiggled the key in the keyhole until I heard the click. I ripped off my jacket and flopped onto the couch, my feet dangling over the armrest. I should have gone to the hospital to check on Winter, but it was late and it took all my efforts to control my rage. And I really needed to talk to someone else.

Chaos was nearby. I could sense his etheric essence emanating from the bloodpath that connected us like a phantom, calling out to me.

Summoning him would be difficult and risky, considering I had to be careful not to alert Horror in the process. The trick was to focus my energy like a shield around the bloodpath, so that only Chaos could sense my intent.

In theory. I had never actually tried before.

Closing my eyes, I stilled my breath, focusing all of my core energy to amplify the connection. The bloodpath responded, winding its way through me like a snake and summoning Chaos.

The darkness outside the window intensified. The moon reached out as if beckoning me closer. I felt myself fading away, drifting further into the blood connection, until finally my brother's voice resonated in my head.

"What do you need, little pest?"

His voice was both commanding and calming at the same time.

I didn't get a chance to answer. The Lord of the Black Demon Hounds materialized in my apartment, wearing his signature black trench coat, a lazy yawn forming on his lips.

"Two days in a row, eh, pumpkin? You're becoming codependent."

Yes, I did it! I summoned his smug ass.

"I can't believe it worked. I got you to show up."

He leaned his six-foot-two, hulking frame back against the wall, arms crossed on his chest. "You're playing with fire. I successfully removed Horror's markings from the elementary skills of telepathic connection that I inherited from him, so he's none the wiser when I use them. Can you say the same?"

I shrugged. "Maybe. Don't care. We're at war."

"I'm sorry, come again?"

"No more pretenses, no more tiptoeing around. It's time I take down Horror. We are officially at war."

He uncrossed his arms. I thought his head would explode. "Fucking fuckety fuck! Are you all the way outside your feeble mind? Did I not instruct you to stay far, far away from Horror? I told you to be smart, to continue with the skittish childish behavior and the constant whining around him. That's not hard for you to pull off. You just had to be yourself."

"Sorry, not sorry."

"You're not ready to confront him, you flighty milkmaid."

Milkmaid?

"You're wasting your time," I said. "He's challenging *me*, not the other way around. And you're the milkmaid!"

He quickly regained composure. "Tell me what happened."

"Where to begin? Let's see. The moment you dropped me off at the hospital, he popped into my head, probing for information, but, if I'm being honest, I haven't a clue if he succeeded in finding what he needed. I was on high alert, kept my thoughts contained and tracked his every move, but who knows?"

Chaos grumbled under his breath.

"He denied involvement in the necromantic attacks, of course," I went on, "then it appears that moments later, he forced his way into the Deep Down, used lethal dark magic against Horpheus and took possession of the crystal tears."

Chaos locked his two steely black eyes on me. "Why the hell would the crystal tears be secured in your fluffy fairy land?"

Right. "Because I gave them to Horpheus."

He thumped his forehead with his palm. "Why in the five realms would you do such an astoundingly asinine thing?"

Exasperation welled as I exhaled hard. "Why do you think? He was the safest option, the only being I could trust not to be tempted by their power."

"The safest option was to destroy them," he huffed.

"Okay, and do you know how to do that? Even the Shadow Master couldn't. If you had a better plan, why did you pack up and leave, brilliant brother?"

He sat on the couch and ran a hand through his hair. "Listen, I don't know *everything*, but I do know that none of this tosses you into a war with Horror."

Give me patience. "That sounds like wishful thinking. Horror can reforge the crystal shield, a.k.a. the Shield of Time, the weapon that can alter reality itself into a nightmare, and he went through me to achieve it. On top of that, he damn well knows of the prophecy where I kill him—or he kills me. Yet, his plans are moving ahead full steam. Wise up, Chaos. I did."

He stopped short of pushing over my coffee table, thinking better of it. "I'm here. You summoned me. Let's hope you have a plan."

"Of course," I assured him.

I so don't have a plan.

"I'm sure it's a doozy," he muttered under his breath. "I'm also sure it will involve me sticking my neck out yet again."

"We can't just sit around, waiting for my mother. We need to reach out. Whatever it takes, we need to contact her immediately."

Chaos gave me a sad smile. It was far more unsettling than all his admonishments. He had become the person I relied on the most when it came to Horror. I had thought it impossible to penetrate his tough exterior, but the gloom on his face proved me wrong.

"Let me see to it," he said.

Now I felt sad for him. Dealing with my mother, the woman he loved and could never have, caused him great sorrow.

I plopped down next to him. "What do you know of a dark rider?"

He shrugged. "You mean like a horseman of the apocalypse?"

I shook my head. "No. Horpheus warned me of a rider who rides the dark, a harbinger of death. A destroyer. I'm not even sure he knew what he was saying. He was delirious, but he said the Eternals will send a *night rider* after me. Yeah. *Beware the one who rides the night.* That's what he said."

That got his attention. "Why would the Eternals want your head?"

"Apparently, the rest of the prophecy dictates that after I slay Horror, I will rule over them."

Chaos burst out laughing. "You? Rule the Eternals? Maybe I should be the one to slay the old bastard then."

I glared at him, unamused. "It's not funny. You're not funny. The job sucks by the way. You'd be stuck in the Eternal Halls forever. You'd be miserable."

"Oh, come on," he said with a smirk on his face. "If we're going to die in this grand folly, at least let's have a sense of humor about it."

"We don't need jokes, we need answers. I need to know

if there is such a prophecy—probably, because apparently there are prophecies for everything—and I need to know what the Eternals know about me, about what I am, and if they are all in on me risking my life to defeat Horror, and also if they plan to reward me with a death sentence, and I need to find out if there's any credence given to this night rider legend and, if so, how can he be defeated, and I have no idea what else we need answers for, but there will be other things, there always are." I blurted all that out in one breathless stream. I was more rattled than I thought.

"Damn," Chaos said.

"What?" I said.

"This shit show just got worse. We have to begin our doomed crusade at the hospital. We must chat with the golden boy *tout suite*."

"Winter? For what? It has to be right now?"

"My old pal was invited to the Eternal Halls more than once. We were not. That means the old boy scout knows things. You'll just have to shake your money maker a little and Mr. Boredom will send us in the right direction."

He shot up from his seat.

"We're leaving now?" I said.

His dark eyes shone with fervor. "Into the fray, little sis. There's no time like the present, especially when the future may never arrive."

"It's after ten," I said. "Visitation hours have ended. They won't let us in."

He grinned as he strode over to open the window. He smiled as the cool night air splashed against his face. "If we cannot get past a few nurse stations, then we are lost already. We're descendants of gods, Luna Mae. Divine blood runs in our veins. I think maybe we have enough tricks up our sleeves to outmaneuver a sleepy hospital security guard."

I rolled my eyes. "So, we're teleporting again?"

If only it didn't make my insides flutter every time.

He waved his hand in dismissal. "You can be so tedious."

I stepped forward, wrapping my arms around him in a tight embrace. "Fine. Whenever you're ready."

My brother hesitated. "Are we absolutely certain about this? There's still time to retreat to my exquisite private sanctuary in Bora Bora."

I looked up into his eyes. "Horror crossed a line. We can't stick our heads in the sand, not even in Bora Bora."

Chaos hugged me tight. I closed my eyes and inhaled his scent of musk and sandalwood. Before I knew it, we were standing on a narrow hospital balcony.

He signaled me to stay put as he picked the lock with magic and glided gracefully through the door like a stealth cat. He waved me over and I followed him inside an empty break room.

We stepped into a busy hallway. The fluorescent lights flickered overhead, casting an eerie blueish hue over everything. The air smelled of hand sanitizer and disinfectant.

We tiptoed past the nurses' station and rounded a corner.

Chaos grabbed my arm and pulled me behind him as he peeked down the empty corridor.

Bringing his index finger to his lips, he pointed down the hall to where Winter's room was located.

A tall woman stood there with her back to us, her head slightly bent. Her long, black skirt elegantly cascaded down to the floor. A shimmering silver scarf was draped around her shoulders above a bright blue and yellow checkered blouse that she tucked into the waistband of her skirt.

It was a peculiar vision—it seemed as if she had stepped out of an antique photograph.

Her aura was prominent around her like a glistening spider web, shifting patterns and colors.

Not human.

Chaos pointed to the woman. I nodded and we both inched forward until we were standing a few feet behind her.

Her neck twisted, and her head snapped in our direction with an unnatural speed, almost as if some mechanism propelled the movement.

The tiny hairs all over my body stood on end. Her pupils were a jaundiced yellow, and the blood vessels beneath them were swollen and almost bursting through the thin membranes.

She fixed us with a penetrating gaze, her head cocked to the side.

My breath caught in my throat. "Chaos, what am I looking at?"

Chaos growled, disgusted. "Fuck if I know."

The woman raised her hands, and a sinister energy spilled from her fingertips. My skin prickled as the air hummed with her energy.

Great, of course she'd have supernatural abilities, too.

Chaos stepped forward, his hands illuminated with a blue light, electricity snaking around him like a writhing serpent.

"Remove yourself from that door," he said, his voice booming.

The woman's lips stretched into a wide smile, revealing two rows of sharp brown teeth. Instead of an answer, she spat at his face.

Ewww!

Chaos went ballistic. His eyes blazed. "You miserable hag."

His hands shot out and grabbed her by the throat, but his fingers started burning on contact. Chaos recoiled. The woman cackled, a chilling sound that sent shivers down my spine.

Bulky lumps swelled beneath her skin, like cannonballs waiting to be launched. She careened back with a sudden jerk and the fabric of her clothes tore as a grotesque shape exploded from within. The creature crashed down, groping the cold floor with her hands, her elbows raised and ready to leap off the ground.

"The fuck..." Chaos said.

Her legs bent at horrific angles like they had multiple knees, covered with thick, bristly hairs, as if she were an enormous spider. She let out an unearthly screech and lunged forward, her hands clawing at the air.

Chaos stepped back as she tumbled onto the ground, and I scrambled away in shock.

What had been a scary-looking woman seconds ago had transformed into a seven-foot-tall monstrosity covered in black and brown scales. Slimy tentacles protruded from her neck and thorax like three extra sets of legs. They wriggled around like eels as she hissed and snarled at us.

Chaos drew his sword from within his coat and charged her, swinging it in massive arcs to keep her away from me. She shrieked with rage, lunging forward and slashing at him with her claws. He blocked each blow expertly, driving her back step by step until he had her pinned against Winter's door.

She sprang forward with remarkable force, scampering off down the hallway to crash through a window and flee into the night.

We stared at the broken window in stunned silence.

Chaos finally interrupted the quiet. "Answer me honestly, did we drop acid before coming here?"

As if waking from a nightmare, I ignored my idiot brother and flung the door open. I blindly reached for the light switch, scared of what I might find. The bed was empty, but nothing else was out of place.

I wet my dry lips. "Where is he?" I muttered.

At that very moment, Winter walked in behind us,

yawning and looking surprised to find us occupying the room.

He arched an eyebrow. "I saw shattered glass all over the hallway," he said. "I should have known you two knuckleheads were behind the mess."

Chaos and I looked at each other and then back at Winter.

"There was a woman in the hallway," I said, my voice quivering.

"Yes, if by woman you mean a creature who will suck the marrow from a man's bones and then lick her fingers to the last drop," Chaos cut in.

"That doesn't narrow it down much," Winter said.

The two idiots laughed.

I shoved Winter. "Not funny."

"Sorry," Winter said. "It's the painkillers. They make me silly."

"Yeah, well, Chaos wasn't that far off in her description. She morphed into a hairy, seven-foot arachnid monster."

"And not the friendly neighborhood kind," Chaos chipped in.

Winter's expression became grave. He stepped out into the hallway to make sure she was really gone. He turned back to us with apprehension.

"Do you know what that was?" I asked him.

Winter shrugged. "Maybe. Did it grow new appendages?"

"Yeah, kind of, they weren't exactly appendages," I said. "They grew out of its thorax, like fucking tentacles."

Winter massaged his temples and closed his eyes as he processed the whole thing. "Best guess is it was a weaver, an attendant of the ancient Egyptian deity Neith."

"Neith?" I repeated. "That must be the one I've seen depicted as a spider."

"The very one," Winter said. "The servants of Neith were quite a wonder to behold. They could shift into the form of a spider at will. They could create doorways between worlds, sometimes even appearing as basic humans to sneak up on prey. A great attribute for skilled assassins such as the Weavers."

"I must have missed that day of ancient study," Chaos said, yawning.

"Yeah, that and a few other things," Winter quipped. "When the Weavers were called upon by their goddess, they would don their black scale armor and set out to do her bidding. They moved through the shadows like wraiths, striking down targets with silent efficiency. Their venomous bites were lethal. In recent times, the few who have survived have had their power greatly diminished, but their old customs have prevailed. Weavers have become supernatural assassins, mercenaries willing to take on any job that pays."

I shuddered in disbelief. "Does that mean you were just now the target of an assassination attempt? And you are in no shape to defend yourself."

Chaos scoffed. "Of course, he was the target, but the better question is *why* he was the target. Was the vile hag sent by Winter's own mile-long list of enemies? Or was destiny's darling, my confused little sister, to blame?"

I forced myself to sound calm. "Winter, if the weaver was here to kill you, then she likely knew you were mortal."

"She knew," Chaos said. "She is no match for him otherwise."

The sincerity of my brother's last words worried me. "We have to move him. He can't stay here. Let's get him somewhere safe."

Chaos shrugged. "There's only one place that would even have him."

Winter flared his nostrils. I expected resistance, but to my surprise, there was none. "Yeah, alright," he said. "To Umbra we go."

That was too easy.

They must be desperate. A dark time is upon us.

Chapter 11

THE LIGHT BURNED. I rubbed my eyes, then opened them again. Either the morning sun spilling in from the window was playing tricks on me or there was a translucent veil of wards right outside. It was almost peaceful, like a guardian watching over me, but I could have sworn it wasn't there last night. The Order of Shadows had taken every precaution to ensure my safety.

Winter had spent the night at the Umbra Infirmary, though I wasn't sure why the Shadow Master had been so insistent on that matter. Winter's wounds had almost healed and he'd vowed to do everything in his power to hasten his immortality's return.

Then again, the devout cultists of the Umbra Order would definitely take offense to Winter spending the night with me anyway.

Magnificent gothic structures with towers, interconnected bridges, terraces, balconies and cloisters sprawled outside the window. My gaze wandered over green pastoral expanses of trees laden with fruits, lush gardens and neatly trimmed lines of shrubbery. I imagined another world in which the future was secure, where I could walk these grounds and let my spirit fill up with peace and harmony.

I studied the protective ward veil, tempted to poke at it to test its potency and limits. My hand reached for the window, but I held back, unsure if my curiosity would be taken as a sign of disrespect to my gracious hosts.

Inside my chamber, the walls featured intricate and ornate designs. A few simple pieces of furniture were scattered throughout the mostly empty room. The vaulted ceiling gave an illusion of grandeur, making the room seem larger than it was and secluded from the outside world.

A silver-plated serving tray with lid waited for me on the mahogany table. I carefully removed the lid, revealing a breakfast feast. Three perfectly poached eggs sat atop a bed of grilled sausage, next to fresh blueberries. A crystal tumbler filled with freshly squeezed orange juice glowed invitingly from the edge of the platter. The familiar aromas brought a smile to my lips.

A melodic tapping came from the other side of the door. It seemed polite but had a firmness that could not be ignored.

The door opened to reveal the Shadow Master, tall and imposing in his robes of gold and purple silk. His smoldering eyes instantly communicated concern but also the assurance that I was always welcome here.

I stepped aside to allow him entrance, bowing slightly in respect. He walked through with both grace and an easy authority developed through many lifetimes of leadership in harsh times.

"I trust you slept well," he said. His voice was warm yet stern—an unsurprising blend for the powerful leader of such a venerable institution. "I had the steward flavor the air with frankincense and clary sage."

I nodded and gestured at the tray on the table. "Yes, I did. And thank you for the breakfast. It looks delicious."

"My apologies for showing up unannounced," he said. "I wanted to talk to you away from inquiring eyes. No one would think to look for me here."

"Of course," I said eagerly. "I've benefitted from your hospitality time and time again. I cannot thank you enough."

He paced the room, lost in his own thoughts.

"Shadow Master," I said, trying to break through his trance. "Did you get a chance to talk with Winter?"

He paused by the window. "Marcus," he corrected me.

"I'm sorry?"

He turned from the window to look upon me with kind eyes. "Call me Marcus. Once upon a time, it was my chosen name."

Doubts stirred within me—could I really bring myself to address the High Master of the Umbra Order by his first name?

He smiled and slowly shifted his gaze back to the window.

"I know what you're thinking," he said. "You're wondering why an Immortal from Western Africa, who's too old to recall the circumstance and the exact place of his birth, chose to go by a Roman name."

"I wasn't going to ask…" I muttered, trying my best to play along despite not having held a single thought about his name.

"Yes, but it was on your mind," he said, amused.

Farthest thing from it, but okay, now I'm interested.

"I do wish people would have the courage to ask me personal questions. I wish they could be relaxed around me," he mused reflectively.

"Well then… *Marcus*, what is the story behind your name?"

He took his time to begin. The silence hung between us like a haze. The air grew heavy with anticipation.

"I woke up to darkness and pain," he began. "I remember I was lying on a shallow mound of dirt, my body battered and bruised, encircled by my loyal regiment, all killed in battle. As I struggled to regain my senses, I pieced together what had happened, bit by bit. I was the last one standing against a throng of Roman legionaries. Like the others, they had mutilated me and left me for dead."

"You fought against Roman legions?"

"Yes," he said with a quick glance back. "And lost. It was during the Second Punic War. I had been forced to fight alongside the Carthaginians. When I regained enough strength, I fled the battlefield. I staggered on, seeking refuge from the incessant onslaught of Roman soldiers, so that my body could fully recover. I was not yet a Shadow Warrior. I had no access to magic or ley line energy. I was left to my own wits."

Been there.

"I stumbled upon a Roman farmer," he continued. "I was still broken, disfigured and covered in dirt and blood. The man must have thought I was going to expire at any moment, for he took pity on me and took me to his hearth to tend to my wounds. I remember his rough hands and gentle touch, the soft way he had spoken to me in a language I didn't understand."

"A good man," I offered.

"Indeed," the High Master agreed. "Before long, Roman soldiers arrived at his doorstep, requesting food. They could have been ten or twenty strong, I don't recall. They pushed in the door and ran a spear through me, then, convinced I was dead, they tortured and killed the kind farmer for giving shelter and mercy to the enemy."

"Bastards," I said under my breath. History was full of them.

"I summoned every last ounce of energy left in me," he said, intensely. "And slowly I pushed myself up off the damp, muddy ground. I stumbled onto my feet—my battered body screamed with pain, but my spirit blazed above all my senses with a determined ferocity. I killed them all, quickly and brutally, until I stood alone and blood-soaked in a silent room."

He stood at the window in front of me, but I knew his mind had traveled back to stand over the dead body of a good and decent man.

"I took his name, the farmer. I became Marcus, an honorable dirt farmer turned Immortal warrior. And from that day on, I vowed to never again allow myself to be dragged into imperialistic wars, not by men and not by gods, no matter the cost."

"Marcus the farmer would be proud of your gesture," I said.

He ignored my comment, still stuck in the past. "When I sauntered through the cobbled streets of Rome, I knew I had been changed, that I was no longer the person I had been. I was now Marcus, a man of unknown heritage and of a new identity. But I also knew that I could never fully escape the destiny stuck to me since birth. I was an Immortal, bound to the weight of my own history. It was then, a few short years later, that I happened upon the Umbra Order; an order to which my fate would be irrevocably tethered."

He retreated into memory.

I was captivated by his words, and my mind spun with questions. I wondered if he thought the grueling journey of becoming a Shadow Warrior was all worth it in the end. And was leadership worth facing relentless internal conflicts and festering politics that came with the position? How many battles? How much death? How much regret? Anguish? Moral defeat?

"It was worth it," he said out of the blue.

Holy shit, can he read my mind or did I just blurt all that out loud?

His eyes shifted to mine and for a moment he seemed almost wistful. "Yes," he said with a smile, "more than worth it. You see, now I'm in a position to help you, the last rider of the mist."

I stared at him. I never really processed being the last of my kind, a remnant of a forgotten legend. I mean, last year I was just an anonymous lunar witch from Astoria.

"Well, help wanted," I said.

His face became somber. "Luna, Darius has been telling tales to anyone willing to listen."

Darius, the notorious demigod whose ambitions had him kidnap Winter in an attempt to manipulate me into doing his bidding, was now a prisoner of the Order after I defeated him in his own domain by absorbing his etheric energy into my own core.

"What nonsense is he spewing now?" I said.

"He claims that you didn't defeat him on your own, but that Horror was there by your side, guiding you. He insists you are Horror's daughter."

I said nothing, trying to look confused while searching for words.

"No one can contain this kind of news for long," he said. "Not even me, neither my authority nor my power can stop gossip."

A sense of dread sunk into my gut. "Your warriors and your initiates have solemnly sworn a code of secrecy. They won't spread tales of this place."

He gave me a fierce look that could have melted steel. "You don't deny it."

"C'mon Marcus, I won't lie to you, but I'll deny it to any other."

"When this gets out, it will spread like wildfire," he said as if talking to himself. "All it takes is one loose tongue."

"Yes," I said with a sigh of resignation. "A matter of time, I suppose."

Not to mention, plenty of people had guessed already, including Horpheus and the Oracle of Delphi.

He stepped closer to lower his voice. "I am not sure you understand the ramifications if the Eternals hear of this."

"You think they may not yet know?" I said, hoping he could somehow provide reassurance.

"I don't know," he said after a few moments of contemplation. "If Horpheus's final words to you are to be trusted, we better hope they don't."

The Shadow Master had clearly talked to Winter. I had divulged every detail of my conversation with Horpheus to him on our way to Umbra.

"The night rider thing," I said. "What can you tell me about that?"

"It's a legend. In all the years I have been alive, I have never encountered the night rider myself nor met anyone else who had the misfortune."

"And what is the legend?"

"We call him the Nightbringer. He is said to be one of your kind, a mist rider who held a legendary status among his kin. His shrouded form—towering, cloaked in darkness, face concealed by a veil—instills terror in the hearts of all who behold him, for his very essence is death and destruction."

"The bogeyman," I said.

"If this is a children's tale, then it is a dark one. The legend states the Nightbringer absorbed a devastating amount of dark energy when he triumphed over the Titans in their revolt against the Eternals. The massive dark etheric transference split his etheric essence into millions of particles, which were locked inside his mist core."

I shuddered. "Perhaps, that eventually killed him? I mean he hasn't been spotted in millennia, right?"

"That has been our hope for many years. However, if that hope runs dry, you must know the Nightbringer is believed to be the most powerful of all beings, a ghost whose insatiable hunger for suffering and ruin would lead to the downfall of countless civilizations. Even the mighty Eternals fear that dark power. But when all options are lost and their fate is dire, desperation could lead them back to their old ally."

A psycho mist rider and an ally to the Eternals? When it rains...

My throat went dry. "How does one store so much evil energy?"

"Mist riders easily absorb energy from every available source. You experienced this yourself when you ventured into Darius's domain. Absorb too much and your magic core will reach critical mass, then something like an event horizon happens in the core, perhaps a reconfiguration or evolution beyond what we can understand."

"Does that mean..." I began hesitantly, afraid to put together the pieces before me.

He quickly shook his head. "No, Luna. It would take eons for you to confront enough evil enemies wielding dark magic to absorb the immense amounts needed to corrupt your core. And Darius himself is not wholly evil. In fact, he was once a great man and a leader. His energy core contains relatively equal amounts of light and dark, even if his ambition has clouded his judgment."

I sighed in relief at the small mercy. "So, the weaver that attacked Winter... could there be any connection to the Nightbringer?"

"There is no obvious connection," Marcus started, his brow furrowed in thought, "but I will investigate further."

I felt compelled to suggest our best bet for getting answers might be to confront my father head-on, but I swallowed that idea. I wasn't confident I could maintain my composure long enough to ask those questions before snapping and attempting to strangle Horror on sight.

The Shadow Master held me in his gaze with a mesmerizing seriousness. "The Eternals are ever watchful. Their reach is boundless." He paused before continuing. "It's best if we keep this conversation between us for now."

Everything inside me felt like it was sinking. The weight of too many secrets grew heavier by the day.

He bowed. "I will leave you to your breakfast." On his way out, he waved his hand over the eggs and sausage to warm them.

Chapter 12

I STUFFED MYSELF WITH poached eggs and savory sausage, then washed them down with the freshly squeezed orange juice. *A girl's got to eat.* Popping one last bite of sausage in my mouth, I made my way out the door and found myself in a silent corridor that stretched out beyond what the eye could see in either direction.

Energy streamed across the floor, subtle yet dense. I let it coil around my feet like a pet snake. The Umbra power grid fed on the mysterious shadow energy that resonated throughout the realm.

Needing to let out some steam, I randomly chose to go right and marched down the endless corridor in search of a staircase or a balcony. I longed to feel the morning dew on my skin and the wind in my hair.

What a shitstorm of a week.

Every day, I found bad news dancing in a conga line. I missed lazy college days of half watching *Grey's Anatomy* reruns on my iPad, sipping on a warm latte while I put off homework.

The direction I chose seemed to be unpromising, so I turned back. As I did, a hand reached out from a door I had not seen and grabbed me, pulling me inside a room.

The morning sun spilled in from an open window, casting a soft glow on Winter's face. His hair formed a golden halo around his head. He looked well rested and healthy, more alluring than ever in the warm early light.

"Where were you off to?" he asked. His voice was impossibly captivating, as if from another dimension. He grinned. "There's grease on your lips."

I licked them clean. "Oh, sausage lip gloss. Food's delicious here."

I tried not to let my eyes drop to the delicious distraction of him standing in nothing but boxer briefs. Instead, I studied his torso. There were no visible signs of injuries or scars. I glided my hand over his abdomen and chest. Surges of intense energy radiated where he had been wounded.

"You left the infirmary," I uttered, my mouth suddenly thirsty.

"I sensed you," he said, his breath heavy and inviting. "I had to come find you. I felt your unease. This wing of the tower is rarely used. Hardly anyone comes through here anymore."

"You might have put on some clothes before you wandered through halls." I walked over to grab a folded black velvet robe from a bed bench.

My breath quickened as he stepped closer to snatch the

robe from my hands and slide it on. The distinct scent of shadow magic filled the air. I saw unmistakable signs of revitalizing energy in his eyes. It was said that the Shadow realm had unmatched powers for healing and cell restoration. One legend stated that the poet Rumi, a basic, had recovered here after being brutally attacked and left for dead on the road to Damascus. The Umbra Order valued his wisdom and monitored his life force.

"Marcus wanted a private conversation, far from curious ears and perhaps far from you," I said.

Winter raised an eyebrow. "*Marcus?* You're on a first name basis with the Shadow Master?"

I shrugged. "I think sometimes he just wants to be a regular dude. You should take him to a ball game or something."

Winter chuckled as he stepped to the window to close it. "You're joking, but I did take him to the Super Bowl years ago and it was... quite the experience."

"Really? Did he have fun?"

"He was amazed. He kept spewing caustic comments about the players and their abilities, deriding their strength, their speed, you name it. I am sure we ruined the game for every fan within five rows of us."

I tried not to laugh. "You see, he needs to get out more. When you lock yourself away in a tower for so long, you lose touch with the real world and forget how to blend in."

"He can't even blend in here. How is he going to blend out there?" Winter said with a grin. "Someone has to be the

Shadow Master after all."

I scrutinized his face. "You look well. Hard to believe you had your gut ripped open by demon claws just three days ago. There's hardly a blemish on you; you've been completely restored to your former glory. Does this mean you're immortal again?"

"Not quite yet. I'm sure I can still die if I were cut in two or a fiend devoured my heart."

An annoyed anxiety escalated in me until I nearly punched him. "Don't you dare joke about that."

His eyes regarded me tenderly. "I'm sorry. Things are progressing and it won't be much longer until I'm my old self. Until then, I'll do my best to avoid necromancers and demons."

I stared at him, full of dread.

"What?" Winter said, furrowing his brow.

"If I leave, do you promise to stay here?"

"You're leaving?"

"Time is running out. We need more answers."

"Luna," he said with his softest voice, "why do I get this sinking feeling that there's more to this than you're telling me?"

I took a deep breath. "Because there is."

A cold gust of air swept through the room as the window swung open with a violent bang.

Winter's gaze hardened. "The wards are tracking you," he said. "They have been calibrated to monitor your every step."

He marched over to the window and shut it, cutting off access to the prying wards.

"Can they listen in?" I said.

"It's possible. We'll go somewhere more private."

I followed him out into the hall where a staircase seemingly materialized out of thin air.

"Ha," I said. "Where did those stairs come from?"

"They've always been here. They're glamoured."

Glamoured, in other words cloaked with invisibility spells.

"And why would your fraternal shadow buddies endeavor to hide staircases from me?"

"Not from you specifically, from everyone. This wing was once used as..." His voice trailed off.

"A prison?" I finished his thought. "Your own sketchy Guantanamo?"

He took my hand and led me down the stairs that opened into a lush garden. We stopped at a line of tall shrubbery. He pushed aside manicured branches to reveal an old tool shed. Its weathered walls seemed to have been left to nature for decades. A thick net of cobwebs hung from the door.

"We'll have privacy in there," he said, his voice low and certain. "At least for several minutes."

We stepped in, and he immediately shut the door behind us. The lock vanished, fused into the wood.

I looked around warily, taking in our cramped surroundings. Stacks of dried-out logs lined the back wall, and an assortment of garden tools were tucked away in one corner. The faint smell of oil paint lingered in the air, and dust motes swirled in the weak light from the single dirty window. A potent aura glimmered, like something ancient had been embedded in the walls and roof.

"Not only a tool shed, is it?" I said.

"It's a tool shed, but it's also a Faraday cage for magic. No supernatural energy can break in or out."

"Not even the Shadow Master's wards?"

He shook his head. "I don't think so, but even if they could, it would make an incredible racket." He rested his hands on my shoulders, his gaze intense. "Luna, what Horpheus said... about the Nightbringer... I won't let that happen. I won't let anyone get to you. Rest assured."

I leaned in. "You will not forfeit your life for me. Don't tell me that or any other noble sacrifice bullshit. That's over. Please."

He closed his eyes. "I am not noble. Any chance of that ended long before you were born. But I do have your back. I won't let the Nightbringer find you."

A wave of claustrophobia washed over me. "The Nightbringer is real and alive? You know that for a fact?"

"He's real. That much I'm sure of."

"And the Eternals control him?"

"Perhaps. It remains to be seen."

"What about the prophecy that I'll become ruler of the Eternals and, by extension, all the realms of magic? Had you heard that one before?"

He hesitated. "I'm honestly not sure. While recovering from my physical issues, it seems my memory needs to recover as well. Most things are certain in my mind, but the prophecy about a mist rider ruling the Eternals... I am not sure. It does sound familiar, but I'm not certain if I am remembering idle gossip or true prophecy."

"You've been through a lot."

"I'm fine," he said. "My job is to go through a lot when necessary."

I grinned. "You should have retired a long time ago. You're really old."

"I'll retire when things like the existence of a dark mist rider no longer threaten you," he said. "Unfortunately, the world never remains static. When massive amounts of energy are transferred between ascended Immortals, there are always unintended consequences—essences are altered, new powers are created, all sorts of weird stuff can happen, including mist riders turning dark."

"And the weavers? Why are they after you?"

"I think they're after our unity. They're like union busters of sorts. They sense the connection between all of us. You, me, Chaos, Kirsi and her Valkyrie sisters... they must feel our alliance is getting stronger."

Ah, the goon squad. Paid agitators. Fucking weavers.

Winter clasped my face in his hands. "What aren't you telling me? Why are you leaving?"

My heart accelerated. "I... will meet with my biological mother. Chaos is arranging it."

Winter stepped back. "Your *mother*? I don't understand."

"Yes. You don't know of her?"

"Your birth records were wiped clean after Chaos brought you to me, but if Horror is your father, that most likely means one thing. Your mother is Horror's wife, known among Eternals and Immortals as Time."

"What impression do you have of her, Jonas?"

"I have no insights to share. Time is an Eternal with strong connections to several ancient deities who favored the Greeks. It is said she has the power to manipulate shifts in temporal dimensions and thus alter the course of time itself."

"And when you say deities, do you mean old Eternals?"

"For the most part, yes. Occasionally, just extraordinarily powerful Immortals." He hesitated for a moment before asking, "Do you truly think she will offer you aid?"

"She is a stranger to me, but I have to ask."

I decided to leave out the part about Time helping Darius in the months leading up to his capture, as well as the fact that she was the one behind the time portals in San Diego opening to let monsters out. I couldn't bring myself to tell him—not before I heard her side.

Winter exhaled heavily, as if he could see through my doubts.

"You don't think she will help," I said.

"Luna, I don't have faith in any of the Eternals. Even the most temperate among them have lost the capacity to reliably access their own emotions. The human concepts of responsibility, empathy or morality are quite foreign to them. Ironically, Horror's volatile temper is the most humanistic trait among the whole lot."

"Well, that's a scary thought," I said.

He softly touched his forehead to mine. I felt his arm slide around the small of my back as he pulled me to him. The warmth of his breath comforted me. The scent of his skin intoxicated me. I gave him control of my body and closed my eyes, savoring his every touch.

"Let me join you," he whispered in my ear.

"Always, but not with this," I whispered back. "She won't let anyone in, not Chaos, not you, maybe not even me. It's all very fragile. I can't risk bringing someone. I don't want to spook her should she grant me an audience."

His eyes reached into my soul to scrape it naked. For a moment, all doubts were erased with a single kiss. His lips were soft and warm, melting away my resolve.

A crazed energy flowed between us. I felt the pull of wild curiosity daring me to abandon all fears, to take on all risks in the face of looming peril.

He released me from his arms. A bitter chill engulfed the space between us—his glacial essence hit me like an avalanche.

I pulled the delicate Umbra silk robe tight around me,

startled by the sudden bite of his icy energy.

"Don't go looking for danger," he warned.

His hypocritical words demanded a quick reality check. "Really, danger boy? That's your sage advice? Run away from danger? What do you even know about that? You couldn't even follow that advice when you were mortal and could die slipping on a banana peel."

He scoffed; a mesmerizing deep blue light illuminated his eyes. I wanted his essence to consume me—a hungry craving that had my skin yearning for contact, for his rough fingers and lips to invade every inch of me. I slipped beneath the surface of that need. Helpless.

"You're still mortal, and we're inside a Faraday cage," I whispered. "We'd be fools not to make the most of it."

His face deadpanned. "Miss Collinsworth, you're a naughty girl."

I shrugged. "And I suppose you're a saint?"

"A saint would refuse you."

"You're not a saint. You're a self-important asshole," I said, perfectly aware that his eyes and hands were starving to explore.

"It's a matter of idiosyncratic interpretation."

"Oh, that's fucking sexy. Say more obscure nonsense. It sounds smart."

He gripped both my wrists roughly, pushing me against the wall. He smiled hungrily before his mouth locked on mine in a long, greedy kiss.

I threw my arms around him, almost unconsciously, to pull him closer, hoping his bones would crush mine to dust. His hands traveled, taking manic inventory of my everything.

He braced one arm on the wall to look at me. His lips remembered my face, first my cheeks, then my nose and then my eyelids. He kissed me so soft it almost felt like a goodbye. A chill ran through my veins, but then his eyes turned fiery. He used his weight to make me feel small, pinning me.

I closed my eyes, hugging him so tight I never wanted to let go. I wanted all his words, all his promises to be true.

When I opened my eyes, my lips met to form a word, but the only sound that came out was a shriek of shock.

The walls of the shed began to quiver, vibrating forcefully as if some unseen force was trying to tear them apart. I heard the door creaking and groaning under the strain, like it might give way at any moment.

With a gasp, I clutched the wall and looked to Winter in alarm. "Is it the wards again?"

"It's not the wards."

An object blurred past us and smashed into the stacked logs. Winter snapped to action, sheltering me in his arms as more objects darted about us.

We hurried out of the shed and into the garden. I felt a crippling ache inside my head that grew more intense with each breath. Winter held me to his chest and put his hand on my head while he looked around, worried.

"Let's get back to the tower," he said, his grip like icy steel.

A familiar energy pierced through the agony in my mind. My headache quickly abated.

"Wait," I said, squirming out of his grasp. "It's Chaos. I think he's trying to reach me. I have to take this call."

Chapter 13

"WHAT ON EARTH IS that?" I said as I peered down the winding path, overrun with thick winterberry and blackberry bushes. The mysterious creature looked like an imp, no larger than a toddler. Its body was covered in fine silver fur. A slender tail swayed over its head like a whip, sparkling with flecks of rose-gold dust. Two yellow stars twinkled in its huge, round eyes.

The little imp slowly blinked at me like an owl before scurrying over to an ancient oak tree. Its feet seemed to barely touch the ground as it moved, scattering a trail of rose-gold powder behind it.

I felt a spasm inside my skull, as though my brain had suddenly been struck numb, and the creature was gone. Then, in a flash, it reappeared on the path, staring me down with contempt.

Chaos yawned. "That imp is a Dustflinger, one of your mother's favorite pets."

I rubbed my eyes, trying to shake off the strange sensation. "Why is it called a Dustflinger?"

Before I finished my sentence, the Dustflinger had vanished again. An eerie melody lulled my mind into a daze, and the imp reappeared.

"Stop staring," Chaos warned, "or it will continue freezing your brain."

Reluctantly, I tore my gaze away from the incredible creature and followed Chaos down the path. I felt the Dustflinger's presence lingering.

"How does it do that?" I said.

"One of Time's reckless creations. The nasty buggers feed off the energy of any moron caught staring, disrupting the temporal flow, so they can slip away unnoticed. And that pink dust their tails fling... it stalls time for a breath or two. Touch it and you'll be crystallized in place, unable to move until the imp decides it has fed enough."

Peachy.

We trekked along the footpath leading to my mother's secret dwelling. The landscape shifted, as the shrubbery slowly gave way to a picturesque canopy of walnut, hickory and sycamore trees, their intertwining branches forming a tunnel of lush foliage which let through only a sliver of sunlight.

The fabric of reality itself seemed to ripple around us. I could feel the mystic power of the land buzzing in my bones.

"How long has Time lived here?" I asked.

Chaos spat out the side of his mouth. "Since she's been with that cretin we call father."

"They never actually lived together in the Eternal Halls

before Horror was banished?"

"Too much surveillance for her taste."

"Horror is the jealous type, huh?"

Chaos gave me a stern look that made me take a step back.

Right. Don't ask him these questions.

He plodded ahead, then spun on his heels to glare at me.

"Horror is a tyrant who will never let go of what he claims as his own. You and Time are on top of that list," he said with venom. "That's why she had to make her realm unbreachable."

This place was her escape, her refuge from Horror's iron fist rule.

Time's imprint on her domain was palpable everywhere. The air was heavy with her essence. The trees swayed with lush, rosy-hued leaves; a subtle, minty aroma filled my nostrils. I felt an intrinsic connection to the land, as if it had recognized me and was offering itself to me.

The more I learned about my mother, the more perplexing it became that she had ever chosen to forsake this tranquil sanctuary to join Horror in his exile. By what inner compulsion was she driven to link their destinies?

Suddenly, an echoing clatter rang out from the trees.

Chaos stretched out a protective arm in front of me, squinting at the sky as he sensed danger. "Dustflingers," he hissed. "A whole horde of them. If we do not avoid them, they'll slow us down for hours."

Jeez! Hadn't we been invited here? Time's welcoming

committee sucked big time.

We ducked behind a pile of timber and scanned the clearing ahead. A swarm of Dustflingers darted about in a frenzied state, their long tails flicking up puffs of pinkish dust which hung in the air like smoke.

The imps formed a column, then made a sharp turn and disappeared into the woods.

"Are they really gone, or have we been time-flung?" I said, my eyes still fixed on the spot where they had vanished.

"Really gone," Chaos confirmed.

"Dude, does she know we're coming? Because it doesn't seem like it," I said, exasperated. "It seems like you ignored her wishes and lied to me."

Chaos scoffed and continued onward without a single word.

A wave of dread washed over me. "This is a wild goose chase, isn't it? I swear, bro, if I left Winter at Umbra because of some bullshit—"

He stopped cold. "Are you fucking serious? He's a Shadow Warrior, not a frail child needing his mommy there to wipe his nose."

I did not honor his foul tone with a response.

I trailed silently behind him; the cheery sounds of birds and squirrels lightened the mood. Flashes of color sparkled and danced on the surface of a small creek. With every step, the brush bristled and snapped under my feet.

"I would not dishonor Time's wishes like that," Chaos

offered out of the blue. "No one would dare. How can you not know that?"

"I'm sorry," I said, "your complete lack of candor worries me."

"No, it's your complete lack of trust causing that."

"Well, whatever, you're just annoying."

He resisted an angry response by taking a breath. "This is what I get for breaking my own rules and sticking my neck out? Centuries of hard-won experience tells me I should be in one of my secret hideouts right now, warded and untraceable, and sipping a good brandy, letting it glide over my palate and linger there with its smoky flavor, but no, I'm here instead, assisting my completely entitled brat sister."

"Fine, you made your point. Jeez."

We reached the end of the path. The overgrown brush in front of us divided with a sudden flutter to unveil a pond of vibrant emerald water, surrounded by smooth rocks and lush rose bushes of every color.

A petite young woman sat on one of the larger rocks. The fabric of her lavender dress that ruffled at her ankles was thin and airy like butterfly wings. Her snow-white hair glistened with silver highlights, cascading in ringlets down to her narrow waist. Her big gray eyes were like shining portals that led back to unfathomable depths containing millennia of intelligence. Her red lips were so full and inviting I was sure they could kiss life into the world. Her aura glittered with an otherworldly splendor, a delicate combination of purple and gold sparkling around her like a full body halo.

When she blinked, it startled me.

How can such exquisite beauty actually live alongside the rest of us?

I clutched my brother's hand and whispered, "Is that..."

Chaos did a double take, his eyes wide with disbelief. "What? Do you think that's Time? Good god, sis, you are of feeble mind."

"How am I supposed to know?" I said under my breath.

"Trust me, the moment you're in her presence, you'll know."

The beautiful woman stood. Her frame was even smaller than I thought. Her skin was delicate like fine rice paper. Her pose was elegant. Her energy soothed me with the lightest touch, like a dying breeze.

She strode past us with a slight bow to invite us to follow. Her lavender dress belled out around her like an ethereal apparition.

"Let me do the talking," Chaos whispered. "Your self-righteous, schoolgirl whine would probably get us escorted out of here in no time."

"This coming from the world's worst diplomat," I smacked back.

The woman bowed gracefully. "Welcome to the Kingdom of Forever," she said, her voice soft and melodic like a lullaby. "I am heartened you have arrived safely. I will join you on the path to the Forever Palace."

I bowed in deference to our charming guide.

"We are heartened by your generosity, kind maiden," Chaos said.

"My name is Chloe, Luna Mae, Daughter of Time," she said, ignoring him, her eyes captivated with me. "Should you have any need at all during your stay, please, do not hesitate to ask."

"Cool, thanks, Chloe," I said. "You're so nice."

Chaos rolled his eyes in derision but kept his mouth shut.

Chloe again bowed and led us on around the edge of the pond to the other side. A trail paved with twinkling gems unfurled before us, snaking its way into an endless horizon.

Total Dorothy moment.

We trudged along the glittery path, feet crunching quietly on tiny pieces of precious stones. The scenery slowly changed. Splashes of color burst from the trees and bushes, painting them in shades of ruby red, sapphire blue and amethyst purple. Branches twisted and stretched, blending and curling together in mesmerizing, fluid forms. The leaves shimmered in the sunlight, fluttering and morphing into energy wisps that radiated rainbow spectrums across the landscape.

"I feel happily drunk, like we're in a kaleidoscope," I said.

Chloe's lips curled into a fleeting smile. "One can forget their troubles when in a new terrain. It's easier to feel free, to detach, but eventually the reason you are really here is remembered."

Point taken.

The bewitching trail curved abruptly. The bright spring colors deepened into rich autumn greens and browns as the vegetation thinned.

Just off the path, a small silver orb caught my attention. It hovered above the ground, twirling and sparkling like a diamond of light.

"What's that?" I asked, pointing it out to Chloe.

Chloe glanced at me before fixing her gaze on the levitating orb. "That's a crystal tear."

Realization set in and my heart fluttered. How could something of such exquisite tranquility prompt the world's ruin?

The orb rotated faster as Chloe's finger brushed its surface. It responded to her touch, unleashing a shower of tiny dancing lights.

"They are fragments of eternity, found everywhere in the Kingdom of Forever and imbued with immense cosmic energy," she continued. "They are composed of particles from the very essence of our universe, carrying within an infinite knowledge of what has been and what will be."

I gazed in wonder upon the crystal tear. It radiated a peculiar energy, a buzz that felt like... transcendence.

"I had thought the crystal tears came from the Horae," I said, surveying the path for a sign of Chaos. Suddenly, I had a hard time recalling when I had last seen him or if he had made the trip at all.

"We don't know where they come from, but we are the only beings who can capture them," Chloe said. "The Horae have the power to manipulate the energy of the tears to unlock their hidden power."

I stared at her in shock. "You... are a Hora."

Chloe nodded. A haunting melody flooded my ears. I knew, in my gut, the eerie voices belonged to the Horae.

In a crystal tear, time does tick
Memories fail, but always stick
Echoes of the past, buzz in its gleam
Forever frozen, caught in a dream

All colors of the realm morphed into a bleak palette of gray; the tree branches stretched for the sky like grotesque skeleton fingers.

The crystal tears hanging in the air like gems for Horror to pluck.

Everything spun around me like a dizzying gray whirlpool.

Chaos, where the hell are you?

I wanted to call out for him, frantically, but my voice caught in my throat. In desperation, I tried to turn to Chloe but only my eyes would move.

Her figure faded from sight, leaving no trace.

Chapter 14

"*FEW THINGS TRULY MATTER.*"

The voice came from my right—a woman's voice, alluring, persuasive. The kind of voice that once heard, you knew could not be disregarded.

The sparkly trail vanished, leaving behind a path of oozing mud. A wall of towering trees with intertwining branches obscured the sky.

Again, the voice resounded.

"*Love, pride, possession—all mere crutches of the weak, ephemeral delusions ever leading to disappointment.*"

I whipped around, an ache rising in my stomach.

"Who's speaking?" I said. My voice echoed off the trees.

I stepped onto the muddy path. The ground beneath my feet squished. It felt like walking on a wet sponge. My feet became heavy.

A spooky feeling took hold of me, as if a thousand eyes watched my every move from behind the shadows of the trees. A gust of wind blew past me, carrying with it whispering echoes.

"Friends make you vulnerable to enemies. Power is a corrupting force. Marriage is a gilded cage. Immortality becomes a burdensome duty."

I spun again toward the voice.

"Mother?" I said, my own voice hollow. "What have you done to Chaos?"

Something rustled amongst the looming trees. Part of me wanted to run away, but curiosity kept me glued in place.

"Mortals don't appreciate the preciousness of life. Much of their time is spent idly, with hardly a thought beyond the moment. There are no earth-shattering battles raging within, no life-and-death choices—just the ordinary and the banal, filled up with disposable items they accumulate over time."

Winter was right. It was astonishing how little Eternals understood the human condition.

"Mortals make profound decisions on a daily basis," I said. "Just getting up and going to work each day is a decision that contains all the weight and stress of the world, and they have to make it every single day. They are hanging on by a thread and they value life more than you'll ever know, because to them everything is so fleeting and one bad decision can send them spinning out of control."

"You are still so young, my daughter."

It sounded like an accusation. I felt my temper rise. I clenched my fists and took a step forward. "Why don't you show your face? Your little magic tricks don't intimidate me."

They do. Everything here does.

My chest churned with adrenaline. I could hear the heartbeat of every living thing in the forest, the quiet rustling of leaves, the swaying of soft blades of grass.

"A purpose," she said. *"A raison d'être. Gods and mortals alike must find that to truly matter. Empathy, strength, determination. Those are the things that give life meaning. Might you be the one to stand tall against the tide of evil as it surges, Daughter? Will you illustrate grace and generosity? Can you use your gifts for a greater good? Are you to become a beacon of hope for justice, freedom and equality to all mankind?"*

"Are you?" I said, fully realizing how rash and immature I sounded. That happened when I got pissed. "You sound like an Army recruiter, by the way."

Her silence pressed down on me. I could feel her gaze, heavy and reproachful. Even the wind had come to a standstill.

I drew a sharp breath to ease my nerves. I was here at her behest. I could stand and trade barbs with her all day, or I could placate her ego so we could move on.

"Forgive my outburst," I said, swallowing back my pride. "I'm trying to be strong and make the right choices, but at times that seems impossible. I could use your guidance."

"There will always be an abundance of choices; moments too, when try as you might, your instincts will fail you—those missteps exist for a reason, not just a test of your resolve, but

an opportunity to reflect and move forward and choose again between equally perilous paths."

An orb of light glowed among the trees. A melodic tinkling drifted across the path like a thousand tiny chimes.

"Crystal tears are the rarest of all enchanted gems," my mother continued. *"Found once on Mount Olympus in ancient Greece, they have now made my kingdom their home alongside the last five Horae. Smooth as pearls, captivating like a raindrop caught in the moonlight, reminiscent of a loving mother's breath, spellbinding like a rippling prism of light. A single crystal tear holds the ability to shape or destroy entire worlds, rewrite history, or twist the fundamentals of physics."*

The luminous orb sprang forth before me, hovering just above my eye level. At its core, a figure stood shrouded in a hooded cloak. He remained still and silent, his face concealed, yet I could feel his uncanny energy buzzing in my ears. I recoiled as my blood recognized Horror's essence.

"Isn't the dark Eternal the reason you're here? Did you not seek me out to inquire how your father can be defeated?"

I drew closer to the suspended crystal tear as the air around me bristled with electricity. Horror's silhouette dissolved, replaced by a purple afterglow.

"I sought you out because of the cryptic message you sent last spring. You said when my destiny arrived, you would soon follow. Well, I'm pretty sure destiny has arrived, Mother, and his name starts with an H. And there's a second reason. I wanted to look you in the eye when I asked…"

My voice trailed off. I decided to resist spewing out all the questions and accusations that yearned to spill forth from my mouth.

"Fretting child, ease your mind. Your father may possess crystal tears, but he cannot unlock their full potential. That task is reserved for the Horae."

I chewed on the implications. "Just to be clear, are you saying Horror could not have forged the crystal shield without help? That would mean you asked the Horae to help him craft it. Huh. That must be why he called it *Shield of Time*. Was it his little homage to you?" I asked, diplomacy be dammed.

"All in due course, Daughter." Her voice was gentle, without a trace of annoyance at my lack of tact. *"For now, I shall count backwards from three. When I snap my fingers, you will be returned to your companions. They will not know that you ever left their temporal plane. In their eyes, it will seem as if no time has passed at all."*

An unnerving thought struck me. "Please, do not erase my memory of our conversation."

"That is how your father behaves. Not I."

The crystal tear spun faster and faster, drawing me into a vortex absent of all light, whirling me around like I was inside a washing machine. Then the centrifugal force stopped abruptly.

I found myself back on the glittery trail. Chaos leaned

against a tree, nibbling on a fingernail, appearing quite bored.

I discovered I was shaking. Chloe's hand coiled around mine. She regarded me with warm, gray eyes. "Abandon your fears, Luna Mae."

"Said Brutus," Chaos mumbled under his breath.

I glared at him.

"How much longer until we're there?" I asked Chloe.

"We will arrive when Time is ready to welcome us."

She glided on, a cloud of dust sparking up behind her. The only sound was the whisper of fabric from her lavender dress bouncing about her feet.

I suddenly understood why my mother had isolated me. She wanted to scrutinize me in every way possible—examine my motivations, assess my character and identify my vulnerabilities. She was looking to gain leverage.

So much for a happy reunion or a budding alliance or even a hint of motherly affection. Even without expectation, I still felt disappointed. People are who they are, not who we hope them to be. She was an Eternal, the farthest thing from a doting mother. She had rejected the unconditional love of Chaos for an alliance with the foulest, most treacherous Eternal of all.

This was not a reunion and there was no time for regret. I was there out of necessity, the starkest of necessities.

Gram is my family, not this bitch.

Chapter 15

THE FOREVER PALACE SAT before a serene landscape of rolling hills, a striking structure made of opalescent glass and jade stones. It was not as grandiose as its name suggested, measuring maybe a hundred feet wide and three stories high. The glass refracted the sunbeams, creating a hypnotic, iridescent web of light around the palace.

I marveled at the finely crafted crystal doorway before it suddenly slid open without so much as a whisper of a sound.

Chloe led us into a large hall. Thin slices of sunlight trickled in through opaque glass windows. I squinted to adjust my eyes to the dim light.

My feet sunk into the plush carpet. The walls radiated with a reflective energy, akin to the surface of a mirror. It was like gazing into a churning ocean of power that fed on my deepest fears and desires.

An imposing woman glided down a marble staircase. The sheer fabric of her gown molded to her elegant curves. Her sleek black hair flowed down her back and around her face in a frenzied swirl, as if responding to a mysterious breeze only she could feel. The glass walls reflected back infinite versions of her, creating a dizzying otherworldly illusion.

A midnight blue aura glimmered around her like a velvet cape dotted with tiny stars. Her eyes were as dark and vast as a winter night, and her lips a deep red like succulent tart cherries. Her power swelled around her, growing with each breath she took.

A blast of searing heat gusted straight to my core. My tongue tasted bitter like old leather. It felt as if I was too close to the sun, a consuming fire sucking every drop of moisture from my skin. I worried my flesh would crumble off my bones, molecule by molecule.

My mother stopped in front of me; her aura had a gravitational pull. I collapsed onto my knees, powerless against the weight of her energy.

I stole a glance at Chaos. He seemed unaffected by the staggering pressure of her presence.

"Luna, forgive the effect my etheric essence has on you," my mother said. "I assure you it is not intentional. The connective pathways between us have grown stronger since I coded them into your cells."

She waved her hand and the pressure abated. I staggered to my feet. My body vibrated as if soothed by a healing energy, and the heat filling my veins quickly cooled.

Chaos fixed his soulful gaze on my mother.

"Old friend," said my mother as she sauntered up to him. "How have the lower realms treated you all these long years?"

There was a simplicity in his expression that I had never seen. "You know me, I travel light."

"Ha!" she said, surprised at her own amusement. "Your charming tongue."

Ah... that was charming? Do I want to be here for this?

His coal-black eyes glinted with satisfaction. "You remembered."

Eww! Make it stop.

My mother's lips curved ever so slightly. She was intoxicating, but her allure was far more than skin deep. Her voice was both confident and soft, conveying warmth and consideration with only a hint of menace. It was no wonder that both Horror and Chaos remained in her thrall. Any man would struggle to resist her pull.

"Emrod, after all these many centuries you have remained as irreverent and sardonic as the day we met," she said with a glint in her eyes.

"Why fix perfect?" he said.

"Right," she said. "I guess each evolves at their own pace." Chaos chuckled.

Time's gaze snapped to me. "My daughter did not venture into my Kingdom to watch me bicker with a depraved Shadow," she said. "I will have a word with Luna in private."

She extended her hand to Chaos. He kissed it.

Their connection was clearly profound. I sensed the immense respect he had for her. I had seen that respect in his eyes every time Chaos spoke of Time, but now I understood its depth completely.

Chloe stepped forward and gave a graceful curtsy. "Please, do not hesitate to call upon me if I can be of service, my lady."

My mother gave Chloe a slight nod before motioning to me. We walked to an exquisite, ornate coffee table and sat across from each other.

I heard Chloe and Chaos's footsteps fading in the distance.

"I know you must be tired," Time said, flashing sincerity.

"I'm fine," I said.

"I'll try to keep this brief."

"We could talk while we walk to the door," I said, my body stiffening. "It's obvious you want me gone as soon as possible."

My words took her by surprise—a flicker of something genuine lit her face. "I was hoping you would stay the night. I've arranged a small get-together."

"Really? A mixer with the Dustflingers? That sounds dreadful."

She considered me for a moment, arching an eyebrow. "Is that a tactic you always employ? Masking your true self with jokes?"

I shrugged, feeling the intensity of her gaze. "My true self is a joke... ever since discovering my entire reality has been completely fabricated."

She took a moment... to reflect or deflect, or maybe to forget.

"You've grown to value your time among mortals, have you not?"

I said nothing, the only way to answer that question.

"Of course, I am the one to blame for that. I placed you in the fifth realm, in the care of lesser beings."

The realm of *basics*, scorned by Immortals and Eternals alike. And why should I be surprised she was a snob?

"Do not trouble yourself, Mother," I said. "It was the one gift you gave to me, a life free from your treacherous, presumptuous world."

She tried to remain calm, but her voice quivered with impatience. "I am pleased you achieved serenity in that simple place, but this fabrication, as you called it, can no longer stand. Your destiny is your only path, and it's bigger than our personal desires. That's why you have come to me."

"I came for answers."

"You came seeking my help."

Same difference.

"And will you help?"

Time drew her lips tightly together as she contemplated. She snapped her fingers. A tall woman appeared, carrying a tray with a porcelain tea set. The cups and saucers clinked against the silver platter.

The sharp angles of the woman's face glinted in the sunlight—high cheekbones, thin lips and a braid of white hair cascading over a shoulder.

Her pale gray eyes triggered my memory. She was the very

woman who had relayed Time's cryptic message after I killed Cerber in his dark realm.

I finally put two and two together. I hadn't known at the time that Horror was my father and had assumed that Cerber acted alone, but it was now clear that Horror had directed Cerber to intercept Time's message, wanting to keep my mother's identity hidden from me.

"Ah, I see that you remember Carpo," my mother said.

Carpo. Another Hora. Maybe Cerber never intended to murder her but rather snatch her away once she left my mother's side and then gift her to Horror.

Carpo set down the tray with a small bow. "It is good to be in your presence again, Luna. Please accept my gratitude for saving me from Cerber."

"You saved me first," I said.

"Carpo delivered my message earlier than instructed," my mother said. "I'm aware it caused considerable distress. The timing wasn't appropriate."

"The time felt right," Carpo countered. "My intuition told me waiting any longer would only hurt our cause."

My mother lost patience. "It doesn't matter, in any case," she said with a tone of finality. "The pieces have now aligned."

Carpo bowed. "With your permission, I will take my leave."

"Wait," I said. "You mentioned something about having the key to defeating Horror. I may not have been ready to know then, but I am now."

My mother cupped my hands with hers. "It is best that we discuss these family matters in private."

Carpo quickly left the room.

My mother poured tea in a cup. "Cream? Sugar?" she asked.

"Yes, thank you."

She offered me the cup once prepared, studying my face as I took a sip.

"I see the questions in your eyes," she said.

"You mentioned your message was ill timed. Why did you decide to send it in the first place?"

"So that you'd know you weren't alone against your father, and that if you sought me, you would find me."

I shifted uneasily in my seat.

"You must be wondering why I married Milan."

"I assume you're crazy. I mean, he calls himself Horror, for fuck's sake."

Her expression hardened. She didn't like my coarse language. "I had no choice in the matter."

"No choice? Please, I don't care how much pressure he exerted, you're practically a goddess, you could have set him straight."

Her brows shot up. "Pressure me? No, that was not at all how it happened, Luna. It was I who did the pressuring. Seducing Milan was no easy task."

My jaw dropped. "You seduced him?"

"It took me years to finally win his affections. Milan was not the type to bind himself to another Eternal; he favored human companions. Their fleeting lifespans meant he could move on without any complications."

"Whoa. You mean that before you, he hooked up with mortal women?"

"Yes, and mortal men, although he favors female companions."

Wow, okay. I guess dear old Dad had let his freak flag fly.

She leaned in, a trace of irritation passing through her eyes. "Emrod was born from such a liaison. Milan had fallen for the daughter of a Phoenician noble. She convinced him to start a family. Unsurprisingly, he changed his mind the moment she became pregnant. Milan kept her in confinement and gave the infant to a pair of Assyrian demons to raise. Then, some two-hundred years later, he felt lonely and thought he'd give the fatherhood thing a try, so he took on Emrod as a pupil and protégé. Emrod learned to channel much of Milan's power. Originally, Milan sought to groom his son as his right hand and chief Warlord for his swiftly expanding army. But eventually Emrod figured out Milan was his father and confronted him. This sparked the feud that has pitted them against each other since that day."

Chaos's mother was mortal and he had never met her—all thanks to our father's cruel whims. It was no wonder Chaos carried such an unyielding resentment in his core.

"Milan concealed Emrod's true identity from everyone,"

my mother continued. "Including me, before we married."

Okay, at least she hadn't knowingly seduced her lover's father.

"Which one spilled the beans?" I asked. "Chaos or Horror?"

"Both. I was unrelenting as I prodded for the truth behind their rift."

"People just tell you things, huh? Do you use compulsion?"

"You might say I have a natural talent," she said, her voice flat. "Eventually Milan discovered my skill and warded himself against it."

I clenched the armrests of my seat with both hands and felt my adrenaline spike. "If you ever use compulsion on me, we're done."

Her long, dark eyelashes fluttered as she blinked. "I would never. Our relationship must be based on mutual respect and consideration."

And now the billion-dollar question.

"So why go to all the trouble of pursuing a dark Eternal who wanted nothing to do with you?"

She thought for a moment. "To set the stage for the prophecy. It foretold that only a child born of the bloodline of the Dark Eternal could wield the power to keep him from unlocking the Vault of Knowledge which holds the key to the universe."

I tried to wrap my mind around her motive. "You had me

to fulfill a prophecy? I am your pawn made flesh?"

"I did what was necessary—even if you deem it inexcusable, it was for the greater good. And you are a wonder. The reason no longer matters. You are here. Existence is no small gift."

"And that gift includes eventually murdering my father?" Despite my best efforts to remain polite, I couldn't hide my irritation.

She nodded. There was no empathy in her eyes, no regrets.

"Then what makes you better than him?" I said.

"The young are always angry at their lot in life, but consider carefully what's at stake, Daughter."

"Don't call me daughter. I can't stand it when *he* does. I don't want either of you to have that privilege. I am Luna Mae, daughter to Clara Mae."

"Regardless of circumstance, you are of my flesh and blood. You are the sole reason I did any of this—why I married Milan, why I accompanied him in his exile while he was most susceptible to my influence. All so you could exist."

"You aided him," I said as the truth dawned on me. "You partnered with the most dangerous Eternal in crafting the crystal shield, and you helped him escape his banishment."

Silence hung between us like a fog. Her eyes transformed into a dark, menacing abyss, hinting at her boundless power. I had traveled here in search of answers, hoping to decipher the motivation behind her choices, but truth can sometimes be the most bitter pill.

"Yes," she said, wearily. "Only the weak are quick to judge. If you had been in my position, you would have done the very same thing. Here prophecy is not prediction, you see. It's a beast that needs to be fed."

For the first time, I truly felt it. *My destiny.* The trap I could not escape. A future coming for me like a freight train. I was overwhelmed.

"Why me? Why not Chaos?"

"Chaos is not a child of pure Eternal blood. There is only you. I do not wish this for you, Luna. The task may be impossible. I would gladly take it upon myself if I could. But if you delay, if you do not act now, we may never speak freely like this again, as mother and daughter."

"Because if Horror prevails, he will rule all," I muttered.

Time became forlorn. "He is not entirely evil. I have seen another side of Milan, a gentler side when his defenses are down. That time has passed. He feels threatened, Luna. And while you hesitate, he will not."

"You mean he'll kill me."

"Though it will cause him great pain, yes, he will."

My thoughts spiraled. *My father might play nice, but when I am no longer useful, when it's him or me, I'll always come second.*

"He will, I know," I said. "And that causes me great pain already."

"I wish this was not the only way."

"I neither want to oppose him nor know how. Everyone

tells me I have to do this thing, but they don't tell me how I can defeat him. I've been in his presence, and I felt his power. It's immense. It haunts me, like a raging tsunami of energy promising to devour everything in its path. Even when he suppressed it with the Thespian ring, I could still hear it roaring like a coming storm. I'm no match for him."

Opening up to her felt surprisingly good, like a weight lifted from my shoulders. But the knowledge of what lay ahead chased away that fleeting sense of peace. With every passing moment, the prophecy closed in on me from every side.

I had to become stronger, somehow. I needed her help, and I needed to find my mist horse. The prospect of facing Horror on the battlefield weakened me, my legs felt wobbly, and my heart contracted. I became drunk with anxiety every time I thought of that moment, the moment before the battle when I would look up into his eyes.

Time reached out and clutched my hands. "Fear not, for I am with you. I will show you how to draw out power directly from him, and I will teach you the secrets of time manipulation, so you'll always be one step ahead."

"Really? It's possible I could influence temporal shifts?"

"With a chronomaster by your side, anything's possible."

"You mean *our* chronomasters in the Deep Down?"

"Yes. Bring me a chronomaster and I'll connect your etheric essences. That will give you access to their power channels whenever needed."

"It sounds very one-sided. Why would they agree to that?"

She leaned in and narrowed her eyes. "To serve me."

"So, the chronomasters are also your attendants? Like the Horae?"

"No, but their power originated from me. Such bonds are hard to break."

She carried her unbridled authority over mortals with such entitlement, but desperate times called for desperate measures. If bonding with a chronomaster meant I'd have a fighting chance against my father, then I had to let a few of my principles get crushed.

"I'll do it," I said. "I'll bring a chronomaster to you."

Time handed me a medallion in the shape of the scales of Themis, the primordial goddess of cosmic order and justice. At its center a ruby stone glimmered like a living flame, its intricate designs writhing beneath the surface.

"Show the chronomaster this," she said softly. "They will know that it is I who has summoned them."

The medallion's force field prickled my fingertips. I looked up at her, my expression blank. "If I do as you ask, you must tell me the truth. What happens after I defeat Horror? What happens to me? What happens to you?"

"The future is never certain, but the prophecy will have manifested. You will have restored balance in the scales of power, and you will ascend the Eternal throne. As for me, I hope I will have a place by your side."

At least, she's giving it to me straight. I think.

I couldn't shake the unease in my stomach. "It's not that simple," I said. "Even if I defeat Horror, I will still have to deal with the Nightbringer."

"Yes, and you will defeat the bringer of darkness as well," she said with unwavering conviction.

"Huh, you're so confident I'll just win back-to-back impossible battles."

"You must believe in yourself the way I believe in you. I have inscribed power into your name."

I tilted my head in confusion. "My name?"

"Your true name is Aurora, for you are the Dawn Rider, and the bringer of light," she said. "Your name is the promise of a new day. I gave it to you so that all who look upon you believe you will conquer darkness and end the night."

Oh, that's all? She's most definitely a tiger mom.

"We will leave it at that for now," she said, rising from her seat. "You should take a moment to gather your thoughts and then rest. We shall speak again at our twilight gathering."

"Mother?" I called out before she left the room. "What is your true name?"

Her entire essence gleamed as the word *mother* filled the space between us. "My name is Isadore. It is so lovely that you're here."

Chapter 16

THE FLAMES WARMED MY face and crackled in my ears. The air in the clearing was infused with the pungent scent of burning wood and the crisp fragrance of wet leaves.

The five Horae—Chloe, Carpo, Thallo, Eirene and Ione—lazed around the bonfire, draped in gowns of delicate fabric fluttering in the breeze that emanated from the heart of the fire.

A group of forest nymphs sang and danced in a circle, their movements perfectly synchronized.

My eyes were drawn to the center of the circle, where my mother stood, her arms raised above her head like a high priestess summoning power from the stars. Her long black hair flowed behind her like a river of ink reflecting the fire-light, and her skin seemed to radiate a transcendent energy, as if she were an embodiment of the forest's essence.

Isadore—the gift of Isis, the ancient Egyptian goddess who was worshipped as the ideal mother and wife.

You have to love the irony.

She spoke in a language I didn't understand. Her eyes

turned in their sockets until they were completely white.

As if in response, the fire roared to life, its flames growing taller and brighter with every passing moment, dancing to the rhythm of the kingdom's magic. The Horae cheered, their voices echoing through the moonlit forest.

I caught Chaos staring at my mother, his eyes fixated like a hawk, entranced by her elegant movements—so much so that he could not look away lest he miss a single detail.

The night bristled with enchantment. I felt the vital force of the Kingdom of Forever stir within me. I watched spellbound as my mother harnessed the mystical energy of the fire and directed it skyward.

I didn't know her true age and I thought it rude to ask. To basics, she would give the impression to be in her mid-30s. She looked magnificent as she twirled around the blazing fire in a white silk gown that accentuated her olive skin and flushed cheeks. I couldn't help but compare myself to her. I had inherited my father's eyes and skin tone, but my nose and mouth resembled my mother's. When it came to beauty, she was literally breathtaking.

Isadore turned my way and stopped dancing. The clearing erupted with rowdy applause, praising the Queen of the Kingdom.

Time seemed to halt as my mother extended her hand to me as an invitation. She beamed and her smile brimmed with youthful joy.

"We must always honor the spirits of Mother Earth before

we begin a gathering with friends," she said softly.

We sat together on a flat boulder. I never thought I'd see her so carefree.

"All your attendants—the Horae, the nymphs, your imps—are you really friends with them?" I asked.

She smiled contently. "Everything that breathes in my land is my friend," she said. "And now not just mine, but yours, too."

"Because I'm your daughter or because I'm a mist rider?"

"Both. Neither. They love you because *I* love you."

Maybe I shouldn't push her, but...

"You love me? Sight unseen? I mean you don't even know me. What kind of love is that? And can someone who has lived for centuries know the same kind of love as those who have lived for decades?"

She fixed me with two shining eyes. "Have you asked your immortal lover these same questions?" she quipped.

I balked at her remark, unwilling to delve into the subject of Winter. I didn't care what she knew or how she knew it. I wanted to bathe in the mystic transcendence of the night and let my mother's realm flow through me like a river of starlight.

The nymphs resumed their singing; their voices carried on the wind like a chorus of songbirds. They spun and swayed to the tune, their hair and dresses flowing like water in a stream. The Horae joined in one by one. My eyes lingered on Chloe. In the orange glow of the fire, she appeared not only delicate but fragile as she danced with abandon. Her movements were graceful, like a liquid ballet, and her feet glided over the ground as if entranced.

Chaos studied Chloe intently, his eyes glinting with an emotion I couldn't discern. He shook his head, as if trying to clear his thoughts.

She swayed closer to him. "You know, fabled warrior, it is considered impolite for a man to stare at a woman for so long," she said, playfully.

Chaos bowed his head, then fully took in her eyes. "You possess an enviable grace of movement, fair maiden. I should think it impolite not to stare at such a gifted dancer."

Her smile widened and she spun around, her long hair swirling. "Well, I suppose I can't fault you for that. We Horae have been known to captivate."

"Movement is made easier when unencumbered by humility," Chaos said, eager to continue their verbal joust.

Chloe stepped closer, her eyes locked on his. "Is this your dance? The art of conversation? Is this how you mean to captivate?"

Holy hell, these two.

Chaos raised an eyebrow. "One who wants to be captive, need only surrender."

"You are quite old for such a cheeky boy."

"It's the best of both worlds," Chaos said, "experience and energy."

As Chloe danced away, I wondered what he was playing

at. Had she truly mesmerized him or was he simply playing the dangerous game of trying to make my mother jealous?

Time walked up to Chaos to sit next to him on the ground, her long white dress draping elegantly around her.

"Charming girl, our Chloe," she said, her voice almost wistful. "Never has a woman lived more pleasing than her."

They sat quietly, watching Chloe dance.

My mother sighed. "The Horae have been here for five centuries. Do you know why I brought them to live with me?"

Chaos turned to her, his face giving nothing away.

"They have become susceptible. They are no longer immune to physical trauma and disease. Their immortality has been compromised. The open world is no longer safe for the Horae."

Chaos leaned in. "Why are you telling me this?"

"We have lost four beautiful souls. An attachment with a Hora may lead to sadness in the future."

"I have been led to sadness before," Chaos said, detached. "Death is not required for that emotion."

My mother stood up, her dress flowing behind her. "I am merely informing you, Emrod. To be reckless is no great virtue."

Oh my god, his plan worked. She's jealous.

Chaos spat out of the side of his mouth. He rose to his feet, taking a tentative step forward. A moment of hesitation seemed to overcome him as he contemplated his next move.

Finally, he nodded to himself and stepped into the circle of the dancing Horae, extending his hand to Chloe. Grasping the small of her back, he pulled her close, towering over her, and their fingers interlaced as they moved together in perfect harmony.

The other dancers stepped back from the couple, their eyes trained on the two as they began to move with a sensual, wild energy. As they spun around, their bodies seemed to meld together as if they were disappearing into each other.

What's even happening?

In the play of light and shadows, Time's eyes seemed wild.

My focus was interrupted as I took hold of a glass of wine pressed into my hand.

Carpo let go of the goblet. "Nectar wine can ease the mind."

I took a sip and immediately a warmth spread through my body. It was like nothing I had ever tasted, rich and full-bodied with an underlying zest. I quickly took another sip and my head tingled with delight.

My feet swayed to the melody, the world around me began to blur, and I realized with a panic that I was getting groggy. I tried to recover my bearings, but everything moved in slow motion. Chaos and Chloe spun into streaks of color. Was this disorientation the wine or something else? My supercharged metabolism usually meant I'd need to drink a whole bottle before I felt any effect. I only had a couple of sips.

Chaos and Chloe pulled apart, their eyes still locked as

Chaos stepped back, a sly grin on his face. The other Horae rushed forward, clapping and cheering as if they had witnessed a performance. As the crowd began to dissipate, Chaos looked to me and laughed at my inebriated state.

My mother took hold of my hand and whispered into my ear, "Would you like to meet your mist horse?"

Dizzy and confused, I raised my goblet. "What's in this stuff? I'm seeing things... and hearing things."

"It's all natural, I assure you. Nature's key to open up all the shut doors of your perception. Everything is fluid. The mind is free."

A sudden unease washed over me. "Did Chloe drink the wine, too? She's whirling around like scarves in the wind."

"Everyone has, except your wayward brother."

"And you," I added, my lips so dry they almost stuck together. "Is this your plan? To compel us to do your bidding?"

"Oh no, nothing like that. Come with me lovely child... let me introduce you to your future."

My mother gestured toward the bonfire. My gaze dived into the flickering blaze.

She chanted a gentle incantation. My senses sharpened, and my mind cleared. The world washed away. Only the crackling flames remained. And then it came into being—a vision of a majestic white horse, its body fashioned by swirling mist, within the slithering flames. Its eyes were silver like pools of melted mercury, and through them I could see mysteries and journeys.

Untamed energy emanated from the magnificent morning creature as if the moment the night meets the dawn created a massive fusion energy. I felt a compulsion to move toward the vision, like a ship to a siren song, beckoning me to my fate. And then, as quickly as it had appeared, the mist horse vanished into the crackle of the surging fire.

I closed my eyes to regain focus. "How did you find it? And how do you know it's my horse?"

"I looked into the past, into the deepest recesses of time. The mist horse you saw was a vision from a time long lost. But it's more than a vision, it's a call. The mist horse has been searching for you for centuries."

My heart filled with wonder as I listened.

"You must find your horse in the mists of this time, Luna. He is to be your catalyst. Together you will bring the morning to life. The Eternals and the Nightbringer will do all they can to stop you, but you must not be stopped. Only then will you ride the mist, only then can you approach your destiny."

I felt the weight of her words deep within my etheric core.

"If there's a horse out there, where will I find him?" I said.

"That," my mother said, "is a question for another day. For now, let us bask in the beauty of the night. The festival has just begun."

I stumbled a bit as I backed away from the bonfire, feeling the effects of the enchanted wine and the trance-like state wearing off.

"Your body is still adjusting to the libation," she said. "In a moment, you will feel complete physical harmony."

"That would be nice, because I was starting to worry I drank something other than the Horae drank."

"The Horae drank much more than a sip. They love nothing more than to frolic and dance."

As the fire pit dwindled, a sense of dread settled over me. Chaos emerged from the shadows. He stood there a moment, watching us, then strode over to my mother and conversed in a hushed tone. I strained to hear what they were saying, but their voices were much too low. His features grew dark as she spoke into his ear.

He bowed to her before strolling off into the night.

Chapter 17

As I climbed the stairs to my studio apartment, a familiar etheric essence invaded my nostrils, electrifying my etheric core and causing my heart to race. The hinges squawked as I pushed the door open to find Winter lying on the couch with a half-smile on his lips.

"Hey," he said, "I must have dozed off. I didn't sense you coming."

A pang of frustration shot through me. "What are you doing?"

"I was napping," he said, rubbing sleep from his eyes. "I stayed up late, worried about you."

"Don't be coy with me. We agreed you'd wait at the Umbra fortress. How can I trust you if you won't keep your word?"

Winter scooched over to make room for me on the couch. "You really look pissed," he said. "I'm recovered, Luna. I'm better than ever."

I dropped my backpack to the floor and slumped down next to him. "That better be the truth."

"Cross my heart."

"Immortals take the crucial *and-hope-to-die* part out of that, huh? Must be why you are all so duplicitous."

"This has hardly been a warm welcome," he said, perplexed.

"You were on the couch. I came in through the door. I get the welcome."

"I think I know how to welcome you," he said with a big grin as he started to lift me onto his lap.

"Cool your jets, big guy, put me down." I exhaled and laid my head on his shoulder. "I'm glad you're here."

A sense of relief flooded through me for the first time in days. Winter was safe and next to me. For now, that was all that mattered. His warm hand found the small of my back, anchoring me to the present. I pressed myself closer to him, tangling my fingers in his hair and savoring the feel of his strong arms wrapping around me. The outside world melted away.

He pulled me onto his lap, his voice a hungry murmur. "I missed you."

"Of course, you did," I said, burying my face in his chest.

We broke apart and I looked into his eyes. They seemed darker than before, like the sea on a stormy night.

"So, you've returned in one piece," he said. "How was your trip?"

"Sheesh, where to begin. I honestly don't know. I think I made some progress with my mother, maybe, but she could have been playing me the whole time."

"Tell me everything, starting from the beginning."

I sighed, trying to organize my thoughts. "Okay, so, when I confronted her about Horror, she confirmed my worst fears. She straight out told me she married him solely to fulfill the prophecy that only a child born of the Dark Eternal could prevent the unlocking of the Vault of Knowledge. Oh, and get this, she also helped with his escape *and* his crafting of the crystal shield."

"Points for getting along with a madman," Winter said with his jaw clenched, "but that's extreme even for an Eternal."

"Yeah, no kidding," I said, popping up to pace the room. "It does seem like everything she has done, from pursuing Horror all the way to cozying up to Darius, was to advance the prophecy like pieces of a puzzle."

Winter stood up and pushed my hair back. "I'm sure she must have presented a silver lining, even if she had to create one herself."

His touch was reassuring, and I let myself relax into it. "She offered to teach me how to draw out power directly from my father and help me master the secrets of time manipulation. Oh yeah, she also claimed there's a mist horse out there somewhere searching for me. Oh, and after I defeat devil Daddy, she told me I'll immediately have to defeat the Nightbringer."

Winter stepped back to stare at me. "Did she tell you how?"

I shrugged. "She said it's in my name. Aurora. That's the name she gave me at birth."

"Aurora? The Roman goddess of dawn?"

"Yep. Apparently, I'm the bringer of light. My mother stopped short of telling me I'm destined to face off with the Nightbringer as well. After that, who knows, maybe she'll want me to fist-fight the Sun."

Winter's face went pale. "You're not going anywhere near him. I don't want you on the same continent as him."

"I would be pretty badass on a mist horse, though," I said, not believing it for a second. "And you could ride a unicorn right next to me."

I remembered the vision I had seen in the flames and imagined the sound of hooves pounding the ground as the mist horse galloped my way.

"The Nightbringer has a mist horse, too, Luna, a mist horse from the pits of the deepest hell. Let me deal with him."

"You know something," I said. "Why else would you think you can defeat that monster when Eternals can't?"

He stepped forward, his hand rubbing my upper arm. "I know enough to stay out of his way. And I know I love you."

I rolled my eyes. "You're such a sap."

He smiled. "Don't be cruel, baby."

"Baby?" I said with a chuckle. "That's a new one."

"Is it really so funny?"

"Yes, I guess. It just sounds so odd coming from you, oh mighty Magistrate."

"Won't happen again," he said. "What did your mother say about the horse?"

"Not much. When I woke up in the morning, she was already gone without so much as a goodbye. She left a message with one of the Horae that she'd get in touch when she returned."

Winter pulled me close. "I'm sure she will. She has a vested interest in you. And Kirsi came by last night. The Oracle of Delphi has a message for you."

"What kind of message?"

"Kirsi will fill you in on the details, but you need to be ready. The time has come for you to meet with the Oracle."

"When?"

"She didn't say, but you need to be prepared to leave at any time."

I leaned on him. "When will it all end, Winter?" I needed a carefree day in the comfort of my own home with the man I loved. Was that too much to ask?

Instead of an answer he kissed me.

"Much of my etheric essence is still suppressed," he said between kisses. "I'm sure I can keep it under control."

"You have that look," I said breathlessly.

"What look?"

"Like you're about to eat me alive."

He laughed. "You have no idea. You've only had a taste. I've restrained myself beyond reason."

"I'm not dignifying that with a response," I said.

"I couldn't sleep last night without you next to me," he said, his hands trailing down my back.

"Really? I slept like a baby." I teased him, but my body was already responding to his touch.

He squeezed my butt and I gasped. Our mouths met hungrily.

"I will guard you with my life," he said, his lips grazing my ear.

"Who's going to guard me from you?" I said, only half-joking.

"You've wrapped me around your little finger, you know that?"

As much as I wanted to resist him, my body betrayed me. Every fiber in me contracted and then released. I wanted us to work out in the end, but considering what was coming, the present might be all we had.

His lips tickled my neck. I slipped my hands under his shirt, pushing it up, then pulling it over his head. He raised his arms to help until the shirt was off and my hands found his sculpted chest. His heart pounded under my fingers and his breath quickened. I loved the effect I had on him, that vulnerability that undermined his arrogance.

I let my hand slide down over the contours of his abs and

then I felt it—a faint pink scar that snaked across his ribs and disappeared around to his back.

"What is this?" I said.

Kisses rained down on me, on my face, my lips, my neck, my chest, and I realized that he didn't want to talk about the scar.

He must have sensed that my thoughts were taking over because now he went straight for the buttons on my blouse. He undid the buttons one by one, letting the blouse hang open on the front.

He slid a hand inside the opening of the blouse, and my mind went blank as a bunch of nerve endings were mercilessly under siege.

He picked me up in one scoop. I wrapped my legs around his waist. He planted a kiss on my nose and then another on my lips. I didn't know why, but I bit his lower lip.

"Such a bad girl," he said. "You need a lesson or two."

"And who will teach me?" I said, laughing in his face.

"All right, that's it." He carried me to the bed like I was weightless. The fresh sheets under my back cooled down my hot skin.

He swiped at my jeans, and they came right off. For a moment, he hesitated above me, his eyes fixed on mine.

Then... the front door lock clicked, and the door creaked open.

Lily yelped. Emmet's eyes peered out from behind her.

Ugh, why must all the curses of the world descend upon me?

Lily turned away. "We'll wait outside until you're decent," she said. Emmet remained stuck in place.

"You texted you'd be away this weekend," I said.

"We wanted to surprise you," Emmet said. "And by the looks on your faces, we've succeeded." He leaned against the doorframe, amused to the point where I would have enjoyed kicking him in the balls.

Lily held up a paper bag. "Soup, your favorite, chicken and wild rice."

"Dude, get out!" I told her.

"Fine, nothing I haven't seen before."

"Just wait out there."

As soon as they left, Winter pulled me down to the bed. "That's why I don't have friends. Or roommates."

"Lily said they were going up to Universal Studios theme park in LA. I told her I was too sick to go. What the fuck's she doing here? And you don't have friends or roommates because you're judgmental and inflexible."

"That's fair," he said. "By the way, Lily and Emmet might have figured out we are more than friends."

"Ah, you remembered their names," I said. "And they knew already."

"Well, I guess they're here now," he said. "There's a cold shower with my name on it, unless you politely ask them to fuck off and come back tomorrow."

I tried to shove him, but it's not easy to shove a tall, sturdy man in a perfect state of fitness. He headed to the bathroom under protest. I quickly buttoned my blouse and pulled on my jeans before collecting Lily and Emmet from outside.

"Finally," Lily said, giving me a quick hug. "You look exhausted. And I doubt it's from that fictitious virus you caught."

"I'm sorry, Lil. I caught a second wind."

"Save it, I saw what you were about to catch."

"We knocked actually," Emmet said. "A couple times. You know Lily, she freaked out and convinced herself you were sick enough to pass out."

"It's all good," I said, trying to move past the awkwardness.

"So, the caveman, huh?" Emmet said with mischievous eyes. "Lily said she tried to warn you about him."

"It just kind of happened," I said. "And no one listens to their friends."

"But they should," Lily said. "Especially when it's me."

"You don't even listen to yourself," I said. "Your past is messy."

Emmet raised an eyebrow. "What past? Messy how?"

Lily hushed him with a glare.

"I'd offer you libations, but the fridge is empty," I said.

Did I really just use my Eternal mother's word?

Lily turned to Emmet. "Babe, go grab some *libations* down the street."

Emmet nodded. "Libations... like?"

She sighed and walked him to the door. "Get soda, juice,

your mineral water thingy, just use your imagination, okay, *mijo?*"

Lily closed the door, then turned back to stare at me. "Are you okay?"

"Why wouldn't I be?"

She set down the bag with the soup on the table. "I don't know, your rhythms are all off."

"Maybe because I was interrupted in mid rhythm by a crazy soup lady."

Lily chuckled. "You could have easily sent the soup lady away if you were that thirsty."

"Nah, if someone who thinks you are sick brings you soup, then you are universally obligated to stop copulating and be a gracious host."

Lily tapped her fingernails on the counter. "Well, that's true."

"I see you worked things out with Emmet," I said. "That's good."

She hesitated, then wobbled her head side to side. "Is it? I still struggle with his nervous energy. That boy's an adrenaline junkie, the monotony of everyday life is never going to be his lane."

"Yeah, wolves be that way sometimes," I said.

"Wolves can be tamed," Lily said.

"I see that. You already have him on a leash."

"Uh huh," she said, distracted.

"Okay, what's going on. Spill it, Lily Herrero."

She filled a glass with tap water before answering. "Cyrus, that's what. I've had a bad feeling about him from day one, but this is next level."

"What did he do now?"

"Cyrus asked Emmet to do something fucked up."

"He didn't ask him to break it off with you, did he?"

"No, that prick asked Emmet to spy on you. I have a terrible feeling, Sophie. Cyrus is dangerous and worse, there's a bad energy all around him. I'm starting to feel it everywhere in San Diego."

I frowned. "Did Emmet refuse?"

"What? Of course, but he'll just ask someone else."

"He's harmless, Lily," I said. "Don't worry about it. And that bad energy is probably just his nasty cologne."

Lily shrugged. "Stop protecting me. This is about you. I don't want anything to happen to you."

I narrowed my eyes. "Lil, take my word for it, I'm a bad bitch. You don't ever have to worry about me."

"Too bad, because I'm always going to worry. It would be easier if there was something, anything I could do."

"You know what, you sexy genius?" I said. "There is something. Tell Emmet, or make him if you have to, that he should meet Cyrus tomorrow and agree to do as he asked."

"What? Spy on you?"

"Yes, Emmet can pretend to spy on me. Instead, he'll tell Cyrus only what we want him to hear, and he'll tell me everything going on at the shifter compound. That will keep us one step ahead of Cyrus."

Lily bit her lip, considering. "I don't know, Sophie. That just sounds like you're asking Emmet to spy as well and take on more risk. And by the way, he's loyal to those people."

"I know, I know," I said. "I don't like it one bit, but it's really the only plan we got. And we can trust Emmet. He'd never let us down."

Lily nodded slowly. "He wouldn't, would he? He's like a knight if you think about it. Hot, loyal and incorruptible. *Mmm*. Okay, we'll try it your way."

"Cool down, lady Guinevere. Lancelot's still down at the 7-Eleven. Let's eat the soup while it's warm. You're such a doll to think of my chicken and rice. It's fucking delish. You're so gorgeous and smart."

Lily's face lit up. "*You're* so gorgeous and smart."

Chapter 18

CARTER WAITED OUTSIDE AS I entered the chronocham-ber. The time lab was usually off-limits to all except the chronomasters, but Helianna, who now acted as first-in-command, had granted me access.

Last night, Carter stopped by the apartment, upset that I had vanished without explanation, and insisted on resuming his squire duties. I refused him at first, but eventually he wore me down, and now I was grateful to have him by my side. As we made our way through the twisting passageways, memories of my previous Deep Down trip to visit Horpheus flooded my mind.

The expansive spherical chronochamber was lined with reflective silver panels. Shelves and cabinets brimmed with peculiar gadgets. At the center, an oversized hourglass was surrounded by an assortment of keys and dials, but it was the pulsating indigo crystal atop a pedestal that caught my attention.

The room buzzed with energy, emitting a low, deep thrumming like a beating heart. Ticking clocks and whirring gears permeated the air, making me feel as if I had stepped inside a giant clock. My eyes widened at the spectacle, and I felt a strange tug towards the crystal on the pedestal. When I touched it, a violent shockwave shot through me.

I shrank back and noticed Anya standing at the entrance. Her gaze flickered between the crystal and me.

"Helianna said you wanted to see me?" she said.

I felt my cheeks flush with embarrassment. "Yes. I'm sorry for messing with the crystal."

I hadn't seen Anya since mid-spring when we faced the daunting challenge of defeating the lethal silver dust that nearly killed Faion. We emerged victorious, but at a great cost for Anya who had lost her love and fellow chronomaster, Grayson, to the murderous hands of Cerber.

I could sense the pain was still raw for Anya. She donned a crisp black uniform with white stripes running down the sides. Her curly locks framed her dark complexion and her features had become more severe than I remembered. The optimism that once sparkled in her eyes had faded.

The vibrant, carefree young woman who longed for a night out in the basic world was no longer here. With Grayson gone, she was now the sole chronomaster in charge of the chronochambers. Her transformation in just a few months was striking.

Anya shrugged. "It's quite alright. The crystal has a way of drawing people in." She walked to the pedestal. "It's an Aeon Quartz, one of our most potent chronostones and the only one capable of temporal projection."

Her words drew me in even more. "Temporal projection? Isn't that almost time travel?"

"Yes, in a way. Temporal projection lingers in the experimental phase, but with the Aeon Quartz we can alter the course of time in the chronochamber without affecting history. We can slow it down, speed it up, or even reverse it. The crystal's extraordinary capabilities allow us to project a person's consciousness into the past, so they can observe historical events without being physically present."

"Isn't that dangerous?"

I watched Anya move closer to the Aeon Quartz. Her delicate fingers ran along its sharp edges as she sized up its power.

"It would be exceptionally dangerous if performed anywhere else, but here within the chronochambers, we have the skill, the technology and the training necessary to maintain a controlled environment." She looked up at me, her voice stern but reassuring. "The Aeon Quartz is the safest way to observe the past without affecting your body in the present."

I'm sold. I want one.

"How does it work?"

"It begins with the selection of a specific past event that you endeavor to explore or understand," she explained. "Once you have a target experience isolated in your mind, you channel that focus into the chronostone, which will amplify and project your consciousness back into the fabric of that time and place until you are witnessing the chosen event."

"That's so cool," I said, my curiosity piqued.

"Yes, it's a profound experience. You are able to watch events unfold as if you were there, but you are invisible and unable to interact. The projection typically lasts only a few minutes before the pathway closes and the chrono traveler is returned to the here and now."

I knew experiments were happening in the chronochambers regarding all facets of the space-time continuum, and I knew that the chronomasters could halt time, but not this... this was a seismic awakening of possibility.

Anya placed her hand on the Aeon Quartz. The chronochamber reverberated with a low hum. The crystal sparked and gyrated; its light intensified until it filled every corner of the room.

Anya smiled for the first time. "Would you like to try?"

My stomach went *whoosh* as if the floor had suddenly dropped out. "I would," I said, nervously smiling. "Why do I feel like throwing up?"

"It's excitement," Anya said, her eyes gleaming as she placed the crystal into my palm. "Focus on an exact moment in time that happened before you were born, something that has always intrigued you. You will feel disorientation as the Aeon Quartz absorbs your etheric essence and your consciousness is transported through temporal rifts. If you need to return early for any reason, simply drop the crystal."

The Aeon Quartz pulsed with energy as I closed my eyes, searching for a moment in history to explore. My mind settled on a date, and I felt the crystal grow warmer in my hand. Suddenly, I was falling through an abyss, my body weightless, my senses scrambled.

Space and time vanished as I catapulted through the void until I landed on solid ground with a hard jolt.

I regained focus. On a bustling street in New York City, women wearing long dresses with lace collars and sleeves, or shirtwaist blouses paired with pleated skirts and bell-shaped cloche hats, marched towards Fifth Avenue, carrying signs that read *Votes for Women!* and *Suffrage Now!*

Excitement and disbelief coiled inside me as I witnessed the celebration for the ratification of the 19th Amendment in 1920. The women linked arms and chanted for their right to be heard.

As the parade passed by, I felt hopeful for the future. If those women could fight so hard and overcome so much, then, surely, I could find the strength to stand up against my evil father.

As suddenly as it began, it was over, and I found myself back in the chronochamber, holding the crystal tight.

I knew that the women couldn't see me, but I felt like I had been part of history—a moment that would shape the future for generations to come.

Anya felt my face with her hands, deep in concentration. "Does your body feel normal?"

I took in and then released a deep breath as adrenaline still coursed through my veins. "Much better than normal. It felt so real, Anya."

Anya became serious as she delicately placed the crystal back onto the pedestal. The clear, smooth surface glimmered in the silver light of the chronochamber, casting flickering shadows on her face as it swirled.

As I gazed at the crystal, a thought entered my mind. "Would it be possible to travel to the future?"

"No, temporal projections only work with events that have already occurred. The Aeon Quartz is powerful, but it can't predict the future. Think of it like a tapestry. Each thread represents a moment in time. The crystal allows us to unravel that thread and witness the events as they occurred, but it cannot create new threads or weave them into a different pattern."

It was the chronomaster principle of time travel. We were only able to observe the timeline, but not alter it in any way. The past was fixed, immutable. The future was an unknown, constantly shifting possibility.

Anya's eyes met mine. "If it's the future you seek, I believe you have plenty of friends among our seers and diviners."

Seers and diviners could tap into the energy of the universe and receive glimpses of what was to come. They could detect the ripple effects of a single action and predict how it might shape the future. The problem was that almost everything my *so-called friends* divulged to me was awful.

"I owe you a night out in San Diego," I said, remembering I promised her a girls' night out back in the spring.

Anya's face fell, and for a moment she said nothing.

My heart sank. "Anya, what is it?"

"Horpheus succumbed to his injuries this morning."

Tears prickled my eyes. A deep sense of loss washed over me. Horpheus had been a father figure and was beloved by all Deep-Down dwellers. His death would leave a void in our hearts that nothing could fill, but his legacy would live on. His knowledge and wisdom had been passed down to the seers and the mages and the witches, and they would all continue to work tirelessly to safeguard our world from harm.

Desperate to help him, I wished I had the power to go back in time and undo the tragedy, or at least observe how the events that led to his death unfolded. "Can I go back to my own timeline?" I asked Anya.

"In theory, yes, but there could be dire consequences traveling back into your own chronology. You could inadvertently materialize in a scene where you don't belong. The gravity of your emotions could pull you through a time wormhole and you'd be stuck in the past, creating a looping paradox that could have catastrophic effects."

Being trapped in the past forever, unable to return to the present, was a terrifying prospect, especially with the doomsday prophecy hanging over me.

Anya's piercing gaze bore into me. "You're thinking about

Horpheus. He knew the risks of meddling with time, and it's the reason why he prohibited chronomasters from accessing the basic world. He understood that the timeline is fragile and even a small change could trigger a ripple effect with far-reaching consequences that could reshape the entire world."

"I get it. I just feel so powerless."

She raised an eyebrow. "Yet, you seem to be itching to take that risk—and you would probably go ahead and take matters into your own hands if I left you alone in the chronochamber for a moment."

I laughed. "You know me too well." Taking a deep breath, I finally asked the question that had been nagging me. "Why have you trusted me with this information about the temporal projection?"

Her expression turned guarded. "With his dying breath, Horpheus instructed the Board of Supernatural Orders to trust you with our lives and to keep no secrets from you."

I frowned. "I wish he hadn't done that."

"Why?"

"For one, I suspect one of the Board members has been compromised. And, also, I don't trust myself with that much power and access."

"If you're worried about the work of the chronomasters being exposed, don't be. We keep it all confidential unless we're given the green light by Horph..." She caught herself. "By Helianna. Luna, what's really going on?"

I hesitated, unsure of how much to reveal. Should I divulge my true identity and my role in the prophecy, or just provide her with the minimum details needed to convince her to join me on a trip to the Kingdom of Forever?

In the end, I decided to let my mother do the heavy lifting.

"I'm here to deliver a message. War is imminent, Anya, and we are both needed to defend our world. To do that, we must bond on an etheric level."

Anya looked at me incredulously, searching my face for clues. "You want me to bond with you? From whom did this directive come?"

With a heavy heart, I removed the medallion of the Scales of Themis from around my neck. I had made the choice to trust my mother and that the medallion was not being used as an instrument for compulsion. Anya had to make up her mind with her own free will—especially since I didn't really know what I was getting her into.

Anya looked at the medallion, then back at me, her eyes wide. "You have the Flame of Justice? Where did you get it?"

"The one who directed me to summon you gave me this. She said you'd recognize it as soon as you saw it."

Anya gazed upon the medallion for a long moment, then snatched it from my hand. I watched as she turned it over, examining it from every angle, her fingers brushing over the blazing-red ruby stone at its center. She glimmered with wonder as if she had long dreamed of holding it.

I knew there must be hundreds of thoughts and questions

swirling in her head, and I braced myself to answer them the best I could, but she uttered only two words, "I understand."

"Anya, you don't have to do this. You don't have to do anything. The choice is yours, and yours alone."

"Chronomasters have known for centuries that we would be called upon to play our part in the war for the five realms. I am holding the Flame of Justice. The war is beginning. I will not deny the call."

As I ROUNDED A corner with Carter, a group of electromancers nearly collided with us, their auras crackling with energy.

Carter's hand went to his sword in a flash, unsheathing it.

"Put that away," I scolded him.

The electromancers barely spared us a glance as they marched on.

Carter grunted under his breath. "This place isn't exactly a haven of welcome for Immortals."

"Control your ego, we're here on business."

Carter sheathed his sword, glaring at me. "You trust too easily."

I smiled. "That explains why I put up with you."

We strolled along the winding pathways to the gate that led back to the basic world. Before I left Anya, I told her we needed to wait for Isadore to make contact. While I felt guilt for involving Anya at all, I also perceived a newfound determination in her, as if the mission had given her a new purpose in life.

"What are your plans tonight?" Carter quizzed. "Going to a party?"

"Huh? Why would I go to a party?"

"Vibe check, it's Halloween. You have to live a little."

"I didn't forget. I remembered all about it... yesterday."

Carter rolled his eyes. "Remember again tomorrow and you can make a Halloween sandwich with nothing in the middle."

"Aren't you a little old for Halloween? How old are you anyway?"

Before he could respond, the air crackled with electricity again. Footsteps reverberated down the path like a frenzied drumbeat.

A band of six came around a bend and blocked our path.

Carter's hand went to his sword, but I grabbed his forearm to stop him.

They were not electromancers, or members of any other supernatural faction residing in the Deep Down. Donning polished silver armor and Corinthian style helmets topped with red plumes, they looked like ancient war gods fallen out of time. We'd seen them before—these were Eternal warriors. How had they bypassed the enchanted gates without sounding an alarm?

"Why are you here?" I said. "We don't want trouble."

They had no interest in talking. Instead, they advanced on us, sparks flying from their swords.

Bloody fucking hell.

Carter and I spun to meet back-to-back, poised to defend ourselves. I could feel the adrenaline swell in my veins as I stirred up my magic. I had handed Eternal warriors their asses on the battlefield in Nightwood and it appeared they wanted a rematch.

As they drew near, their icy eyes blazed with an obsessed malice. We were on a collision course, but just before we clashed, a deafening explosion thundered down the pathways, causing the ground to shake.

A ferocious thundering reverberated in the tunnels, rattling the very foundations of the underground infrastructure. The sound surged with a menacing magnitude, stirring up a primal fear that disconnected rational thought from emotions, disarming all capacities except instinct.

When the dust settled, a sudden breeze chilled the back of my neck. I turned around to witness a portal materializing, enveloped by raging flames.

So, that's how the Eternal assholes bypassed the wards. They are mistaken if they think a few portal tricks will give them an advantage.

As the portal stabilized, a rush of wind filled the air. A steady stream of warriors emerged from the portal, and their numbers grew at a shocking rate.

Carter's confidence faltered. "We're screwed."

The thought of grabbing Carter and summoning the blue smoke to teleport us to safety crossed my mind, but the consequences were too dire to consider that. If we fled, those ruthless invaders would be left to pillage the Deep Down to their heart's content or, worse, pursue us into the basic world.

I worked up a tsunami of sizzling energy in my hands, pouring into it everything but the moisture in Carter's eyes.

"Take cover," I warned Carter.

I braced myself to unleash a cataclysmic blast that would undoubtedly leave a trail of destruction and body parts in its wake, and engulf Carter and me in its aftermath, but what other option did I have?

The energy dwindled in my hands as an unfamiliar essence completely took hold of me, sucking the air from my lungs and leaving me gasping for breath.

The portal crackled and expanded, pulling me in. A warm glow wrapped around me, ensnaring me in a swirling whirlpool.

Carter's voice called me from far away. "Luna!"

The truth struck me with a jolt of terror. This wasn't a portal. It was a fucking exile vortex—a one-way ticket to the land of no return.

I focused my magic, determined to resist the vortex's pull, but the force was too strong, dragging me relentlessly towards the swirling portal. I fell onto all fours, digging my fingers into the earth as I struggled to hold on.

I tumbled head over heels through the vortex, and I felt my magic dripping away, as if the portal was feeding on me like a parasite. My screams of defiance were swallowed up by the maelstrom encircling me.

From nowhere, a colossal figure materialized, shrouded in a swirling cloud of blue smoke.

The walls vibrated with the impact of a thousand force fields. Eternal warriors were lifted into the air as if swept away by a tornado.

Horror let out a deafening bellow, his wild hair a fiery red mane. He resembled a roaring lion. At nearly seven feet tall, his naked torso a brick wall of muscle, he looked like an amalgam of human, animal and demon. I could have sworn his fingers were tipped with razor-sharp claws.

With a booming roar, Horror unleashed a torrent of blood magic that rippled through the air like a nuclear blast wave, snatching two more Eternal warriors with its force and shattering their bones like glass.

As my father surged towards me, his massive hands scooped me up. The vortex spun faster, its sheer force slicing through me like a dagger. The stinging wounds were excruciating. My very essence was being torn open.

My father's hands dissipated into tendrils of vapor, and I was alone. The vortex took hold of me, and even the mighty Horror could not stop it.

Before everything went black, I caught a final glimpse. Two Eternal warriors seized Carter. A third slit his throat.

Chapter 19

As my eyes flickered open, a piercing headache assaulted me. I tried to move, but my body refused, locked in place by a wave of pain rippling through me. Gritting my teeth, I willed myself to sit up an inch at a time, only to be met with a crippling vertigo that sent me crashing back to the cold, hard ground.

After some time, I opened my eyes again to take in my surroundings. Ancient stone walls in a dimly lit room. A high ceiling. Old furniture. Dust on everything. The stale odor of mildew lingered in the air, like the one usually found in damp basements or neglected bathrooms.

Swallowing hard, I forced myself first to sit up, then to climb onto my feet, swaying precariously all the while. For a moment, I felt like I was floating, my limbs weightless. There was no sign of Carter or the Eternal warriors. Panic seized me as my last memory of Carter flashed in front of my eyes.

No, I can't think like that.

Carter was resilient, a fierce Immortal who had survived brutal battles. And then there was my father—he wouldn't risk alienating me by going back on his promise to keep my friends safe.

Right, and then he'll adopt a rescue dog. Get a grip, Luna.

If my father had orchestrated this whole thing to present himself as a hero, I would gladly kill him. He would never break me. He'd never convince me to help him or step aside so that he could take control of the world. No way. Uh-uh. Not a chance in hell.

This isn't my first rodeo and it won't be the last.

I took a few deep, measured breaths and slipped into a sort of robotic calmness. It's what Winter always did, his way of maintaining a level head when things went sideways.

My fingertips tingled with an electric charge when I tried to touch the wall. The room was warded, I expected as much, but what threw me off was that I hadn't sensed the wards before poking them. Some force had dampened my supernatural abilities. I had encountered such rooms before, and it never boded well.

I focused on my surroundings again, taking in every detail with a keen eye. Gradually, my instincts began to kick in, and subtle signs of magic emerged in the room. The air hummed with a fragile energy. Faint lines of light traced a complex pattern around me. It was an intricate network of wards set up by someone with considerable skill and experience.

I took a step forward, extending a hand to test the boundaries of the wards. Before my fingers could make contact, an invisible force pushed me back, throwing me off balance.

The fuck. I was a lunar witch and a mist rider, and I was not so easily deterred. I prowled around the edges of the room, my eyes scanning for any flaw or weakness in the wards. My instincts screamed that the longer I stayed in this room, the harder it would be to escape.

I closed my eyes to summon the blue smoke. Nothing happened. The wards wouldn't let anything through. Not that I knew how to control teleporting with the finesse and skill of Chaos anyway, but anywhere was better than here.

I gathered all the energy I could muster and pushed against the wards, but they didn't budge. I tried every ward-breaking spell I knew, but they just bounced off the walls like rubber bullets.

Frustration mounted as I conjured a blasting force field and aimed it at one of the wards. The magic crackled through the air, and the ward shattered, only to be replaced by another ward instantly.

This room was designed to hold the strongest users of magic. Going directly at the wards was pointless. I needed a new plan, and I needed it fast.

Footsteps echoed outside the room. My body tensed and my senses heightened as the sound drew closer. The tread was measured, deliberate, each footfall landing with a solid thud—the unmistakable gait of someone who knew exactly what they wanted and how to get it.

The footsteps stopped at the door, which flew open like it had been kicked in. A middle-aged man strode into the room, tall and imposing, his form draped in a simple tunic, embroidered with symbols I recognized to represent the cycles of life and death. His long hair shimmered with streaks of silver and gold. His piercing eyes held eons of knowledge.

He moved with royal grace and poise. His demeanor was that of a man used to giving orders. Most importantly, he exuded an otherworldly etheric essence.

A lump seized my dry throat as I felt my captor's ancient magic.

His eyes scanned the wards. A wave of his hand shattered the remnants of my failed spells. "These wards come not from the Deep Down nor from any place in the world that is known."

I quivered at the sound of his voice—deep and resonant, vibrating with the depth and density of the entire cosmos.

The voice of an Eternal, but what else was he?

He turned and left the room, leaving the door open. I followed. Two necromancers in dark robes flanked me as soon as I stepped out of my holding cell into a narrow hallway.

We came to a stop in front of a large door made of dark, heavy wood. One of the necromancers pushed it open to reveal a spacious room bathed in warm, flickering light. A roaring fireplace cast a cozy glow.

My stomach rumbled as the tantalizing aroma of mouth-watering food wafted in the air. A long, sturdy table stood in the center of the room, laden with dishes overflowing with succulent meats, freshly baked breads, and colorful fruits and vegetables. The plates and utensils were made of the finest porcelain and silver. I marveled at the opulence of it all.

The room was decorated in deep, rich shades of blue, with plush chairs and a cozy sofa arranged near the fireplace. The curtains were drawn back, revealing a magnificent starry view of the night sky.

I felt a pang of confusion at the luxury of the room. It seemed at odds with my current predicament. Was this some sort of mind game? A ploy to lull me into a false sense of security?

The necromancers left. My abductor gestured for me to sit, and I hesitated before sinking into one of the chairs. The plush cushions received me with a warm embrace as if the room itself was trying to ease my concerns.

He broke the silence. "You no doubt have questions, and I will answer them in time. But let us first enjoy this meal. When there is much to discuss, I find that a feast is the best way of bringing people together."

"I'm good, thanks."

I immediately regretted saying that. I hadn't realized how hungry I was before walking into the room. Could it be compulsion?

Refusing the food would impress no one, but the last thing I wanted to do was let my abductor enjoy all his psychotic plans.

He sat back into his chair. "Should you change your mind,

feel free to dig in at any time. Let me apologize for the unpleasant chamber in which you landed." His expression was almost remorseful. "It was in error that the vortex delivered you there. I assure you, you are not a prisoner here."

"Really? Well, your Yelp review is going to suck."

"You are a guest. Ask if you need anything."

"A guest?" I said, dumbfounded. "Do you know what that word means? Do you murder all your guests' friends before kidnapping them into your hellish guest room? What happened to Carter? There's your first question."

He ignored my words, his gaze unflinching. "Do you understand why you are here?"

I just stared at him.

"No? I allowed myself to hope you might have worked that out. You see, I have reason to believe that you possess certain... abilities."

I frowned, deciding to play along. "What type of abilities?"

"The type that make you both a great value to certain people... and a threat to others."

I wasn't about to let that asshole intimidate me. "Dude, who are you? What do you want from me?"

"Very well, we can skip the pleasantries. All you need to know about me is that I am a Timekeeper and I need the Seventh Council Seal."

Son of a bitch.

"It was you," I said. A homicidal rage welled up inside me.

"You sent those necromancers and the mutant badgers or whatever the hell they were. You're the one who's been after the Seal."

He towered over me with a malevolence I could feel in my very core. "You possess great power, young rider, but it is feeble compared to the power of the Timekeeper. One wrong move and your potential will be lost. Tell me where the Seal is kept while you still can."

"If I knew where it was, why would I share it with you? You're obviously fully and completely deranged."

The mask slipped off his face and a faint frown creased his brow. "The Timekeeper knows your deepest secrets, the things you keep hidden even from yourself."

"You're the Timekeeper, right? So why do you refer to yourself in the third person? Oh, I know, because that's what crazy people do."

"I suggest you not rely on your paltry charms with me. I know you are aware of your most dangerous secret. Should you choose not to comply, I will bring the matter of your deceit before the Great Eternal Magistrate. His fury would surely make you regret denying my simple request."

A knot formed in my stomach at the mention of the Magistrate. "You make a rotten first and second impression. I don't know you from Adam. Why should I trust anything you say?" I said, stalling for time.

"This is your choice. If you want your secrets to remain undisclosed, all you have to do is aid me in retrieving the Seventh Council Seal."

I flashed an innocent smile. "So, tell me, what's so special about this Seventh Council Seal?"

His eyes seemed to sizzle. "It's an artifact infused with far too much power to be left in the hands of scoundrels and rogue Immortals." He paused, letting his words sink in. "While your mother, Isadore, may be able to bend time to her will, it is my duty to ensure that the timeline remains secure and never deviates from its natural order."

My goose is cooked.

If he knew about my mother, he knew about my father as well.

I raised an eyebrow. "And what does that have to do with me?"

"It has everything to do with you," he snapped back. "You know what I see when I look at your world today? I see slaves to technology. You make yourselves complacent by relying on machines and gadgetry to interpret your existence. The natural rhythms of life are stunted and mutated. Your wisdom is digitized vomit repackaged into viral fortune cookies. My purpose is to restore balance, to remind the living of the infinite impulses within the electric life force of their bodies and their intrinsic connectivity to the natural world."

All words meant to feed his hungry ego. I yawned. "I loved the part about the digitized vomit. That was a sick bar. We just need to find the right beat and upload it to SoundCloud."

Two can play at making word soup.

"Have your fun, but you need to make this choice wisely, for there are forces beyond your understanding that will stop at nothing to undo you."

I rolled my eyes. "Been there."

His voice thundered. "You are what I feared, a product of your diseased culture. Help me secure the Seal, or the Magistrate will learn that you are the prophesied child, the spawn of the Dark one. And when he does, he will go to work on you. First, he'll break you, then mold you, then weaponize you into a fiend most heinous and foul."

"While you're at it, tell him he's going to be sorely disappointed, because I don't break. And I'm already a weapon. And if he catches me on the wrong day, I can do that whole heinous and foul thing, too."

I knew I sounded delusional, but I wasn't going to give a single inch to that bastard—not intentionally and not accidentally. I had been burned before and I wasn't about to make that mistake again.

He leaned forward, his face inches away from mine. "Do you want the Dark one to get his hands on the Seal? We are natural allies."

I chewed on that for a moment. If he wanted the Seal to banish Horror, it could be an answer to all my problems. But something told me that his intentions went way beyond that.

I opened my mouth to respond, but part of the ceiling shattered with a deafening thud, raining rubble down on our heads in a thick cloud of dust.

A figure landed on the floor, surrounded by a bright red aura.

Horror sprang to his feet, towering over me like a demon from the deepest, darkest vortex. The fire flickered, casting eerie shadows on his bloodied face.

I scrambled to my feet and pressed my back against the wall.

The Timekeeper spun around, dragging Horror to him with a staggering magnetic force field. Horror's red aura exploded in a shockwave that smashed the force field into pieces that fell to the ground.

Shadows in the shape of human skeletons emerged from the walls, trapping Horror inside sticky webs of dark magic. When the shadows pounced on him, he grabbed them by their throats.

Horror fucking grabbed the throats of shadows!

Undeterred by the sticky webs ripping at his flesh, he spun about quickly and tore the shadows to shreds. His face was savage.

The Timekeeper conjured a mighty death spell, but Horror swiftly countered with a string of ominous incantations that sent tremors rippling through the room.

His formidable blood language.

I watched in awe as the Timekeeper's power faltered for just a moment. Horror seized the opportunity to physically grab his opponent and launch him headfirst into the wall.

The Timekeeper's eyes sparkled with an unearthly light as he chanted a frantic incantation. A blinding flash shrouded him, and the Timekeeper vanished in the blink of an eye, leaving only a faint afterimage behind.

Horror's voice cut through my stupor. "Now!" he commanded.

I grasped his hand, then coiled my arms around his thick neck.

He pulled me into an embrace. As soon as his arms were tight around me, the room started spinning, and a kaleidoscope of colors swirled us away.

Chapter 20

I STUMBLED ONTO THE rocky ground beneath me, my head spinning from the abrupt spatial shift. We were standing on an elevated plateau, with an endless horizon of milky sky stretching out before us. There was nothing to break up the barren landscape; not a single tree or boulder, just a monotonous wasteland as far as the eye could see.

My throat was parched. I licked my dry lips, my tongue rough against them. "Where are we?"

Horror tugged at my hand, guiding me down a steep incline towards a narrow gorge.

The immense power of the place was unmistakable, almost tangible. Primordial magic pulsed within every rock and pebble, as if the very soil beneath our feet was alive.

We came to a small spring, nestled deep inside the gorge. The water was crystal clear and rippled with a gentle current. Horror crouched down, scooping up a handful of water.

"Drink," he said, offering me his cupped hand.

My reflection on the water's surface appeared distorted. "What is this?"

"An eternal spring. You must drink to erase the imprint he used to mark you."

The dickwad marked me?

"You can't linger in this sanctuary forever," Horror continued. "The moment you leave, he would know where you are, unless you drink from the spring to wash away the imprint."

Winter had bathed in an eternal spring to purify his etheric essence against the darkness threatening to consume him.

I eyed the water warily, uncertain whether I could trust my father. But exhaustion and frustration won out, and I took a hesitant sip, feeling the cool liquid slide down my throat. My mind felt clearer, my senses sharper, as if a veil had been lifted.

"Better?" Horror asked.

Not knowing what else to do, I nodded. "How'd you find me?"

"There is only one way to reach beyond the boundaries of the Eternal Halls—third eye vision."

I gasped. "I was in the Eternal Halls?"

"The lower levels, yes."

"Escaping the Eternal Halls is impossible. Why did you risk coming to find me? People who go there never return."

"You are surprised? I am your father."

"Okay, you must really need me, huh? And on the day that I serve my purpose, you'll have the pleasure of killing me yourself."

Horror regarded me, puzzled.

"Don't give me that look," I said. "You're a master manipulator, and you'd do anything to protect your interests. You won't hesitate to eliminate your own daughter. Be honest."

"You make a good point. I hadn't considered it... You're very convincing, though. *Hogwash!* Who fills your head with these daft ideas? Why would I kill my own child? You are a mist rider. I take pride in that."

The prophecy, my potential, mother's grand design. That's why.

I stepped back until the rocky wall poked my back. "You expect me to believe that you have scruples? You tried to kill Chaos, remember? Or doesn't he count because he's a bastard? That's what you call him, right?"

His eyes flashed with disdain. "When did I try to slay that wretched brother of yours? That ill-bred mongrel ought to be put down, but rest assured it won't be by my hands."

I dropped my head and covered my ears to block him out. "Please, stop. I can't take this anymore. I don't know who to trust, who's lying, who's being real. Everywhere I go, it's all deceit and corruption." The air felt thick as I took a deep breath, trying to focus on what mattered. "Where's Carter?"

"Carter?" Horror sneered. "You mean that dainty degenerate who follows you around like a sickly goat?"

I shot him a sharp glare, my patience wearing thin.

Horror sighed. "I dispatched the warriors trying to drain his essence. And do you know, that ungrateful cur fled without so much as a word of thanks."

My heart fluttered. "He's alive?"

He tapped his foot impatiently and sighed. "He breathes, unharmed, but I would not regard him as alive. He appears to be nothing more than a mindless, chattering blood bag."

"I swear, Father, if this is some game of yours…"

He waved a hand dismissively. "Your bodyguard is fine. Your father on the other hand… took a great risk for you, my flower. Gratitude, or at least a civil tone, would be appreciated."

"You want a medal? Or what, a participation ribbon? I'm the one who's screwed. That creepy psychopath threatened to reveal that I'm your daughter to the Great Eternal Magistrate."

I swear, he almost laughed. *Almost.*

"That would be some feat to see, considering that creep *is* the Great Eternal Magistrate."

Say what now?

"He has been busy," Horror said. "He was also the architect of the attack on the exquisite Valkyrie's shop. I was on my way to inform you when the bloodpath alerted me you were yet again in peril."

My joints tensed in anger. I knew my kidnapper was behind the attack at the shop, but I didn't know he was the Great Eternal Magistrate. I had been warned that he would take an interest in me once he knew what I was, but it never occurred to me that he would actually go after me himself.

Horror leaned in, his expression grim. "Indeed, deceit is everywhere."

My thoughts swirled in disarray. "Did he steal the crystal tears from the Deep Down?"

Horror hesitated. "That was me."

And just like that, he had confessed as if it were nothing.

Blood rushed to my face. "You bastard," I hissed. "You killed Horpheus."

"I did no such thing. I left him alive."

"Well, he's dead," I shot back.

"Perhaps old age finally caught up with him. Your venerable mage was drawing life from places he shouldn't have. I used no lethal force. I simply induced a temporary deep sleep meant to last for hours."

I stared at him in disbelief. He genuinely believed he had done nothing wrong.

"You shouldn't have used any kind of force," I said. "You had no business being in his vault, no business stealing the crystal tears."

As I spoke, I could see his anger simmering. He stepped closer, his hand balling into a fist. "He tried to kill me," he spat out. "*Me*. A god. I would have been within my rights to crush him like an insect, but I controlled my wrath."

"I don't believe you. You are either the biggest liar in all the realms or dangerously paranoid, and you're a cold-blooded killer."

"You dare accuse me of such treachery? I may be your

father, but I am also a First Eternal and I will not tolerate insolence."

"Horpheus was found dying as soon as you left. The facts are the facts and considering all you've done, why wouldn't you take one more life?"

His expression softened. "I restrained myself for you, my flower. Your heart is too tender for this treacherous world. I won't do anything to hurt my own flesh and blood, even if that means sparing those you value."

"Oh, and putting Horpheus in a coma while stealing the crystal tears was supposed to make me happy?"

Horror's gaze bore into my soul. "I needed to protect you," he said. "I need to remake the crystal shield to keep us both safe from the festering nest of wasps that are the Eternals."

I clapped. "Well done, I feel *soooo* safe right now. News flash, the moment you escaped your exile, you sicced the magistrate on me."

He shot me an irritated glance. "The magistrate has wanted to eliminate you since the day you were born."

"What? Why?"

"Because he is none other than Chronus, who also happens to be your great-great-uncle."

"Chronus?" I asked, dumbfounded. "The same Chronus who ancient Greeks believed presided over the cycle of seasons and the movements of the stars and planets is my relative?"

He nodded.

"Ah, yes, he mentioned having something to do with the concept of time, which makes sense now. He referred to himself as the Timekeeper. So, I have an uncle who wants me dead, too? Why? What's his end game in all of this?"

"He has been gunning for me for centuries. Always trying to find a way to banish me from the Eternal Halls until he finally succeeded. I anticipated that he would eventually come after you and I had plans to protect you, but then Isadore and Chaos defied me in the most appalling manner."

I stared at him, unsure of what to say. My great-great uncle was a god, and he wanted my head. Yet, if he wished my father harm and he knew about the prophecy... why wouldn't he want me to live—at least until I dispatched Horror? It was almost too much to take in all at once.

"He must be related to my mother," I muttered to myself. "The time-controlling thing runs in the family."

Horror's lips twisted into a bitter smile. "He is her great-uncle, and there is no love lost between them."

My life had always been a big fucking mess, but now, with Chronus on my trail, things were about to get even more chaotic.

The truth dawned on me. "That asshole was the one who tried to kill me when I was four and ended up putting my adoptive mother under a potent spell that kept her trapped inside her own mind, unable to move or communicate."

Horror was furious. "You see now why we have to use

every weapon we have at our disposal?"

"Right, because you're so much better than him. I can't let you reforge the crystal shield, Father. The last thing anyone needs is a more powerful you."

"I do enjoy your delusions, but it's not up to you, my child."

No, it's up to Time and the Horae, but it's not for you to know I've caught wind of that fact.

"Your father needs you, Luna. At great risk, I recklessly breached the Eternal Halls with my essence uncloaked. I can no longer hide. I can be tracked. Even the necromancers shifted their allegiance to Chronus after I killed Cerber for you. You see, I'm the one who's *screwed*, not you."

Before I could respond, Horror raised his hand, conjuring a swirling blue smoke that encircled me. The air crackled with energy, and I barely had time to register what was happening.

"Wait!" I protested, but it was too late. The smoke enveloped me completely and within seconds, I felt myself being yanked from the gorge, hurtling back toward my own world, powerless to change the course of events that had been set in motion.

A nagging thought persisted. If Horror hadn't killed Horpheus, who had?

Chapter 21

I sat on the couch in Winter's living room, replaying the recent events in my mind. The sounds of the Pacific Ocean crashing against the shore outside the window did little to calm my nerves. I hugged an oversized throw pillow and focused on my breathing, but my thoughts kept derailing to dark places.

Winter was on the phone, pacing back and forth. His voice was hushed and tense. I didn't catch most of what he was saying, but it didn't matter. The Seventh Council Immortal Magistrate had resurfaced and was in full swing, reaching out to all his sources to collect information on Chronus in an attempt to verify Horror's wild story—a story that had left me reeling.

Questions pecked away at my mind like vultures. Who had dealt the final blow to Horpheus as he lay in a deep sleep? Why did Chronus try to kill me as a child, when I was the one destined to defeat Horror, his sworn enemy? How the hell was I supposed to prevail against not one, but two lethal Eternals?

A knock on the door snapped me out of my trance. Winter shot me a worried glance before answering the door. Kirsi strode in, her striking auburn hair flowing down her tight blue leather jacket. She had on the cutest high waist orange corduroy flare pants I had ever seen. Kirsi always command-ed a room's attention, but it was the man who stepped in behind her that made my breath catch in my throat.

Carter.

"The prodigal son returns," Kirsi said with a grin.

I launched myself from the couch and into his arms, but then I thought better of it and pinched his arm instead. Hard.

"Ouch! You're like a rabid raccoon," Carter protested.

"That's for being so reckless. Next time we're jumped by Eternal meatheads, you'll run the other way, got it? I thought you were fucking dead."

"Oh, I'm sorry, did my supposed demise cause you undue stress? Just try watching your friend get sucked in by a vortex strong enough to consume a fucking cruise ship."

"Fine," I said, my voice conciliatory. "We'll call it a draw."

"It's a draw?" Kirsi said. "This isn't tic-tac-toe. You both made it back in one piece, that's a huge win for you both, not a draw."

I stared at Carter. "Did Horror help or was he feeding me BS?"

"He did," Carter said, spitting the words out like bad milk. "I'll spare you the gory details of how he dealt with the meatheads. Let's just say there wasn't enough meat left on them to initiate cell regeneration."

I rolled my eyes. "That's not sparing the gory details."

"Really? You weren't there, but I'd be happy to go into more detail."

"Don't you dare!" I said. "And I know you didn't have the stomach for the aftermath. I heard how you ran off. Horror thought you were rather ungrateful, by the way."

"That father of yours is a bloody nightmare," Carter said.

Facts.

"Him wanting me to believe he's on my side is the only reason you are still breathing."

"That's like bubonic plague being on the side of the living," Kirsi said.

I grimaced. "You have news for me, Kirs?"

We settled on the couch. I finally enjoyed a moment of peace.

"The Oracle of Delphi reached out to Herja," Kirsi said. "Pythia is eager to grant you an audience as soon as possible."

I leapt off the couch. "How do I get there?"

Winter gently pulled me back down. "You won't be going anywhere tonight, tiger. You've already covered immense distances through vortexes and portals. So much long-distance teleporting in such a short timespan severely drains your etheric core and leaves you vulnerable. You'll stay here and you'll rest."

He was bossy but right. The past twenty-four hours had

been a lot. I took in a deep breath to calm my surging adrenaline. "So, how will I make it there when the time comes?"

"The *Pyramid of the Sun* in Teotihuacan hosts a portal that can teleport you right to Olympus," Kirsi said. "From there, you can traverse the ley lines and make your way to Delphi."

My eyes widened in wonder. "You mean the portal can actually transport me all the way to Greece?"

"It's usually kept shut because it churns tremendous earth energy and with new human scientific devices it is harder to keep a secret, but the Oracle will make an exception and open it for you."

I glanced at Winter. "Will you join me? Or am I the only one who's allowed to go through the portal?"

"We're all going," Kirsi said. "Herja, too. You'll need all the help and protection you can get."

"We don't know what we're up against, Luna," Winter said. "But I need you to promise to not take matters into your own hands."

"Yeah, of course, I promise."

"I never thought I'd be saying this," Kirsi said, "but you should consider bringing in Chaos. His crazy ass is far from stable, but he does command a shitload of power."

I mean, yes?

Kirsi stood, her tight leather jacket creaking as she stretched. "Okay, I'm going to jet. Let's go over the trip itinerary in the morning."

Carter slowly rose from his seat and cracked his knuckles. "I'd offer to stick around, but you'll turn me down," he said with a grin.

I grabbed his hand. "Don't vanish again, okay?"

His smile widened. "You sure about that? Didn't you compare me to a mosquito trying to get inside your ear in the middle of the night?"

"Dude, really? You're still a pest, but you're my pest." I turned to Kirsi. "Thanks for everything, Kirs. See you two tomorrow."

She flashed me a mischievous smile. "Don't forget to recover tonight. Get your beauty rest. That's not always easy with a needy Viking around. He might say he wants you to rest, but he'll want something else more. He's thirsty."

I was too tired to laugh. "He'll be a good boy."

At last, I was going to Greece—only instead of exploring its magnificent ruins, savoring its exquisite cuisine, or experiencing its lively nightlife, I was destined to play peacekeeper for perhaps the most ill-conceived, motley fellowship ever assembled on my way to receive a dire prophecy and move ever closer to the ultimate battle for the five realms.

THE INGREDIENTS WERE SPREAD out on the kitchen counter: flour, milk, butter, eggs, sugar, cinnamon, nutmeg, vanilla extract and two large Japanese sweet potatoes. The first step to making the sweet potato pie was to boil and mash the potatoes, according to the online recipe.

Baking was not one of my strong suits. I found myself easily distracted and overwhelmed, feeling lost amidst measuring cups, baking pans, and the complexities of combining ingredients and setting oven temperatures.

I put the sweet potatoes in a pan with cold water and placed it on the stove. Thirty minutes of boiling should do the trick.

While the water boiled, I started mixing the dry ingredients with my diced butter and cold water to make the pie crust.

Winter found me bending over, looking for a baking pan of the right size and shape in his cupboards.

"Your water is boiling," he said.

"What?" I got up to find the sweet potato pan overflowing, frothy water spilling all over the stove. My disappointment almost turned to tears, but I kept myself together.

Crying over spilled potatoes... seriously, Luna?

"Let me get that for you," Winter said, turning off the stove and moving the pan to the sink. "You okay?"

"I can't even boil potatoes anymore."

He added cold water to the pan and returned it to the stove.

"It happens to the best of them," he said, unable to hide a smile.

"The best of them have issues with boiling? Really?" I

said. "You're such a bullshit artist."

"You say that like it's a bad thing. Did you know that farmers use bullshit to fertilize their crops?"

"Yeah, and bullshit is also ruining the ozone."

He wrapped his arms around me from behind so he could adjust the pans on the burners. "All things can be mastered with practice," he said, softly.

I closed my eyes and enjoyed his lovely scent. "Are we still talking about cooking?" I said, unable to mask the pleasure his proximity stirred.

He pulled away to grab a bag of carrots from the fridge and quickly crunch into one. "Yeah, what else? Someone has to say this, I think you might be a sex fiend."

I waved him off. "You're an idiot."

"What is all this for anyway? Are you cooking for me?"

"I don't know. I felt like baking a pie. I don't want to leave San Diego without ever having baked a pie."

He untied my apron and tossed it on the counter. "Let's go out."

GOING OUT WAS A great idea, a way to distract ourselves from the looming storm. We ended up at Cucina Urbana, our favorite cozy little restaurant in the heart of San Diego; the familiar scents and sounds of my city gave me a sense of normalcy amidst the madness.

The food was delicious and comforting. For a moment, I forgot about evil Eternals, ominous prophecies and deadly forces meaning to destroy me.

We lingered outside the restaurant, breathing in the brisk evening air. Winter's arm gently draped around me. "A stroll or a drive?" he said.

"Let's drive. I want a panoramic view of the city."

We hopped in the car. Winter drove to the Cabrillo National Monument, where the cityscape unfolded before our eyes. As we stood at the edge of the lookout point, the lights of San Diego shimmered in the darkness. The Coronado Bridge gracefully spanned the bay like a ribbon of steel against the night sky, connecting the city to the island. A salty wind rustled through my hair, carrying the smell of the Pacific. I knew this city, the streets and the people like I knew myself.

"I've called San Diego home for so long," I said.

Winter brushed a finger against my cheek. "The magic of the city has always pulled me back, even before I surrendered my weapons to a lunar witch." He placed his arms around my shoulders. "This isn't a final farewell, baby. We'll be back. It's our home."

"Yes, we will," I agreed.

I leaned into him, finding comfort in his warmth. The skyline stretched on forever, touched by the moon's glow. Each light was a memory, a part of this place that was mine. The ocean's roar was faint and far away, like the tall tales that children whisper. The palm trees swayed and soothed, casting long shadows across dark paths.

I held on to every detail, each piece of San Diego I had collected over the years. No matter where I traveled, the rhythms of this city would stay with me, beating in time with my own heart.

Chapter 22

I JOLTED AWAKE, MY heart racing as I sensed a presence in the room. The first rays of dawn filtered through the curtains, painting the walls with a warm, golden hue. Winter's arms were wrapped around me, his breath slow and steady in sleep.

I sat up, pressing against the headboard, when a burst of purple light revealed Carpo standing at the foot of the bed. I slid out of Winter's embrace, my feet landing softly on the carpeted floor.

"Carpo?" I whispered, careful not to disturb Winter. "What are you doing here?" My voice wavered between apprehension and annoyance at this invasion of my privacy, undoubtedly sanctioned by my mother.

"I bear a message," Carpo replied. "Your mother requests your presence in her realm."

She stepped forward and held out her hand. A gleaming crystal lay in her palm, shimmering with a kaleidoscope of colors.

"The chronostone will take you to her," she said.

I stared at the chronostone, feeling its power resonate within me. "What, you mean now?"

"Time is of the essence."

"I can't just walk out on Winter like that."

"We're inside a fluid cocoon where time doesn't move, Luna. He won't know you've gone. You'll return before he awakens."

She pressed the chronostone into my hand. "Close your eyes and think of your mother. The stone will do the rest."

I did as she said. The floor shifted beneath me, and my body swirled. When the sensation of movement stopped, I opened my eyes to find myself in the Forever Palace.

My mother and Anya lay on chaise lounge sofas, their faces illuminated by the warm glow of a hearth fire. I glanced down at my clothes—my sleepshirt was gone, replaced by a long, flowing gown, similar to the one I had worn at the bonfire during my last visit.

My mother smiled at me. "Welcome home, daughter."

Anya's expression remained unchanged. She too flashed me a warm, reassuring smile. My mother must have explained our familial ties to her, and likely more.

"It sounded urgent," I said cautiously, studying my mother's face to discern her intentions.

"Oh, it is," she confirmed. "I have conferred with Anya, and she has kindly agreed to participate in the bonding ritual."

"And have you explained all the details to her?"

"Of course. My faith in the young chronomaster is absolute."

"Luna," Anya said, "please believe me when I say I will do anything to help you."

"You might not feel that way if you knew the extent of what we're up against," I countered.

Anya reached out and squeezed my hand reassuringly, her touch a comfort in an otherwise overwhelming moment. "It doesn't matter. I've suspected for a while that you are more than meets the eye. I think you have that effect on everyone. We will not let you face this enemy alone."

My heart ached like a storm cloud about to burst. "You've already lost so much," I muttered.

"And now I want to make sure they pay. Every one of them."

I had no retort for that.

"Everything is prepared for the ceremony," my mother said, her voice commanding. "Please, ladies, follow me."

The circular ritual chamber had walls made of polished obsidian that reflected the flickering light of the countless mounted torches. A magnificent domed ceiling displayed a shifting, iridescent mural of the cosmos. Gold and marble floor tiles formed an intricate pattern that represented the interconnectedness of time.

The air was scented with exotic spices. A crystal altar at the center of the room stood on a raised dais, surrounded by five hourglasses, each filled with sands of different colors representing the power of the five Horae.

"Stand before the altar, my daughter," Isadore instructed.

I stepped forward; the weight of a mystical power pressed down on me.

The five Horae stepped into the chamber and formed a circle around me, each standing next to their respective hourglass. They closed their eyes and extended their hands, palms touching, to create a continuous ring of power.

Anya stepped to the center of the circle, positioning herself directly across from me at the altar.

My mother began to chant in the ancient language of the Eternals, the words resonating with power, filling the room with tangible energy. The Horae joined her, their harmonies rising and falling in a haunting melody. Their combined voices summoned the very essence of time, bidding it to bend to their will.

Anya's transformation was arresting. Her commanding presence evoked Medusa, with her hair coiling and writhing like a nest of snakes, emanating a palpable aura that left those who beheld her unable to look away.

My mother stood just outside the circle, her arms raised, gathering force like a cyclone. A brilliant light filled the chamber, arising from the center of the circle. Anya's eyes snapped open and locked onto mine. Our spirits entwined and I could feel the force of chronomancy flowing into me.

As the ritual reached a crescendo, the light at the center of the circle exploded outward, enveloping us all in a blinding radiance. And then, just as suddenly, the light receded, leaving us standing in the aftermath of the powerful ceremony.

Anya reached out to me, her fingers brushing against my forehead. The connection between us was electric, a bond that transcended the limits of mortal understanding.

"You can now access the magic of the chronomasters," she said.

"Use the gift wisely," Isadore said, her voice heavy. She was tired but satisfied, maybe even a little proud.

I followed her out. We walked down lavish corridors and halls until we reached a set of ornate double doors. Pushing them open, we stepped out into a stunning garden.

A vibrant symphony of colors with flowers of every shade arranged in harmonious patterns greeted us. A gentle stream wound its way through the lush foliage. The air was filled with the sweet scent of blossoms and the gentle sound of rustling leaves.

Isadore led me to a stone bench beside the stream. "Something is troubling you," she said. "A new worry on your mind since last you visited."

I sighed. There was no point trying to hide things from her. "Chronus kidnapped me," I said, "and Horror came to the rescue. I don't know what his end game might be. He had interesting things to say."

Concern flashed in her eyes, the first sign that her self-confidence and poise weren't boundless.

I rehashed all the events that had taken place since being

pulled into the vortex, the stuff about the Seventh Council Seal, and everything that Horror had to say about Chronus. She listened without interruption.

"How much of that is true?" I asked. "Is Chronus the Great Eternal Magistrate? And is he really family?"

"What Chronus did was most inappropriate. There must be a deeper motivation behind his actions than the one he confessed. He is my grandmother's half-brother, but we do not share any familial affinity. We maintain a polite distance and stay out of each other's way."

I raised an eyebrow. "There is no way he approves of you or your union with Horror."

"Chronus is a traditionalist who adheres to the letter of the ancient laws rather than their spirit. He presumes I use my powers far too freely."

"I know he wants to get rid of me eventually because, if the prophecy rings true, I will take his throne from him."

"Chronus doesn't have a throne. The Eternal Throne has been unoccupied for millennia."

"He still doesn't want Horror's daughter to sit on it."

"Chronus may be a textualist and a formalist, but his integrity is intact. That's why he was chosen as Great Eternal Magistrate. He controls time vortexes and is an unwavering timekeeper. He would not murder a mist rider under any circumstances."

"Yeah? Well, he sure as hell had murder in his eyes when I refused to give him the Seal."

She considered my words for a moment. "If he wants the Seal, it is to banish you, not to kill you."

I rolled my eyes. "That doesn't make me feel better. He would kill my life rather than killing my body. Same difference."

She grasped both my hands and locked her eyes on mine. "I will tear Chronus apart limb by limb if he ever dares lay a finger on you again."

Her intensity shocked me. "Let's hope it doesn't come to that."

"I will inform him in no uncertain terms that you're not only under Milan's protection but mine as well. In the meantime, your priorities should be learning to access chronomancy, exploring your bond with Anya and mastering the depths of your own magic."

"I will, I promise, but not today. I must travel to Delphi to receive an important message from the Oracle." I rose up, brushing off some pollen from my gown. "Will Carpo return me to San Diego?"

Isadore nodded. "Luna, a word of warning."

A dark premonition rose in the pit of my stomach.

"This intrigue you have going with the Seventh Council Chief Magistrate has to come to an end," she said. "Nothing good can come from it."

Great, another one who wants me to give up on Winter.

"This again," I said. "Are all Eternal parents so adverse to love? Must every relationship have an ulterior motive? You are both so ancient. Have you ever been in love? Could you walk away from it?"

A look of surprise crossed her face. "Does Milan hold the same feeling on this subject? It's good we can agree on something. In our world, love always leads to regret," she said. "Winter's etheric essence is not stable. He will dry up *your* essence by consuming your power if you continue sleeping with him."

I simmered while I resisted the urge to channel Anya's power and instantly teleport back to my own timeline in San Diego.

"That can't be real. Why would that happen?"

"I don't know. A magic very old and very dark left a residue inside of him. You are not physically compatible. When together, he is like a black hole feeding on your morning magic."

"Have you met Winter?" I asked, irritated. "He's not perfect, but he's sincere and has a true sense of justice. He respects rules and authority, but unlike Chronus and the lot of you, he still retains his humanity and acknowledges his feelings."

Her manner hardened. "As your mother, I would be remiss if I didn't warn you, but ultimately it is a choice only you can make."

"That's right. Now, Mother, excuse me, but I really must be going."

She nodded, her eyes full of worry. "Just be careful, dear.

Do not put your full trust in him or any man."

I wandered back inside to search for Carpo when I came across Chloe arranging flowers in large vases in the great hall.

"Luna, it was such a transcendent ceremony. I'm very pleased it worked," she said, her face beaming.

"Was there any doubt it would work?"

"Oh yes, much, it rarely ever does, but you have inherited your mother's predisposition."

I opened my mouth to respond when Chaos entered the room, carrying a delicate Ming vase adorned with a beautiful dragon design. Its vibrant shades of blue contrasted brilliantly against the crisp, white porcelain.

When Chaos spotted me, his expression soured.

"What are you doing here?" I said.

"What are *you* doing here?" he retorted.

"Clever," I said, rolling my eyes. "Shouldn't you be off somewhere corrupting women or abusing your hounds?"

"My business is not your business."

"Chaos!" Chloe admonished him gently.

"I'm just lending a helping hand," he grumbled.

"With what exactly?"

"There's a banquet tonight."

"And they needed your help?" I said, incredulous.

To say my questions irritated him would be an understatement.

"Yes."

It was like pulling teeth. "Who asked?"

Chloe raised a hand. "I did."

I stared at her, dumbfounded. "Why him?"

Chaos handed Chloe the priceless Ming vase and seized my arm, leading me outside to a terrace. "Will you just chill?" he snapped. "What I do is none of your business."

I regarded him in shock. "You're flirting with Chloe... oh god!"

"Please refer to my earlier statement."

"Huh, what are you up to, big brother?"

"Why does it matter to you?"

"It matters, because if your little games cause my mother to change her mind and remove her protection, I might end up with my head on a spike."

"What a shame that would be," he said, his mocking tone suggesting he didn't find that deadly prospect troubling at all.

"This thing with Chloe needs to end," I insisted. "You had your fun, now wise up."

"Have you ever been in love? Could you walk away from it?" he said, his expression deadpan.

My cheeks flushed. "You heard me talking to Isadore?"

He started to move away. I grabbed his arm. "Then you heard I'm going to Delphi. And you know I need you."

"Sorry, no can do, pumpkin, I have better plans."

"Plans? Is that what you call fooling around?"

He pried my fingers off his arm one by one.

"C'mon, Chaos. Don't make me beg."

"You can beg all you want, sweetheart, I'm still not going."

Ugh.

"Why are you so muleheaded?"

"I have a banquet to attend."

"I'm asking for twenty-four hours of your time—forty-eight tops."

He grabbed my shoulders with force. His irises glowed red, like the eyes of a demon. "Luna, I told you I can't go."

"But you never gave me a reason."

"Because Chloe is dying." The moment the words left his mouth, he turned away from me.

A storm of feelings raged inside me—sorrow, disbelief, guilt. Chloe, the bright, beautiful Hora, was nearing death. Suddenly it all made sense—why he had grown protective of her and didn't want to leave her side.

"She's dying?" I said, my voice drifting through the air like an echo.

He flared his nostrils in anger. "She's been infected with the vicious virus of mortality, and I can't do a damn thing about it."

"Is that what Isadore told you the night you took off?"

He said nothing, but it was clear that fragile Chloe with her slender frame, her luscious snow-white hair and her radiant gray eyes had won his favor. What might have started as a misconceived attempt to prove a point—maybe to my mother, maybe to himself—had turned into something he had not anticipated, something real, and now something all-too-real.

Chloe joined us on the terrace. The tension was obvious, and it caused her a moment of hesitation.

Chaos turned to her, his demeanor shifting in an instant. "Ah, fair lady, have you come seeking my talents in napkin folding? I suggest the Bird of Paradise fold, the perfect first impression," he said, a smirk playing on his lips. "Or perhaps you require my keen eye in the art of flower arrangement? Ah, I see it now. You want me to bake up my white and gold rustic cupcakes."

Chloe grinned. "I must admit I was skeptical at first, but after having tasted your soufflé... You have a certain... flair for domesticity. Who knew a demon lord could have such a delicate baking touch?"

Chaos feigned offense, placing a hand over his heart. "You wound me, cruel maiden. My talents extend far beyond the kitchen, I assure you. I can also expertly sew a button or hem a garment with the utmost precision."

Chloe laughed—light and genuine glee and utterly contagious. It was as if her laughter peeled back the layers of time, revealing a glimpse of the carefree girl she once had been. It was the power of love. It shattered the mold of who you were and opened up a world of infinite wonders.

"You two have a wonderful night," I said, heading for the sliding doors. "I'll be on my way. I have a thing."

As I stepped away from the terrace and their smiles, the enchantment of the palace tugged at my heart, urging me to linger a while. The bittersweet longing to do just that reminded me I could not linger anywhere.

Everything in my life had been so temporary and ever changing.

Chapter 23

THE TEMPLE OF APOLLO at Delphi was perched on the slopes of Mount Parnassus, surrounded by a landscape of rugged cliffs and fragrant olive groves. The air, cool and crisp, brimmed with the aroma of pine trees, as if the very essence of the land could be inhaled. Awe-inspiring stone columns guarded the entrance; their time-worn surfaces chronicled the centuries they had endured.

My heart swelled with reverence to be standing at the threshold of Delphi, about to meet the most renowned Oracle in history. Just a month ago, I had believed Pythia's divinations to be mere fabrications, a guise for kings and generals to fulfill geopolitical agendas. Even though I was star struck to be meeting the Oracle of Delphi, I had to remain vigilant and trust my instincts. She, like everyone else, could very well have her own ulterior motives.

The sound of metal sliding against leather echoed behind me as Winter unsheathed his sword. Carter, Kirsi and Herja followed suit, flanking the entrance.

My own personal order of knights.

With a deep breath filling my lungs with the early morning Greek air, I approached the entrance to the ancient temple. A flat portal shimmered before me like a mirror. I reached out and poked it with a finger. Its surface rippled like a still pond disturbed by a pebble.

The portal swallowed me whole. My body stretched like I was made of playdough and then snapped back together. I tumbled out of the portal and onto the marble floor of the ancient temple. The air inside was heavy with the scent of burning incense and laurel leaves.

I scrambled to my feet. The temple's interior was dim, lit only by torches mounted on the walls. Frescoes adorned the ceiling, their once-vibrant colors now muted.

I ventured deeper into the temple, my footsteps echoing in the vast chamber. As I rounded a corner, I came upon a massive stone door etched with characters of the Greek alphabet. I pushed the door open, revealing the heart of the temple.

There, at the center of the room, seated on a tall tripod up on a platform, her back straight and her eyes closed in meditation, was Pythia. Her hair was tucked under a white cap. She was surrounded by a golden aura.

Above the platform, a mural depicted the radiant figure of Apollo, the Greek god of light, music, and prophecy. His golden bow and lyre were prominently displayed, symbols of his divine power.

A towering figure stood behind the Oracle, half-hidden

in the shadows—a cave golem, his body hewn from the very rock of the temple.

His limbs were thick and powerful, the muscles of his arms and legs carved into the stone with painstaking detail. The ceiling of the temple nearly grazed the top of his head.

Half his face was hidden behind an exquisite golden mask, the contours of the metal perfectly melding with the golem's visage. The exposed half of his face revealed a stoic expression, his eyes narrow slits that seemed to see through me.

Pythia's lips curved. "Welcome, seeker of truth and daughter of the morning. You stand in the presence of the Oracle, where the veils of time are drawn back, and the mysteries of past, present, and future are revealed, and all languages are known."

Her voice resonated throughout the temple with a three-dimensional quality like it was built with the echoes of many voices.

Pythia slowly opened her piercing eyes, fixing me with a hypnotic gaze that seemed to penetrate the depths of my soul. Her form began to waver and blur, like a mirage shimmering in the heat of the most arid desert.

Gradually, the mirage dissipated, revealing not one, but three separate figures in place of the singular Oracle who had greeted me moments ago. Each woman represented a different stage of life: the maiden, her countenance unblemished and alight with the curiosity and innocence of youth; the matron, her features etched with the wisdom and experience acquired through life's myriad trials; and the crone, her silvery tresses framing a face that bore the heavy imprint of time, her eyes fathomless pools of arcane secrets.

In unison, their voices thundered off the chamber walls.

"We are the embodiment of the feminine triad, encompassing the full spectrum of life, bequeathing guidance and enlightenment to those who fervently seek our counsel."

To underestimate the Pythia would be to court disaster, for I now stood within the sanctum of Apollo, and the arcane magic that swirled around me might well be beyond my skill.

"You have ventured forth to implore our guidance, and it shall be granted. No sacrificial offering shall be demanded of you, for the lifeblood we require must be drawn from the living. You are tasked to procure the blood of a Shadow. We serve as conduits for the power of divination, and the diviner requires payment."

As their voices blended, the three women melded once more into the singular figure of the Oracle. Her face was beautiful, haunting and wise.

A low, grinding sound filled the chamber as the golem stirred to life. Each step he took sent tremors through the ground beneath my feet. The sound of stone scraping against stone made me shudder.

Halting mere inches from me, the golem extended a massive stone arm, the sinewy fingers of his hand curling delicately around a diminutive flask.

"By nightfall, you must return with the blood," the Oracle decreed.

"You want the blood of a shadow warrior?"

"Indeed."

"Why?"

"The Temple thrives on magic. We would petition for your own blood, but it holds too great a value, and the Temple may become a beacon for malevolent forces."

How convenient that I had a shadow warrior waiting outside. Did she know? Of course. She was the Oracle after all.

I reached out and took the flask from the golem's outstretched hand, my fingers brushing against his rough stony palm.

The golem withdrew to his post behind Pythia.

"The timeline reflects our intentions, a looking glass into the depths of our souls. Dismiss not the chronology, O rider of the mist, for the mind's confines are the sturdiest of prisons, and dogma begets the death of reason. Heed our divinations not with your intellect, but with your very essence, unblemished and liberated from preconceptions, akin to a pristine parchment. Only then shall the truth I impart resonate within you."

"I am prepared," I said, my voice barely a whisper.

"In three days, when the Cretan sky is graced by a full moon of radiant superlunary potency, He who is the Dark must meet his demise. The threads of destiny have accelerated, heralding the advent of the prophecy. The storm of war shall descend upon you, and flight is no longer a viable option. The hour to alter the weave of time has come and gone."

A mere three days. I am far from ready.

I desperately needed clarity, but my instincts screamed she wouldn't give it to me. "Is my victory foretold? How might I ready myself in a mere three days without a mist horse? How will it all start and where?"

Pythia's gaze penetrated my very being, her eyes ablaze with enigmatic fervor. "The tapestry of the future is a labyrinthine mystery, its threads interwoven by myriad hands and aspirations. To divulge excessive detail would jeopardize the precarious equilibrium of destiny. You alone must traverse this path."

Great. We might as well call the whole thing off.

Her voice assumed a resolute tone. "Once the Dark One is vanquished, you must prepare to ascend the Eternal Throne. For it is foreordained that the one who overcomes darkness shall herald the dawn of a new age."

That's not as cool as it sounds.

"Ascend the Eternal Throne? That's not a path I'm prepared to walk."

Pythia regarded me with an inscrutable smile. "You are still young, and the true extent of your own intentions remains concealed, even from yourself. The desires of one's essence lie shrouded behind the veils of uncertainty and fear."

I cloaked my mind with an impenetrable barrier and stayed quiet. I could never make the Oracle understand that I harbored no ambitions. Maybe if I was raised by my Eternal parents, but I was brought up an unassuming witch by a loving Grandmother who taught me the value of small things.

"What of the Nightbringer? I've been warned that the Eternals will unleash him on me as soon as I defeat Horror, when I'm depleted."

"The Nightbringer is already here, scrutinizing your vulnerabilities. And therein lies your greatest advantage. For while he seeks to infiltrate your spirit, he shall inadvertently reveal his own nature to you."

Is that supposed to make me feel better?

My mind swirled with unanswered questions.

The Oracle raised a hand, forestalling my inquiries.

"You have been granted all knowledge the diviner can share with you. You must not falter, Last of the Riders. Trust in the path."

As her words faded, the golem stirred to life once more. Its massive arm swung deliberately, striking a gong with resounding force. The sound reverberated through the temple, and the world around me shifted.

In the blink of an eye, I found myself standing outside the temple, the ancient stones now silent behind me.

I stood there, still reeling from the Oracle's words. This whole time, I had hoped for a different outcome every time I spoke to Isadore or Miss Celia or Horror himself, but the

Oracle had cut right through my denial.

Winter's eyes filled with concern. I must have looked terrible. He wrapped his arms around me like I was a child.

"How did it go?"

"As clear as mud. I..."

A sudden rush of air stirred around us and Chaos materialized, his expression a blend of annoyance and resignation.

I raised an eyebrow, more than a little surprised. "Am I hallucinating from all the incense?"

"I demand it to be known that I didn't want to come," Chaos huffed, crossing his arms. "But Chloe insisted."

"You told Chloe?"

He kept at it. "It's not like I didn't have anything better to do. I could be lounging on a beach and sipping a mojito. But no, you had to show up and pull the sky-is-falling card and add a good guilt trip to the mix."

Kirsi feigned coughing. "We appreciate your... unique brand of support."

Chaos regarded Kirsi with disdain. "Killer Kirsi and her tepid enthusiasm. Oh, joy. Let me just dive headfirst into an inferno with you all."

Herja shot him a lethal glare, as if to warn him she'd cut his tongue out and fry it as bacon if he said another word.

Carter stepped forward and pointed off into the olive grove behind the temple. "A watcher is just there, obscured in the grove."

I followed his gaze and discovered a cloaked figure behind

an olive tree, its body made of gray stone, a leather hood over its head. A cave golem, much smaller than the one sitting behind Pythia inside the temple.

"Why would a cave golem spy on us?" Kirsi said. "And badly?"

Herja's eyes narrowed. "I don't know, but we must proceed with caution. The Delphi golems report directly to Apollo."

"He's not here to harm us," I said. "He wants something."

Carter crossed his arms. "And what might that be? Skin?"

"I had to promise the Oracle something for her service."

All eyes were on me.

I hesitated for a moment. "The Oracle wants Winter's blood."

Winter's face contorted. "My blood? Why would she need that?"

"Not yours specifically," I said, "she requested the blood of a shadow warrior." I retrieved the flask from my jacket pocket. "She claimed it's to maintain the magic of the Temple, and she couldn't take mine because it would make the Temple a target for dark forces."

Winter shook his head. "Absolutely not."

"Please, Winter," I pleaded. "We might need her again one day."

His expression darkened. "You like to ask the impossible."

He turned and stalked away, his posture a picture of rigid anger.

I scurried after him.

"The answer is still no," he said.

"Help me understand. Why this? It's such a small ask."

He spun around to face me. "Their magic is weakened, and they want to leech off mine. What delusion made you think I'd agree to that?"

"I don't know, maybe because we're about to get obliterated? Who the hell cares if they get a little power boost from your precious blood?"

"My blood holds potent magic, opening its channels would…"

"I promised," I cut him off.

He shot me a sharp alpha glare. His blazing eyes swallowed up the space around us and any chance I had to convince him.

I attempted to unleash a similar soul-crushing gaze. "I can't go back on my word, Jonas!"

"But I can."

His body became so rigid I thought he would turn into a stone golem.

That's it. He's not changing his mind.

I turned on my heels and marched back towards the temple. I could feel his eyes on my back, that stubborn man of mine.

Carter, Kirsi and Herja exchanged uneasy glances.

"We need to find another way," Carter said.

"Agreed," Kirsi chimed in. "We can't force Winter to do

something he refuses to do. We'd sooner get water from a stone."

Herja nodded. "There must be another way," she said, eyeing Chaos. "We simply need to be clever. Where, I wonder, might we find another Shadow?"

Chaos sneered, but his defiance quickly dissipated. Kirsi and Herja, faces set with determination, swung their swords to rest on each of his shoulders.

Resigned, Chaos grumbled, "I left the Forever Palace for this shit."

Chapter 24

THE INKY WATERS SHIMMERED, set alight by the reflections of a seemingly endless row of bonfires that lined the seaside promenade. The smoky aroma of burning wood entwined with the briny essence of the ocean overwhelmed my senses and made me feel like a gothic heroine.

We flew to Crete aboard Aegean Airlines, indistinguishable from the ordinary tourists that filled the plane. To be honest, I welcomed this mundane mode of travel, a respite from the draining experience of traversing through portals. Each time I used one, I felt my very essence dim ever so slightly.

When I relayed to my companions what the Oracle had foretold about the outbreak of the war happening in just three days under a Cretan full moon, Herja's face had darkened. She was convinced the prophecy was linked to the Seventh Council Seal and had promptly taken off for Ideon Andron to consult with the Kouretes, the demons entrusted with guarding the Seal.

We didn't have much to do while waiting to hear from

her, so Winter took me out for a night in Rethymno, an enchanting seaside town, to make up for our silly fight over the blood thing. Vibrant bougainvillea draped over the quaint, whitewashed buildings, and the cobblestone streets were alive with the laughter and chatter of locals and tourists alike. The picturesque harbor, framed by an imposing Venetian fortress, was a testament to the rich history and culture that thrived within this charming corner of Crete.

Winter held my hand as we strolled down the bustling, fire-lit promenade, making my insides purr and growl at the same time. He appeared every bit the Greek god in a burgundy buttoned shirt and black jeans. The interplay of flames and shadows only served to accentuate his chiseled features.

"I bet this is not what you expected when we came to the island to prepare for war," Winter said, pointing at a band of traditional street musicians on a slightly elevated platform.

"What's going on?" I said, utterly captivated by the crackling fires and the exuberant mood of the crowd.

"Not sure, a traditional celebration perhaps."

A group of elderly men and women in folding chairs watched the comings and goings of young couples, boisterous teenagers and excited children.

Winter led me to a quiet bench facing the sea. From there, we had an unhindered view of the small boats adorned with glowing lanterns as they crawled across the water. To our left, the street musicians serenaded us with traditional melodies played on clarinets and violins. To our right, children diligently stoked the flames of the bonfires with fresh wood.

"Gram would love it here," I said, my thoughts drifting. "She gets so mesmerized by a good bonfire. She just stares into the depths of the flames and sees faraway things no one else could see."

A pang of longing always accompanied thoughts of my grandmother. I missed her so much. I missed her warm hugs and kisses on my brow. I missed her clear and unique way of seeing the world, and I missed how she could set me straight so lovingly when I made mistakes.

Winter's eyes twinkled with amusement. "It is unwise to let Carter and Kirsi roam the town on their own. Locals are bound to hit on the Valkyrie, and knowing those two hotheads, they'll cause mayhem and end up in a cell."

"I'm more worried about Chaos."

"Nah, he'll sleep to recover from the lost blood. He's weird like that."

"Back to what you were saying, do you think Kirsi is so beautiful that any man would hit on her?" I said.

He picked up a pebble and threw it into the sea. "I don't think about Kirsi like that."

"Apparently, every man thinks about Kirsi like that. Why should you be any different? She's a lot of woman."

"Kirsi is not a woman."

Did I hear him right?

"What does that mean?"

"You make me say the strangest things, Luna," he said, licking his lips.

"I did that? I made you say Kirsi is not a woman?"

"You know what I mean."

"No, I surely don't."

Not sure I enjoy where this conversation has gone.

"Kirsi is a friend, a companion and a fellow warrior. She has my trust and gratitude. That puts her above the realm of the flesh. There's nothing I wouldn't do if she asked me."

"That's precisely how men think about women they find attractive."

"No, that's what mortals think of goddesses."

I couldn't help but laugh. "You're so full of shit. Just say Kirsi is attractive and be done with it."

"I'll meet you in the middle," he offered with a sigh. "She is intelligent and that makes a woman attractive in my humble opinion."

"Jonas Sandell has *humble* opinions? Who knew?"

"Opinions should be humble. Only facts are certain."

I nodded. My hot warrior was quite smart himself. "And am I intelligent enough to be attractive in your humble opinion?"

He raised his hand to brush his fingers against my cheek. "You, Luna," he said, his voice trailing off. "Any man would agree that your intelligence is a certainty."

Every time Winter let his guard down, I was struck with an irrational fear that he might somehow be saying goodbye.

"And you?" he said. "Do you find Kirsi attractive?"

I covered my mouth, stifling a laugh. "You're ridiculous, you know that? But, oh yeah, she's a straight fox."

"I'm ridiculous, that's certain, too."

"You also might be the devil."

"I might just be," he agreed and tenderly took my hand.

No matter, this devil already has my soul.

There were times when talking to him was a maddening rollercoaster, but, strangely, it often brought me a sense of calm.

He tightened his grip on my hand and pulled me up.

I wrapped my arms around his neck. He remained still, unyielding beneath my touch, making no move to embrace me in return.

He grasped onto my wrists instead.

"Luna," he whispered. "All I do is feel things for you. Too many things. Messed up things... pure things... and everything in between. I don't intend to dump them all on you. You're more important to me than my own feelings. It's my intention to keep you unscarred."

"Too late for that."

He stared into my eyes, pressing my hands against his chest. The moment got swept away by a loud bell announcing the start of the festival.

A cheerful middle-aged woman suddenly seized my hand. I was taken aback by her boldness, but Winter nodded in approval, urging me to follow her lead.

She led me to a large clay jar brimming with water; an array of trinkets—rings, bracelets and earrings—floated on the surface.

Teenage girls stood around the oversized jar, smiling at me.

"What is this?" I asked.

"Place something in the pot," one of the girls told me. "Tonight, the stars do some magic, and you have dream of the man you marry."

"Oh," I said. "If I'd known, I'd have visited sooner."

Winter put his arm around me. "Do it," he said. "You can't defy tradition."

Still unsure, I removed one of my earrings and tossed it into the jar. "That's one lost earring," I said, as we walked away. "Now what?"

"Now we swim. But not here."

WE WALKED BAREFOOT ON the sand, holding our shoes in our hands. The beach was deserted. Two old pedal boats sat forgotten by the water's edge. My skin shuddered as Winter's arm brushed against mine.

"It's perfect here," I said, when he stopped to stare at the dark sea.

He quickly took off his shirt, taking my breath away. He was a shining excellence under the pale starlight—a hypnotic spectacle of masculinity and self-confidence. I doubted there was a single moment in his adult life where he felt insecure around women.

"Well?" he said, a slight impatience on his handsome face.

I shook my head before taking off my t-shirt and unbuttoning my shorts. "So, this was your grand design?"

The night air was unexpectedly warm, but the water was not. I dipped my toes cautiously... or would have if Winter hadn't decided to lift me up and toss me out into the deeper water.

"What the hell?" I said, climbing to my feet in shoulder deep water.

"Embrace the unexpected."

"Embrace a kick to your balls."

"From you, I would, Luna Mae," he said as he forced me back into his tight embrace. "If I hold you close, you won't have room to kick."

"Don't be so sure," I said. "Mist riders have hidden talents."

He laughed. "You'll never believe you're ready to be thrown into the deep, but you are more than ready, mist rider."

My heart stopped as he leaned in for a kiss. His powerful chest rose and fell rhythmically against my body as his tongue did its magic. His right hand moved to the back of my head, pulling my wet hair in a tight grip.

I wrapped my arms around his neck, lifting one leg to force his hips closer to mine. The world vanished in the darkness and the salty fullness of his lips.

He untangled his lips from mine, gently tracing my face with his fingertips. "Are you sure?" he said, breathing unevenly. "There will be some energy reverberations, but we're already on a warpath and I don't give a fuck who knows what we are to each other."

It took me a second to make up my mind. "Oh yeah! I want this."

Everything I was ached for his touch. That thought played on a loop in my head as he scooped me up to carry me from the water. We were so hungry and needy we barely made it onto the sand before we attacked each other's mouths again.

My body shivered under his weight as I lay on my back. The soft waves rolled onto my toes in time with the gentle swaying of his hips over mine.

I ran my hands up and down his shoulder blades while my lips stayed glued to his lips. I didn't know how either of us was able to breathe or how we managed to keep our tongues tangled and hot like that for so long, but I wanted it to last forever. I was ecstatic to have his fingers running through the wet, messy strands of my hair.

All of it. Forever.

When we finally came up for air, his right hand fell down to trace my jawline and neck before his thumb landed on my throat, which he stroked gently while staring into my eyes.

"Give me permission," he said.

"Permission?" I repeated like an echo.

"Yes," he said, nibbling on my earlobe. "Permission to do anything."

"You have it," I said with a sigh, not quite sure to what I had agreed.

His fingers left my throat as his tongue drew a hot, glistening trail across my neck and chest down to my bellybutton before moving to unexpected places like the back of my knees, my calves and my feet.

One by one, he nibbled on my toes, gently, deliberately. He crawled slowly back up my body when he was done.

"That's it?" I said, rolling my eyes.

He chuckled. "You'd be surprised how many women don't enjoy having their toes nibbled on like that."

"The fools."

"It would have been cruel if you kept them from me. Such exquisite, delicious little treats."

I raised an eyebrow. "Are you trying to scare me?"

"No," he said. "I don't have to try."

He was right. My whole body yearned for his touch with a mixture of delight and dread. Sleeping with him while he was mortal was one thing, but now that his immortality was back, intimacy might prove too much. It scared me to know I was giving up all control of myself to this man who dragged centuries of violence behind him, who always took what he wanted.

When his name landed on my lips, I stopped caring about any of that. I decided to just be, to just live in the moment.

Hearing me call out his name triggered something inside him.

It felt so good, I never wanted it to end. My body played along the melody he was humming like a well-tuned violin. I dug my nails into his back, wanting to feel him closer, lose myself in him completely. I gasped so loud I might have scared the fish away from the shore.

And then everything detonated inside me and around me as if a cosmic fuse had ignited. Literally. It felt as though a star had collapsed and a supernova exploded in the very core of my being, radiating outwards in a cascade of emotion and energy.

The once calm waters surged forth in a tidal wave, crashing onto the shore with unbridled force. The ground beneath our feet shuddered and convulsed, as though the earth itself were waking from a deep slumber, ready to unleash its geothermal fury.

We ran for the bluffs beyond the shore with pandemonium coursing through our veins. We stumbled and fell on the way, only to scramble back to our feet, propelled by the intoxicating blend of fear and exhilaration, the sheer joy of being alive in that wild, orgiastic instant. We had unleashed mayhem upon the universe and reveled in the wild, untamed beauty of it all.

We rolled onto the ground, breathless and laughing.

"Did I do it right?" Winter whispered.

It wasn't a serious question. He knew the answer.

"You arrogant prick," I whispered back, barely able to speak.

He fell on top of me, his forehead rested against mine, an unguarded smile on his face. Seeing him completely happy made everything right. To reach a moment of total peace is the purpose of every beat of our hearts.

Is this his first peace? Is it mine?

I think so.

Chapter 25

THE GAPING MOUTH OF the Ideon Andron cave, nestled high up on Crete's untamed Mount Ida, loomed before us like the jaws of a primordial behemoth, inviting us to delve into its shadowy depths.

Herja emerged from the cave clutching a splintered spear, a strained smile on her face.

Winter's voice boomed. "What mischief have you seen?"

Herja glanced down at the shattered spear. "The Kouretes are on edge. They mistook me for an intruder," she said, her voice raised until she walked closer. "There have been disturbances in the shield around the cave; they suspected a paranormal entity to be probing the cave's defenses. They reacted aggressively upon my unannounced arrival."

Winter scoffed. "That's what you get with fucking demons."

Kirsi glared at him. "That's not helping."

"Those demons want out, that's why I asked you to meet me here," Herja said.

"Want out?" I said. "And what of the Seal if they leave?"

"They don't care," Winter said, disdain dripping from his words.

Man, he really has demon issues.

I turned to Carter. "Stay outside and keep watch, just in case."

"I'll stay with him," Kirsi said, tapping her fingers on the hilt of her sword.

Winter and I trailed Herja as we descended into the cavern. Our footsteps echoed off the rough, limestone walls.

Here, the veil between the realms ran thin, allowing an otherworldly aura to infiltrate every crevice, every alcove, saturating the cave with a festering energy that threatened to spill out into the basic world.

The cave extended deeper into the mountainside, its shadowy recesses rich with an air of mystery and intrigue. The soft, rhythmic patter of dripping water echoed throughout the cavern.

In the very back of the cave, a serene pool of green water lay undisturbed, reflecting the faint light that struggled to arrive in the mountain's depths.

The ceiling above unfurled a canvas of intricate stalactites. They hung like crystalline icicles, their sharp tips glistening with moisture—a testament to the slow, patient artistry of geological forces that had carved and shaped this subterranean realm.

From the shadows, two Kouretes emerged near the pool. Their eyes flickered like molten embers, set within high, sharp cheekbones. Their sinewy forms were peppered with coarse, raised quills of hair, and their skin gleamed with the hue of polished bronze. Their hands and feet had a sixth digit each, tipped with razor-sharp talons.

They gestured for us to follow them into the pool. Herja moved forward without hesitation. I trailed after her.

The water was cold, first rising up to my calves, then my hips, as we waded further until we reached the center of the pool. There, the water began to swirl and ripple around us. The Kouretes disappeared beneath the surface.

"It's a gateway," Herja said. "Trust it."

I hesitated, my gaze meeting Winter's. He stepped forward to take my hand. With one shared breath, we took the plunge together, following the Kouretes down.

As we sunk deeper, the temperature increased. The sensation of being underwater was disorienting yet oddly serene. My lungs remained filled with air though I had no idea how. The Kouretes ahead of us glowed with a green light, their forms distorted by the rippling liquid.

The water guided us towards an opening and, once through, we emerged from the gateway into a concealed chamber. We stumbled onto a stone ledge, inhaling fresh oxygen into our lungs.

In the center of the chamber, five Kouretes were assembled in a circle, their intense focus directed on the symbols etched into the stone floor.

The two Kouretes who had guided us through the

gateway joined the widening circle.

Winter's eyes narrowed as he scrutinized the symbols. "They're trying to reinforce the shield," he said, his voice hushed. "But there's a problem. The energy source is unstable. If the shield fails, the Seal's essence will be exposed."

The Kouretes continued their work, their focus unwavering as they traced and retraced the lines of symbols.

I took a step forward to get a closer look, only to stumble against something very hard and very invisible. A configuration of small stones bearing runes materialized around me.

The head Kourete, dressed in a red cloak and towering over the others, snapped his head toward me. A smug grin played upon his face.

Yes, I get it, I'm not stupid.

The runes were acting as wards, but not just any wards—these were demon spells that only unbridled dark magic could dismantle.

Winter tried to step inside the circle of wards and was shocked back instantly. He blinked at me, slowly, as if to say, *you got this.*

The head demon taunted me. "Break free if you dare, for if you cannot, imprisoned you will be, measly being."

He thrust his hand. Stalagmites erupted from the ground, reaching upward, nearly grazing the cavern's ceiling, forming a transparent wall around me that cut me off from Winter and Herja.

Is this a fucking twisted game? Alright, I'll play.

I assessed the integrity of the wards—remarkable yet not invulnerable. For a fleeting moment, it occurred to me that the diplomatic thing was to wait until the demon decided to release me, but demons did not strike me as the diplomatic type.

To test the resilience of the runes, I hit them with small blasts of magic.

The Kouretes sneered at my efforts, their incessant, cracked laughter grating on my nerves.

"Persistent yet fruitless and pitiful," the head Kourete mocked.

With renewed vigor, I harnessed my mist magic along with the elemental energies of water and earth abundant within the cave.

This will be child's play.

I used all that magic not to crush the wards but the demons themselves, tapping into their very essence to drain their innermost reserves of dark magic. My power surged, the mist and the darkness coalescing into a tempestuous whirlwind around me. With an eager focus, I cracked open the confining wards and splintered the stalagmite wall.

Shock and disbelief marred the demons' twisted expressions.

"Her skinny self she has freed, yesss, yesss, yesss," they howled, dancing frantically around the chamber and baring serrated teeth.

Winter moved to my side, his enchanted sword at the

ready, wisps of smoke swirling around the blade.

"Enough!" he thundered, his voice resounding through the cavern like a bell gong. "You have the nerve to toy with us? You are only allowed here in the surface world because of the noble Valkyries who advocated for you at the demon trials."

The Kourete leader scraped forward, revealing an axe in his hand. "To enter our domain, great challenges await."

Winter's grip on his sword tightened, his knuckles whitening. "We have come to secure the Seal, not to indulge in twisted whims."

Herja placed her hand on Winter's arm. "We're not here to fight."

Winter hesitated, his anger waning under Herja's soothing touch. He reluctantly sheathed his sword and its tendrils of smoke drifted away.

The tension eased, and when the head demon spoke again, his voice was serious. "We cannot mend the shield. We depart now."

Winter and Herja exchanged glances.

"We can help you repair it," Herja said.

The demon raised his hand, only to lower it again. In his eyes, I saw trepidation. "No time. An Eternal draws near, seeking the Seal."

Not just any Eternal, Chronus, the Great Eternal Magistrate.

Deep within, I felt it. My great-great-uncle, ancient

beyond measure, had managed to discover the Seal's location without my help, and he was coming to claim it. *Brilliant.*

"You must stay," Herja urged him. "The Valkyries defended you when we had nothing to gain."

"The Seal dooms us. The Dark craves the power of the Seal. Stand against the Dark if you choose to die. Our debt is settled."

Once a demon said *no*, nothing could change their mind.

The Kourete stepped back. He lifted his hands. Dark energy spread around him like wings. The ground trembled.

He gazed intently into my eyes. "*Seh kseroh, peh-thee to troh-moo. Toh teloss sou pleseah-zee.*"

The foreign words slithered from the demon's mouth. A viscous black liquid welled up from the stone ground and spread out. The demons vanished.

Winter had grasped the meaning of the demon's parting words—it was evident in the somber way he looked to me.

"Was that Greek? What did he say?" I asked.

"He called you child of Horror."

"Seems word travels fast," I muttered.

"We must secure the Seal," Herja said. "We have to gather allies."

Winter clenched his fists. "I will inform the Shadow Master. The Umbra Order won't refuse the call." He stormed away and sank into the green waters.

"I'll summon the Valkyries and the Sisterhood," Herja murmured.

"Something's not adding up," I said. "Why would Chronus go to such lengths for a Seal that can send Eternals into the exile vortex? He has banished Eternals before, Horror included, without it. And he can control time vortexes."

Herja sighed. "Kirsi thought it best not to tell you. She worries you have too much on your plate."

"Tell me what?"

"The Oracle called Kirsi back after we left Delphi. She's the guardian of the Seventh Council Seal, so the Oracle thought she needed to know."

"Herja, just spit it out."

"Regarding the Eternal language cyphers that Düsternis embedded in the Seal's core... they hold a power far beyond the banishing of Eternals. When spoken aloud they imbue the Seal with the seductive power of illusion. The possessor of the Seal will have the ability to create the most potent illusions, the kind that can drive both mortal and immortal beings to the brink of insanity."

My confusion deepened. "How the hell did Düsternis pull that off?"

"He didn't." Herja crossed her arms. "Chronus tricked Düsternis. He was the one who provided the cyphers."

It started to make sense now. "Chronus intended to use the Seal on someone and let Düsternis take the blame."

"Maybe, but that's not the worst part. Every Seal belonging to a Council has a key that can unlock its full potential. If the Seventh Council key is inserted into the Seal now that it carries the Eternal cyphers, it will unleash a hidden layer of power, granting the ability to the key holder to open the Vault of Knowledge."

I recalled my mother's words. The prophecy predicted I'd keep Horror from unlocking the Vault of Knowledge, which contained the key to the universe. The Seal of Banishment was now at the center of a brewing conflict between Chronus and Horror as they raced to reach the Vault first.

"Luna," Herja said, concern etched on her face, "use every ally."

I took her advice to heart. "I need to speak with Chaos."

I SAT WRAPPED IN an old blanket that Herja had found among rockrose shrubs near the cave, gazing at the starlit sky above. Never in my life had I seen such a multitude of brilliant constellations.

A fire crackled before me, warding off the bone-chilling cold of the night. Kirsi and Herja had fallen asleep on a makeshift cot inside the cave while Carter patrolled the perimeter, ever vigilant.

Winter sat beside me, his silence betraying the thoughts that churned within his mind. I could see the unease in his eyes as they scanned the darkness, anticipating unseen threats.

"You are tense," I said. "Why not get some rest?"

"Being tense keeps me alert and sharpens my mind."

"Okay, but you're making me tense, too, and I don't need it right now."

"Is this your way of telling me you want to be alone?"

"No... maybe, sort of. I need some space to process everything, and your constant teeth grinding isn't helping."

He remained silent.

"Besides, when I'm this close to you, all I want to do is curl up in your arms and tend to my wounds," I said.

He smiled. "And what's wrong with that?"

"Nothing, I'm just... I don't know, I need to be able to control the flow of my thoughts and impulses."

He studied the flickering flames. "We could leave now, regroup and confront Chronus on our own terms."

"Even if it means being on the run constantly burdened by the Seal?"

He nodded.

My gaze met the fire. "Could you really do that?"

Silence again.

Yeah, I didn't think so.

He rose to his feet. "Enjoy your stargazing." He leaned down, his breath tickling my neck. "But if you're not in that cave within thirty minutes, curling up in my arms and tending to your wounds, I'm coming to get you."

"Deal."

I watched him walk away, drawing the blanket closer. He glanced back, his eyes searching my face, and my heart swelled with affection. Everything I felt for him surged within all at once. Winter made me better. He frustrated me to no end, but I cherished even that. I loved his fathomless ocean eyes, and the way he furrowed his brow before he lectured me. I loved his strength, his resolve, his faith in me. He revealed my limitations while inspiring me to strive for more.

But tomorrow might tear us apart.

Chaos popped up beside me. "I thought he'd never leave," he said. "For someone who despises the art of communication, our golden boyo sure knows how to stretch a goodbye into a sappy manifesto."

"You're forgetting I saw your soft side, too, Mr. Flower Arranger. And you're not fooling anyone. I know you care for Winter."

Chaos snorted. "The first boy scout? Have you ingested opium?"

"You play at being polar opposites, but I've seen too much. You both camouflage yourselves to hide your similarities. And if he disappeared tomorrow, you wouldn't know what to do with yourself."

"I'd know exactly what to do with myself."

"What do you have for me? Did you speak with Isadore?"

He settled next to me. "Indeed. She was not thrilled to see me again, but she listened."

"And what did she say?"

Chaos regarded me with heavy eyes. "She agreed. She will

aid you in locking away the Seal in a hidden dimension, but it will come at a cost."

"Everything does."

"Isadore can't create stable time pockets for inanimate objects," he said. "Someone will have to accompany the Seal and stay with it at all times."

I nodded. "That will be me."

Chaos shook his head. "She will not agree to that."

"Then she won't know until it's too late."

"Stupid are the brave. Luna, once the new dimension manifests, the power it will generate will be on a nuclear scale. The dimension will not reopen for centuries or the energy sustaining it will implode, tearing apart several other dimensions."

A lump rose in my throat. "Which is why Winter can't know. Because he would not allow it and I don't want to deal with that right now."

I could see Winter's eyes in my mind, hard and unyielding, as he told me it would be over his dead body that I would go ahead with my plan.

Chaos sighed. "Are you certain of this? Do you really want to be trapped in a frozen dimension? There's a reason Antarctica is not a vacation spot. You will be suspended in a loop of endless tedium, likely losing your sanity over and over again while your mind fights to restore itself. And then when it's over, all your friends in the basic world and the Deep Down will be dead and gone, and you'll emerge in a world likely gone to hell. The basics' only magic being their ability to consume and destroy the natural world."

"I hear you, brother, but unless you're willing to take my place…"

He opened his mouth, but no words came out.

"Relax, you fool, this is my fight. I intend to see it through. Chronus will have to pry the Seal from my cold dead hand."

"We have options," he insisted, his voice rigid. "We can fight, negotiate, run for the hills, or—"

I cut him off. "I'm aware, Chaos, this is a last resort kind of thing. I won't just toss the Seal into a different dimension unless all is lost."

"This is like speaking to a mule. Time for me to catch some z's."

I grinned. "You'll miss me when I'm gone."

"I'm more than willing to test that theory."

Kirsi materialized at the entrance of the cave, her voice slicing through the stillness of the night. "Don't mind me, I'm here to take over for Carter."

I waved to acknowledge her, but then a staggering force crashed into me, enshrouding me like an icy fog, threatening to consume me in its suffocating grip. A wave of hostile energy lanced through me like a dagger.

I pushed back and the pressure receded but lingered at the edges, poised to strike the moment I let my guard down.

"Kirs, no worries," I said. "I'll take this shift. I'm wide awake."

"Are you sure?" Kirsi said.

"Completely, go get some rest. I'll wake you up when I get tired."

With a slight bow, Kirsi retreated into the cave.

Chaos regarded me for a long moment.

"You too," I told him. "I could use some alone time."

I found Carter perched on a lookout spot above the cave. "I'm taking over," I said. "Go on, go inside."

Carter peered at me, his brow furrowed. "You sure?"

"I can't sleep. I'm going to sit on your perch and have a long conversation with myself."

As soon as he left, I sprang to my feet and hiked down the mountain trail. The gravel crunched under my every step. The night air was thick with the scent of wildflowers. I strode past overgrown bushes, steep rock formations and tall fescue grasses to stop at the site of an old holm oak tree.

Chronus stood under the tree wrapped in a long cloak that was darker than the night. He inclined his head slightly. "You heard my call, mist rider."

"What can I do for you, Uncle?" The words escaped my lips before I had a chance to think.

If he was surprised, he didn't show it. "You know why I came. Place it in my hands and I shall depart as fast as I arrived."

"I can't do that."

I almost told him to go fuck himself but caught myself in time. Anger was not a useful weapon when faced with such an experienced adversary.

His eyebrows arched. "Force my hand, and I will summon the Seal with a flick of my fingers."

"Then why involve me at all?" I snapped back.

His voice was as icy as his demeanor. "I have an offer. Surrender the Seal and I will allow you and your companions to walk down the mountain. As long as you stay out of my way, I will tolerate your presence in the human realm."

"And if I refuse the offer?" I inquired, my heart pounding.

"If you defy me, you will be banished to a realm where existence is but a mere shadow."

Way ahead of you.

I fought to keep a level head. "I get it, Uncle. You want the Seal to do your dirty work, that way you don't have to expose your despicable actions. You don't want anyone to know that you would banish your mist rider niece summarily without a trial."

I'd be damned if I let him know that I knew about the secret cyphers.

"A trial would only result in your execution," he said with loathing. "My offer is an act of mercy."

"And what is my crime, Uncle?"

His gaze narrowed, intensifying. "Mist riders are an anomaly. Their existence is a rare variable, a recessive mutation that comes about every thousand years. You are an unreliable catalyst who unsettles the equilibrium of the power structure. Despite this, you hold remarkable sway over gods, compelling them to adjust to the capricious changes you are prophesied to bring about. You are a loose screw in the cosmic order."

Another aggressively tossed word salad. I stood my ground, staring him down. "I'll play along. A screw usually has a place it belongs, and once it finds that place and it twists itself back into just the right spot, the cosmic order becomes more finely tuned."

"You do not understand metaphor," he said, losing patience.

"Okay, let's put this in plain talk," I said. "I will never surrender the Seal to you because you would use it to shape the world to your megalomania."

A bitter laugh escaped his lips. "You are your mother's daughter."

I shrugged. "I wouldn't know. She had to give me up to protect me from toxic assholes like you."

His magic radiated like a sinister aura. The fury he had struggled to contain burst open. "You disgrace yourself. You are unworthy of your heritage or your name. The very air you breathe has been squandered on you."

Alright then. "If we're going to act childish, I should really tell you that words can never hurt me."

The magic he let loose felt like a punch to the abdomen. His voice erupted like a sonic boom, assaulting my eardrums.

"SURRENDER THE SEAL OR SUFFER THE CONSEQUENCES. DO NOT MISTAKE MY MERCY

FOR WEAKNESS, AURORA."

His threat hung in the air. The scent of brimstone clung to him like an overbearing cologne.

"And don't you underestimate me, Eternal Magistrate," I said, forcing confidence into my voice. "I will protect the Seal, no matter the cost. And you better hope you don't see me mounted on a mist horse anytime soon."

He regarded me with fresh eyes, assessing my determination. A flicker of something akin to begrudging respect dashed across his face, gone as quickly as it appeared. "I have seen the birth and death of stars, civilizations rise and fall, and the coming and going of great kings and magistrates. Time rules over them all, and we are all of us but ticks on the clock. I will restore harmony for that is the vision of the Timekeeper."

"Well, I'm not a fucking Timekeeper and you're not a clock. The world is not yours to envision, nor is it mine. Your vision is oppression, a construct I cannot abide. Your so-called guiding hand is holding a fucking leash and every time you tug on it you choke the wild spirit inside all living things. Your condescending concern is just straight tyranny, Uncle."

His mouth contorted grotesquely as he cackled. "You are beyond saving. Your pride is its own megalomania. I will, how do you say, pop some popcorn and simply observe from afar while you and your father knock heads in the most brutal of fights, like two savage beasts in the arena. I am quite sure that would prove a most tantalizing and bloody show."

He detested me, plain and simple. He hated me because I was my father's daughter and because I challenged his authority when I was so young and undeserving. I had not put in the time. Chronus would do anything in his power to take me down. The Seal was only the beginning.

"Be gone," I said. "Shoo. You're annoying me."

His eyes flared with malice, pure, cold hatred. "You will never ascend the Eternal throne, my niece. Your weaknesses are too many."

"Take your throne and shove it up your exit vortex."

A cyclone of energy flew out of my entire body. Electricity danced in the air around me as the gusts of my storm picked up strength. The holm oak tree groaned and swayed perilously. Chronus visibly shivered as my elemental force swept over him.

Damn, that feels good.

I hastily pulled back my magic. I didn't want to provide him a single clue about my real capabilities.

His voice rumbled like a distant thunder. "YOU ARE YOUR FATHER'S CURSED SEED. IN TWO DAYS, WHEN THE NIGHT'S LUMINARY REACHES ITS ZENITH, I SHALL RETURN, COMMANDING AN UNSTOPPABLE FORCE. BRACE YOURSELF, AURORA, RIDER OF the DAWN, RUN IF YOU WANT, BUT KNOW THIS: THERE IS NO SHELTER, NO SANCTUARY ON EARTH FOR YOU, FOR A

BETRAYER WILL SOON BE DISCOVERED AMONG THOSE YOU CALL ALLIES."

With a swirl of his dark cloak, Chronus dissolved into the night, leaving me alone under the old holm oak tree.

The night was colder now, the darkness more oppressive. I took a deep breath, inhaling the clean, earthy scent of the mountain.

This is how it begins.

I traced my way back to the cave, guided by the fire's warm glow that called me forth like a beacon. Ready or not, this was happening. We could take the Seal and run, but I was exhausted. I did not want to live a life of running... from prophecy, from Chronus, from who I really was.

Chronus ran away, reluctant to raid the cave of Zeus on his own.

I'm going to stay right here where I'm needed until the end.

If nothing else, I was eager to take on the challenge, even if I didn't know how Horror, my father, the Dark one, fit in all of this.

I slipped into the cave, tiptoeing cautiously, careful not to rouse my slumbering companions. My gaze scanned the shadow-laden space, searching for Winter, but not finding him. He had vanished, leaving no trace behind.

THE SECONDS TICKED BY slowly, but my mind spun too fast, disorientating me. Carter stormed into the cave, his coiled muscles ready to strike. He cleared the last steps in a single bound, tension sparking in his violent eyes.

I tried to understand the lines and shadows that etched his features. "What happened?"

"Not a thing, there's no trace of him. Vanished into the ether."

I forced out my next words. "What if he's in danger? He could have been taken against his will."

Herja shook her head. "Our combined powers shielded the cave. The meteor that wiped out the dinosaurs could not have breached the wards."

An exaggeration for effect, but her point hit home.

"So, you're saying… he just left us without a word?"

"That's exactly what she's saying." Chaos emerged from the back of the cave. I had sent him to inspect the secret chambers, pointlessly, for the third time. "The boy scout never set foot back there, Luna. But we knew that, didn't we? I can smell his shadow trail like my hounds smell blood. It ends right here." He jutted a finger at the entrance. "He walked out like a boss, cloaked in invisibility spells. There are no signs of other essences or even the slightest indication of a struggle. He fucking ghosted us."

"What possessed him?" I said. "It makes little sense to walk away now."

Herja sighed. "It does lack logic and is out of character."

"Winter does not betray," Kirsi said. "You all know this. He lives by a code of honor. If he left without a word, rest assured, he has his reasons."

"Sure," Chaos said. "If it were me, you'd already be sharpening your knives, but when it's the stoic stooge, let's give him a free pass while he's jamming it up our backend."

Kirsi flashed menace and breathed a low growl.

She might have a point. If Winter had left of his own will, who knew what harebrained scheme he was cooking up? No doubt some quixotic, heroic nonsense.

"What news is there of the mobilization of the magical world?" I asked, eager to change focus.

"The Shadow Master and his Warriors are due here by morning," Carter said, looking like someone had kicked his puppy.

"The Valkyries are rallying as we speak," Kirsi chimed in.

Barely enough time to brace for the storm rolling in.

"Okay," I said. "Carter, secure the perimeter."

Carter nodded and slipped into the night. Chaos slung his sword over his shoulder with a smirk that made me want to punch him square in the face.

"Back when we thought you had kidnapped Emmet," I said, "Winter mentioned there was a path to find you through your connective shadow channel."

Chaos frowned. "That would only work if he left the channel open. And if I attempted to connect through it, he'd be able to read my mind."

"So? What is it you're hiding?"

He said nothing, but his face spoke volumes. He didn't think Winter had left any paths open.

Carter jogged back into the cave. "Someone's outside." He hesitated to continue.

"Out with it," I said.

"She claims your mother sent her."

I rushed outside to meet Anya. The chill night air did nothing to cool down my nerves.

"We got the call," she said.

"I won't lie, it doesn't look good," I said. "You don't have to be here. This isn't your fight."

"Where else would I be? The whole point of the bonding ritual was to strengthen you. We have two days left to fortify that bond."

Two days until the final battle—it would never feel like enough. "When will Isadore join us?"

"She said she'll come when the time is right."

Great. More cryptic non-answers.

Anya took my hand. "Isadore said you wanted a hidden time pocket to shield the Seal. I'm ready to cast it and guard the Seal within."

I shook my head. "That's kind of you, but I can't agree. If it comes to that, I'll go in to guard the Seal."

"Luna, your mother has granted me the power to create the time pocket. It's arranged. I want to do this."

I blinked. "You have the power to create a hidden

dimension yourself, without Isadore's help?"

She nodded.

"Finally, some good news," I said, taking a deep breath. "Then it's settled. You'll cast the time pocket, and I'll go in with the Seal."

Anya paled. "Isadore would never forgive me."

"At least, you'll be alive. I can survive this, Anya, I'm immortal and a mist rider. It will be agonizing, but I will come out on the other side. For you, it would be a death sentence."

"I know, but it's my duty," she insisted.

I held her gaze, willing her to understand. "I need you to do this and Isadore can't know until after the fact. I need you to give me your word."

Anya's mouth opened to argue but closed the moment she saw the resolve in my eyes. Her shoulders slumped as she nodded. "You have my word. There's more. Isadore has a message for you."

What now?

"Go on."

"She said that the mist horse is closer to home than we thought."

I rubbed my eyes, exhaustion sinking in. "What else?"

Anya shook her head. "That's all she said."

Home—whatever the hell that meant. If Isadore was serving me riddles, things were dire indeed.

I glanced at the darkening sky; mere hours remained

until morning. "Get some rest," I told Anya. "You will need all your focus and energy."

She headed into the cave without a word. Alone under a sea of stars, I inhaled deeply. The night felt heavy as if the world itself held its breath. The mist horse was close to home but Winter was not. In two days, I would fight the hardest battle of my life with or without them. But for now, the night remained, stars shone soft above and for a handful of heartbeats, at least, the world stayed whole.

Chapter 26

Two days later, I stood outside Ideon Andron at dusk next to the Shadow Master. The last rays of sunlight cast long shadows on the ground and a gentle breeze rustled the surrounding foliage. The mountain was so peaceful, yet the air was heavy with the anticipation of the upcoming battle.

Channeling the primordial energies of Mount Ida, the Umbra Elders had performed a ritual to cloak the enchanted domain of the cave and its environs, almost as if creating an alternate reality, a hidden dimension accessible only to those initiated to the supernatural. No matter what happened here tonight, the basics would remain blissfully oblivious.

Behind us, a group of five elite Shadow Warriors guarded the cave entrance, their silhouettes blending seamlessly into the surrounding darkness. Hundreds more lurked around the slopes and the fields below us, along with the bulk of our other forces, now hidden from sight.

Two days had come and gone without any news of Winter. Chaos had attempted to reach him through their shadow channels to no avail.

Chaos assured me all that meant was that Winter wanted to avoid detection, but his reassurances did little to quell my rising anxiety. Not to mention how much it bothered me that I had no fucking clue where Horror was—or Isadore for that matter.

"You should at least consider the possibility," Marcus said.

"What do you mean?"

"That there's a traitor among your allies like Chronus suggested. We thought there was a mole on the Board of Supernatural Orders, but what if it is someone here instead?"

I grinned. "Should I put you on the list of suspects, Marcus?"

"It would be the wise thing to do, but..."

"But I'm not known for my wise choices," I finished his sentence for him. "In fact, I'm terrible at it. But sometimes that's what's needed, a crazy bitch willing to burn everything to the ground."

Marcus and I exchanged amused glances, then his gaze shifted to the field below where edges of an interdimensional portal had started to form. Despite our best efforts to halt its progression, the portal kept growing.

Chaos had used the third-eye vision to peek at the Eternal gates and the Aetherway bridge, which provided the swiftest passage in and out of the Eternal Halls. It had taken him so much energy he'd slept for 24 straight hours. I worried about him, but I was mostly worried about what he had seen—Chronus had amassed a force of Eternal Warriors numbering in the hundreds, as well as tens of thousands of other fearsome beasts, strong enough to decimate an army five times their size.

"Did you invite the shapeshifters?" Marcus said.

"Not directly, but they responded to the call that went out to all supernatural factions."

Marcus nodded. "We can't turn anyone away."

No, in fact, we should beg.

We were seriously outnumbered, despite the mobilization of shifters, shadow warriors, Valkyries, and Deep-Down fighters and mages who stood united in this fight, hiding among the recesses of the dark mountain, ready to take on Chronus and stand their ground.

We all knew what was at stake; if we failed to stop Chronus, everything we cherished could be lost.

Cyrus McDonnell approached us with a trot, his naked torso gleaming under the surging moonlight like flesh armor. All his people were half-naked so they could shift at a moment's notice.

"Hey, Cyrus," I said.

He flashed me a toothy grin. "From day one, I've been asking what you really are, and you never gave in. Finally, I know."

"Marcus, could you give us a moment," I said.

The Shadow Master bowed and walked away.

"Bravo," I told Cyrus, clapping my hands. "I think you might have won a big burger of nothingness."

"I'll take a Balboa burger," he quipped. "Anytime."

"Why did you ask Emmet to spy on me? Please, do us both a favor and start with the truth. We might all be pushing up daisies by morning so we might as well avoid the bull."

His eyes turned serious. "A rumor was out that Darius had managed to contact his Immortals at their camp. I wanted to make sure you'd be safe."

"Okay, I believe you, and thanks. It doesn't really matter now."

He gazed out at the darkening mountain, flaring his nostrils as if sensing bad weather brewing.

"Having second thoughts?" I asked.

"I'm already on fourth thoughts, but I'd never let you Deep Downers have all the fun. I'm here to dance with the devil whenever the fiddle plays."

"I'm grateful you didn't involve Emmet, by the way."

He shook his head. "Kid's got too much to live for. The pack was never his thing. Your generation is fucked, a bunch of low-fi loners basking in the glow of lifeless screens."

I *was* grateful. I could never face Lily if something happened to Emmet.

There was someone else I wanted to shield from the rubble of the battle—Anya. I'd asked her to stay in the cave with the mage healers, but I wasn't sure she would listen.

A bright crimson streak slashed the sky, splitting it into two halves. Our scouts hastened back to the cave, their breaths ragged and urgent. Trees and bushes crumbled to the ground in the distance under the weight of a fierce storm that seemed to be miles deep. Bursts of lightning rose up from beyond the horizon. My uncle's army marched forward, spilling out of portals, following pathways and crossing bridges. They conquered whatever stood in their way—be it of land, water or air.

Above us the full moon hung in the bleeding sky, brimming with lunar energy so brilliant it illuminated the night as if it were day.

"Here we are at the omega as the Greeks say," Chaos said.

I almost jumped out of my skin. "Dude, stop sneaking up like that."

"If that scared you, I'd suggest wearing adult diapers for the rest of the festivities I see coming at us like the proverbial freight train."

"Okay, that was funny," I admitted. "Why are you funniest at the most inappropriate times?"

"Like my little sister, I use humor as deflection."

I mean, yeah.

The storm loomed ever closer, fueled by my uncle's devouring power. Its staggering ferocity threatened to annihilate any brave soul who dared stand in its way. It was like standing on a beach, waiting for the tsunami to hit.

I had no mist horse, no Winter, but I had a mega-shit-ton of fury.

Winter... wherever you are, whatever drives you right now, please, stay safe.

Carter materialized beside me, his body coiled as if ready to spring. Kirsi and Herja would lead the formidable Valkyries into battle. Chaos and I would try to hold Chronus back as long as we could.

The first Legion of Eternal Warriors thundered across the field on stout warhorses, their silver armor glinting under the eerie red sky. They were each so like the other, with cold, unyielding hate burning in their eyes.

Chaos gripped my hand tightly, his gaze locking with mine in a silent moment of understanding. Our kindred energy surged through our intertwined fingers, giving birth to an immense force field that radiated outward, forming a dome of protection around the cave and our fighters.

As the Eternal warriors advanced, they sensed the impenetrable barrier and skidded to a sudden halt.

The earth beneath our feet quivered as if seized by the violent shift of a massive quake. The ground heaved and buckled, threatening to tear itself apart as it reverberated with a deafening roar. The interdimensional portal cracked open and solidified, spewing out a horde of monstrosities.

"The Supernal Vanguard," Chaos said.

These nightmares made flesh were as fearsome as the legends that preceded them. Among them were Pyroskulls with flaming skull-like heads and wielding fire-whips; Galeswifts, winged beings whose aerodynamic forms allowed them brief flight; Umbrastalkers, who could meld into shadows and move undetected, rendering them virtually invisible; and the most formidable of all, Terraclaws, hulking behemoths with stone-like skin, possessing colossal strength and resilience, able to manipulate the very earth beneath their feet, creating tremors, sinkholes, and walls of stone.

Amidst the tumult of colliding energies and the warping of reality, Chronus descended from the sky, tearing through our force field as if it were nothing more than beams of light. He loomed over the battlefield like a huge dark vulture, floating just above the ground.

Casting a shadow over both mortals and immortals, humans and beasts alike, Chronus glided towards Chaos and me. He was draped in a cloak of shadows that seemed to devour light itself. His eyes blazed with a blinding intensity that scorched the soul. A malevolent grin stretched across his face as he surveyed the battlefield below.

His feet touched down. With each step he took, the air grew colder. The specters clinging to the mountain trembled in fear. As he raised his arms, the skies above thundered in response, reflecting his command over the elements.

Chronus halted before us, grinning as if our futile resistance amused him. The god of gods had come to claim the Seventh Council Seal, and only we stood between him and the end of all things.

I clenched my fists, struggling to steady my nerves. The brilliant light that suddenly burst forth felt overwhelming, and I fought the urge to avert my eyes and kneel before Chronus.

"SURRENDER TO THE GREAT ETERNAL MAG-ISTRATE FOR YOU LIVE AT HIS PLEASURE," he bellowed with a voice that made my eardrums ache.

"Then why is it that you are shaking in your boots?" Chaos yelled.

Chronus unleashed a wave of power, but it splashed off the invisible boundary of the shield that Chaos and I had quickly forged.

"I WILL ONLY SPEAK WITH THE MIST RIDER, NOT HER VALETS."

"Unless you've come to beg for forgiveness, we have nothing to speak about," I replied.

"THE GREAT CHANTER DIDN'T HAVE ANY-THING TO SAY EITHER WHEN I GAVE HIM THE SPELL OF DEATH. NOR DID THAT UNFORTU-NATE, PUNY LUNAR WITCH, CLARA MAE."

He wanted to provoke a reaction—I had prepared for that. I kept my lips sealed, but inside, my rage boiled over.

I fortified the shield and launched an attack, channeling ley line energy strong enough to knock down a skyscraper. Smoke spiraled from his hands, forming serpentine tendrils that snapped and hissed as they struck at my force field like long forked tongues.

My arms trembled under the strain as I pushed back with all my might. Chronus deflected my assault, countering swiftly with a surge of earth energy that made me stumble. I regained my footing and unleashed a lunar wave upon him, a screaming torrent of moonlight and magic.

He retaliated in kind, hurling one devastating energy wave after another in an attempt to throw me off. Our energies clashed and danced in a deadly ballet, force fields manifesting and dissipating in rapid succession, each seeking to dominate the other. Yet neither of us could gain the upper hand.

Chaos laughed, apparently bemused by this bloody stalemate. "This looks like it might take a while. I might go grab a coffee," he yelled out.

Chronus's patience finally frayed. "I WILL STRANGLE HORROR'S SPAWN WITH MY BARE HANDS."

With a deft flick of his wrist, he tore a hole in our main force field. His face contorted with effort as he held it open, allowing his warriors and monstrous beasts to pour through the breach.

The bellow of a battle horn reverberated across the battlefield and our fighters surged forward like wildfire. The air filled with the sounds of clashing steel and the screams of battle-hardened warriors.

The night sky bled crimson, and the full moon cast an otherworldly glow over the carnage down the mountain. As the clashing steel deafened, the Valkyries appeared, zipping through the air, their high-pitched battle cries somehow rising above the din with wrath and defiance.

Throughout the mountain, the earth quaked, its tremors reflecting the magnitude of the energy forces at war. The elements themselves seemed to be warring, a mirror of the titanic battle for the Seventh Council Seal.

Summoning the full moon, I drank its enchanted energy to the brim, letting it saturate my core. The power flooded out of me in shimmering lunar beams, ensnaring Chronus within its numbing silvery grasp.

"Are you afraid, Uncle?" I taunted, watching as he struggled against the energy that bound him. "This is what it feels like to be powerless."

He snarled at me, his eyes burning with rage. "YOU DARE MOCK AN ETERNAL GOD? YOU THINK THIS PITIFUL TRICK WILL HOLD ME?"

"No," I said, "but it sure as hell feels good."

"YOU WILL LOSE, NIECE."

"Fine, as long as you join me, Uncle."

Chronus's smirk mirrored my own as he shattered the lunar prison with a violent burst of dark energy and retreated towards the battlefield below us.

Relying on magic alone was a losing proposition. He would counter everything I threw at him until I was utterly spent. He was merely biding his time, waiting me out until he had the last magic standing.

It was time to join the fight and confront him in the heart of the battlefield to probe for chinks in his armor. Sword in hand, I marched down the blood-soaked slope, Carter and Chaos at my side.

The battle raged on. Monstrosities clashed with shifters and shadow warriors, their blood spraying the earth. Bodies flew through the air in every direction.

Chaos, a wicked grin plastered across his face, launched himself into the fray with a zeal both terrifying and mesmerizing. His deadly artistry was fluid and swift, his limbs a blurry ballet as he met his opponents with graceful precision. He seemed to feed off the vicious turmoil that surrounded him, the death energy, as if the battlefield was his own personal playground.

Each strike he delivered was a work of brutal mastery, a macabre dance of the dead that left his enemies reeling. As he moved, his form flickered and shifted, a living shadow that danced in and out of literal chaos, toying with those who sought to take him on.

A strange sensation prickled my skin. An unmistakable aura permeated the deathly air. My heart hammered in my chest. *Horror's essence.*

I skidded to a halt, Carter colliding into my back. I searched the battlefield for my father. There were no signs of him, but I couldn't shake the feeling that he was near, lurking just out of sight.

The battle raged on around me, a maelstrom of violence that clanged and crashed everywhere at once.

Three Pyroskulls ignited into existence directly in my path, flaming skulls and fire-whips included. If they thought their little tricks would intimidate me, they were sorely mistaken.

My magic pulsed in response, latching onto their cores like

a steel trap. The Pyroskulls recoiled in fury as I took control of their fire source and guided it against them, lashing their faces with their own whips.

Carter watched the spectacle unfold with a smirk, nearly bursting into laughter. In the next breath, he dove into the battle.

Yeah, okay, it's a little funny.

I clenched my fists, slowly sucking the fire out of the Pyroskulls' cores. Two collapsed as their whips fizzled out. The third recovered and lunged at me. Its whips spun out of control, roasting a couple of unsuspecting Galeswifts into barbecue.

The Pyroskull's eye sockets glowed with malice as it opened its jaws. I slammed my sword through its skull and guided the whips to tangle up its legs. Mist magic surged out of me, reducing the fiery beast to a smoldering pile of ash.

Three beasts down, a few thousand more to go. The night was still young.

A ball of fire burned across the sky like a comet. Horror descended from the clouds above. His eyes scanned the battlefield until they met mine. Every sort of emotion stirred within—fear, anger, hope. Hope he would help keep Chronus from getting to the Seal, anger he had taken his sweet time while good people fought and died, fear that his presence meant the prophecy was marching toward its inevitable conclusion and Chronus was just the catalyst.

Horror unleashed a torrent of incomprehensible syllables

that cascaded from him like a vocal hailstorm. The Eternal warriors keeled over as if their legs buckled beneath them, teeth clenched, eyes bulging.

All around the battlefield, humans and beasts fell to their knees. Chronus, Chaos and I were the only ones left standing. The blood language had no ill effect on us.

The bloodpath that connected me to Horror and Chaos lay wide open. Chaos's gaze snapped to mine, his expression a mirror of my own apprehension. He had felt it too.

"Please, Father, don't screw this up for me," I pleaded.

Horror's voice came in a whisper. *"Your dad is here to help squash that Eternal shit stain, my precious daughter. Our family matters can wait."*

"Daddy wants the Seal," Chaos hissed inside my head.

"Better him than Chronus," I hissed back. My own words startled me, perhaps more than they did Chaos. *"Father, don't make me fight you."*

Horror laughed.

The energy around us shifted. Chronus had focused his attention entirely on Horror. As Horror's feet touched down on the blood-soaked soil, the kneeling fighters seemed to hold their breath for a moment, anticipating the cataclysmic clash that was about to unfold.

Horror reached behind his back. "Looking for this?" he said.

In his right hand, the Seventh Council Seal glowed like an amethyst stone. A whirlwind of energy hummed around it.

How in hell?

With a sly, knowing grin, Chronus raised his hands and muttered an ancient Eternal incantation. The words reverberated like the mournful toll of a funeral bell.

The massive Terraclaws surged to their feet, liberated from Horror's hold. More erupted from the earth, hewn from stone and clay, each one pulsing with the dark energy of Chronus's spell.

They advanced upon Horror, a relentless tide of beastly earthen forms. My father unleashed a devastating bolt of raw energy, aimed to obliterate them, but Chronus's spell veiled them, repelling the forceful attack.

They lashed out with razor-sharp precision, tearing at Horror's shield. His power crackled and flashed like lightning, but the sheer number of Terraclaws threatened to overwhelm him.

"Father, it's a trap." The warning shot along the blood-path, but somehow failed to land. Chronus had managed to intercept it.

The Terraclaws forced Horror back, step by grudging step. His magic flared, slicing through Chronus's spell and reducing the first line of beasts to rubble.

Still more came—an endless, churning tide under my uncle's command. His eyes ignited with a violet flame as his hands wove intricate webs of dark magic to entrap Horror.

Panic gripped me. I tried to move, but my feet might as well have been rooted in place, as Chronus's staggering spell clawed at my very essence.

Caught between the ravenous horde and Chronus's pulsating force, Horror spun, searching for an escape route as his shield began to crack under the unrelenting pressure.

Invisible shackles encased his limbs, winding like chains around his wrists and ankles. Even as he struggled, the restraints held fast, lifting him off the ground. Horror was suspended in midair, rage twisting his features.

A roar shook the mountain as Chronus, face lit with triumph, drove his Terraclaws into a final surge.

Chronus commanded not only the combined power of the Eternals but also that of the entire necromantic sect. He had meticulously crafted a trap, and Horror had walked straight into it. Isadore had the right idea staying away.

My own magic felt stifled, suppressed—I was no match for Chronus in this weakened state.

If Horror didn't find a way to counterattack, we'd be done for. And if he did manage to retaliate, would he take the Seal and flee? Worse, would he try to murder me?

He met Chronus's gaze with defiance. "The Eternal Magistrate has turned to the foulest dark arts. And they call *me* the Dark One? There can be no mercy for you when it is known by all," he bellowed.

"YOU SHOULD HAVE VALUED THE LOYALTY OF THE NECROMANCERS INSTEAD OF CASTING THEM ASIDE FOR YOUR UNWORTHY DAUGHTER."

Chronus cared nothing for rules or restraint anymore. He would reorder the entire universe to suit his purposes.

He whipped his hand in the air. Boulders and earth took flight as gaping chasms erupted, disgorging fresh legions of Terraclaws. The conjured abominations stormed onto the battlefield. Their imposing forms, wrought from the land itself, trampled onward, heralding devastation with every thunderous step.

Petrified, I watched as the Terraclaws set their sights on Chaos. His deafening roar cut through me, and my chest tightened with the urge to defend him. They tore into him as one, their jagged limbs ripping through his flesh.

I pulled all the magic still left in my core to unleash an electric torrent upon them, but their shield held strong.

Chaos ignored his injuries and kept fighting. He crushed the skull of one Terraclaw with a thrust of his sword and swatted another away with a powerful backhand punch, but the Terraclaws kept coming, unrelenting and tireless, inflicting excessive damage on his body.

In an instant, Chaos vanished, only to reappear a moment later as his blue smoke fizzled out, strangled by the dark magic of the Timekeeper. The Terraclaws swiftly assembled walls of rocks, entrapping Chaos within.

Chaos bellowed his rage.

Sensation rushed back to my frozen limbs. Adrenaline surged through my body, igniting a primal fury that sliced through Chronus's spell. I bolted across the battlefield, racing to reach Chaos, navigating the mangled bodies and jagged wreckage scattered in my path.

200 feet. I can make it.

Chasms opened under my feet. I dodged them as best I could. Rocks tore free from the slopes, thundering down on me. A huge boulder smashed onto my path. I crashed against it, stubbing my toes and smacking my knees and face directly into its hard surface.

Damn! That hurt.

I got up, ignoring the searing pain, and sprinted on.

100 feet.

Chaos exploded out from the rocky prison. The Terraclaws pounced, their gargantuan forms obscuring him from view. The ground fractured and split, barricading his escape path.

No! 50 feet.

Chronus lifted his hands, unleashing a stream of necromancy that ripped the flesh open on Chaos's face and hands.

I vaulted over a gaping sinkhole and rolled onto my feet next to my brother. The sight of his mutilated body rattled me.

"Chaos!" I yelled, my heart breaking.

The Terraclaws shifted their focus to me, their momentary hesitation mirroring Chronus's uncertainty. Going after Horror and Chaos was one thing—targeting a mist rider presented a much more complex challenge.

A thin wisp of mist swirled around Chaos's eyes and

mouth—a sign of his etheric essence slipping away. Chronus had poisoned him with toxic magic through the Terraclaws' blows.

His lips quivered as he tried to speak.

I gripped his hand firmly. "Don't talk."

"The Seal... get the Seal..."

Chaos's essence flickered, fluttering away. Desperate, I tried to grasp it and force it back into his body. Every ounce of magic within me strained to keep him alive, but I didn't have that power or knowledge.

I let my thoughts cease. I was all raw, bleeding instinct now. My essence stretched up the slope and into the depths of Ideon Andron, latching onto Anya's etheric core.

I tugged at her magic. Time crawled to a near standstill. My own breath echoed in my ears, drawn out and distorted.

Chronus stared aghast as I harnessed the chronomaster's power to wrap a time veil around Chaos and me. The Timekeeper's lips parted, but no sound came out, powerless against the devastating effect of halted time.

Chronomancy surged into my core. I absorbed it all, melding it with my own magic. With painstakingly slow tugs, I pulled at the temporal thread, rewinding it second by excruciating second, determined to reverse time all the way back to before Chaos was mortally wounded. I didn't give a fuck how it would affect the timeline.

Time inched backward at a glacial pace.

Three seconds, four seconds, five...

I breathed slowly, my exhales resounding in the stillness.

Horror observed me through half-closed eyes, unable to break his invisible chains to intervene. The Terraclaws continued to assail him, but they couldn't damage his etheric essence.

That's right, only I can kill Horror.

He'd have to wait his turn. First, I'd tear my great-great-uncle apart.

Seven seconds, eight, nine...

A scraping sound echoed behind me—again and again, like the repetitive pawing of a hoof against the earth. My head swiveled slowly, as if submerged in a sea of jelly.

Across the battlefield, leaves, grass and branches turned black. A rider astride a massive black steed emerged from a portal. Clad in ebony armor, visored helmet, boots and epaulettes, the rider advanced, each hoofbeat ticking like the hand of a clock.

The steed's nostrils exhaled a viscous dark mist. Behind the rider, a trail of black smoke unfurled like a sinister river.

The rider removed his helmet. My breath caught as his familiar features came into focus, his unfeeling eyes piercing my very soul.

Winter.

He unsheathed the heaviest sword I had ever seen, its obsidian blade gleaming like black silk.

The Nightbringer is already here, scrutinizing your vulnerabilities.

The time veil had no effect on him. He was a living night-mare, a harbinger of doom and destruction. He raised his sword. His face was blank without a single trace of the affection he once held for me.

My defenses faltered, and before I knew it, Chronus had breached the time cocoon.

He sneered at the Nightbringer, arrogance dripping from every word. "Kill all three, the entire cursed bloodline. Start with the rider."

The Nightbringer leveled his blade at me, slowly, as if deliberating which part of me to chop down first.

"Do you know why he is here?" Chronus taunted. "I summoned him right after our last conversation. I gave you the choice, Aurora."

A betrayer will soon be discovered among those you call allies.

"You promised to protect me with your life, Winter," I said. "You said that your feelings were profound. If any of it was real, remember, I love you."

I spoke the words, but their meaning drained away. My heart was winding down. I could not withstand much more of this pain.

Despite my repeated attempts, I failed to summon my mist magic—his oppressive force was paralyzing.

The Nightbringer remained unmoved. His glassy eyes darted about in their sockets.

"You said I was more important than your feelings," I

went on through welling tears. "I believed you. I thought you'd move heaven and earth for me."

The cruel killer moved closer, the tip of the blade aimed at my chest. In a blur, the sword flew out of his hand.

I closed my eyes, anticipating the icy steel piercing my heart.

Chronus gasped, pinned now to a tree, impaled by the very sword I expected the Nightbringer to plant deep into my chest.

And therein lies your greatest advantage. For while he seeks to infiltrate your spirit, he shall inadvertently reveal his own nature to you.

Winter dismounted. He snapped his fingers. A magnificent white horse walked through the mist of the portal.

A mist horse!

Winter, already back on his own horse, locked his wild eyes onto mine before rocketing away. He was not the man I knew and loved. I didn't know if he would ever be.

The mist horse approached me, its ethereal silver mane flowing in an invisible breeze. As I reached out and touched him, a surge of morning power flowed between us, forging an instant bond that felt like an electric shock.

My heightened senses alerted me to movement behind me. I spun around. Chronus had unpinned himself from the tree, the sword that had impaled him now clattering to the ground.

He conjured a sphere of pulsing light in his hands so

bright it almost blinded me. With ruthless precision, he directed it at Horror.

Horror's essence dimmed for a moment. The Seal leaped from his hands into Chronus's grasp as if summoned by the light. With a triumphant laugh, Chronus tore his way out of my time cocoon.

He brought his hands together, the Seal shimmering with energy. Aetherway, the mystical bridge between our realms, materialized with an ominous hum—a spectacular arching structure of wrought iron and glass, stretching towards the sky.

If Chronus crossed into the Eternal Halls in possession of the Seal, the world would fall.

Vaulting onto the mist horse's back, I felt our magic intertwine. My spirit soared with the burgeoning potential as I drank in the comforting warmth spreading throughout my body.

Isadore pierced through the time veil, splintering it into fragments. The frozen timeline began to chug along again. She spotted Chaos and ran to him.

"I halted time for him," I told her. "He was dying. What took you so long?"

"If Chronus sensed me on the battlefield, he wouldn't open Aetherway."

Right, the damned prophecy.

Chronus had reached the bridge. For a moment, everything went still. His figure was framed by the glowing gateway which shimmered with a brilliant silver light.

"He's out of our reach now," Isadore said. "The only way to stop him is to seal the bridge after he crosses it, so he can never cross back."

"How?"

"Leave Emrod to me," she said. "Go."

I urged the mist horse forward, and he tore across the battlefield at a breakneck speed. The landscape blurred around us. A horde of beasts stood in our way. With a ferocious neigh, the mist horse burst over them like a bolt of lightning.

I was nearly at the bridge when I spotted Horror sprinting across it, chasing after Chronus and the Seal.

No, Father! Get off the Aetherway!

My mother's voice penetrated the mists of my mind. *"Seal the bridge."*

I hesitated as Horror charged further up the bridge.

This is how I stop him, a fate worse than death, stripping away his access to the mortal world.

I didn't want that. I couldn't.

"Time is running out, Aurora," my mother pleaded. *"Chronus has the Seal."*

The mist horse snorted, his ancient power surging through me to infuse every fiber in my core. I reached out and grabbed Chronus's mind. It was so easy I laughed. I could have crushed his mind like an eggshell. I felt his initial resistance dissolve into panic.

He turned around, and our gazes locked. In that brief

moment, he understood that I held complete control over his fate.

You are a small god, engorging yourself on hate, and I am humanity.

I drew his magic to me like pulling the string on a ball of yarn. I could sense the individual threads of magic as they spun like a pinwheel around his essence, surrendering their secrets to me.

I directed all that magic at the Aetherway bridge. It began to spark and shimmer, quickly turning into a colossal exile vortex. The vortex swirled around the bridge, absorbing every bit of its matter.

Horror froze as I met his gaze. His etheric essence traveled across the bloodpath like a kiss on my face. He smiled coyly, his hand coming to rest over his heart.

Tears spilled down my cheeks.

Goodbye, Father.

The Aetherway collapsed in on itself in a violent storm of splintering light until nothing remained but emptiness.

The vortex sealed itself shut, cutting off access to the Eternal Halls and effectively ending any chance Chronus would have to use the Seal.

Chronus's troops fled in a panic as shifters, shadow warriors and Valkyries secured the mountain. In the distance, I caught sight of Winter slicing the Terraclaws in half like they were made of butter.

Isadore walked to me with Chaos trailing behind with

a limp. I fell into her arms, unable to stop the tears from coming. She embraced me gently, cradling my head against her bosom as she ran her fingers ever so tenderly through my hair.

"I'm so sorry, my love," she said, her voice soft as air.

I hugged her so tight for this heartbreak and all the heartbreaks she had missed, all those lost years and all those lost dreams. Mine and hers, my dear mother, the lone Eternal spared the unbearable loneliness of the banished Eternal Halls.

Chapter 27

THE BRIGHT SUNLIGHT STREAMING through the windows of the Forever Palace felt too harsh. I shut my eyes to ease the unsettling feeling in my stomach. My ears still rang with the fading echoes of a hard-won battle.

I should feel relieved—I was alive, I wasn't sitting on the Eternal throne, Chronus no longer posed a threat, and the prophecy had been fulfilled without a direct confrontation with my father. For a second, at the end, I could have sworn he had accepted the inevitable. When he looked at me from the Aetherway bridge, something in his eyes told me he was almost at peace with it.

Yet, nothing felt right. My skin prickled. The battle cries in my ears blurred into a buzz. When I opened my eyes, the grandeur of the palace felt oppressive instead of comforting.

I forced myself to walk around the room. One step, then another. *Don't think about the haunting sights and sounds of what happened. Don't think at all. Just move.*

I blinked fast to clear the salty threat of tears. A crystal clock hung on the wall across the room. I stepped closer. The hands on the face of the clock moved erratically, pausing, speeding up, then slowing down, as if responding to my shifting emotions.

I was drowning in a sea of contradiction and unvoiced guilt. Part of me held out hope that Winter was not the Nightbringer, not in the unfeeling way the legends had painted him, and in that tiny corner of my mind, he strolled through the palace gates to offer an explanation.

The rest of me knew better. I had seen what he had done, witnessed the cold, dismissive glance he had cast my way. He had embraced the role of the night rider completely.

The clock ticked on, uneven and unsteady, measuring time I no longer kept. I had no choice but to accept the obvious—I never really knew Winter at all.

I tensed as Isadore approached behind me. She smelled of spring rain and dew-kissed grass at dawn, much like her kingdom.

"Did you get any sleep?" she said softly.

I turned to face her. "Does it matter? I'll survive even if I never sleep again."

"Even Immortals need sleep to maintain their vitality, Aurora."

I shook my head. "That's not my name."

"It is a name that carries immense responsibility. In time, you will come to see it as the extraordinary gift it truly is. Use it well, Daughter."

I bit back the bitter laugh that tickled my throat. "A gift?

I just condemned my own father to eternal banishment. I know he was awful and dangerous, but he cared for me in his own way. I see that now." My voice sounded hollow to my own ears.

She cupped my face with her hands. "It was the only way to shield the world from darkness—to safeguard those we hold dear."

"Did your scouts... any word of Winter?"

"No." There was some sadness in her eyes but mostly relief. "He's gone."

The harsh truth echoed through my heart with every breath. Winter was the Nightbringer through and through.

"Now you know the truth about him. You can move on," Isadore said.

"Move on? Do you understand love? Trust? Ever cared for someone deeply, genuinely, when you were young, maybe?"

She sighed. "My mother counseled me once and now I'll counsel you. Power is a beast that you can either tame or reject. Whatever path you choose, be certain it's one you can walk every day, Aurora."

Every word she uttered felt like an ending. I should feel grateful, make an effort for her sake.

"Where is Chaos?" I said.

"Gone." She paused, her gaze unfocused as if forgetting my presence.

"What is it?" I said.

She offered a wistful smile. "I asked him to stay with me."

So, he had turned her down. Whatever they once shared, he wanted none of it now.

I saw myself in her silence. I was wrong. Isadore understood both love and loss.

A WEEK LATER

My eyes snapped open, taking in the details of my dim apartment. A sliver of sunlight slipped through the curtain. The patter of rain mixed with the screech of tires echoed in the background, causing me to tense.

Too loud. The window was open.

I tried to stay calm as my hand reached for the enchanted sword next to me—Winter's gift from our little heist of the Swedish History Museum in Stockholm.

Ears perked, I listened as soft footsteps neared my bed.

I spun and landed a kick to the intruder's stomach, my muscles flexing, before leaping off the bed, sword ready. A hand grabbed my left arm. I pressed my sword to his throat, our eyes locking.

"Winter?"

My kick had barely fazed him. His eyes pierced mine, his chest close, as we both breathed heavily.

The blade nicked his throat and a ribbon of blood dripped

down his shirt. His eyes looked feral, but otherwise he looked totally... Winter.

"What the fuck are you doing?"

"Checking your reflexes," he said, his grip on my arm unwavering.

"I could have killed you."

"That's right, you can kill Immortals now."

"And corrupted mist riders."

He loosened his grip. "Ouch. I walked right into that."

"Where have you been?"

"At the Eternal Springs in Norway. They've kept me in the light for centuries, staving off the darkness."

"And when the connection between the Springs and the Eternal Halls is fully severed?"

He averted his eyes. "I don't know. I came to say goodbye."

By wrapping the Eternal Halls inside the exile vortex, I had essentially damned Winter to eternal darkness.

I stepped back, still clutching my sword. "What are you exactly?"

"Not your average Joe," he said with a bittersweet smile.

"No, you're not even an average Jonas. You should have told me."

"You had enough on your calendar, Luna. The weight of that information would have pulled you down."

"Nothing would have pulled me down. We were in this together. I could have helped you. It was my place to help you."

"But that's just what you did. You helped me stay on the path of light. And there was never anyone less deserving than me."

I stared at him intensely. "That's a true fact."

He grinned, wiping the blood from his neck with the back of his hand to reveal unblemished skin underneath. "I like that you don't hold any punches, Luna Mae. By the way, that term *true fact* is redundant, don't you think?"

I hated that he sounded so much like Winter still. "Not as redundant as your constant deception."

I sheathed my sword, my eyes never leaving his.

Silver sparks danced in his gaze. "You can ask me anything."

"Where would I even start?"

"I don't remember what happened to me or when," he offered. "In case you're wondering. It's true, I was a mist rider once, but I have no recollection of that time. I absorbed too much dark energy when I fought against the Titans and the ancient gods of evil, but I'm not the terrifying Nightbringer the legends describe. It's taken me an immense amount of willpower to keep the darkness controlled. I never lied about that part."

No, I guess he didn't.

My head was spinning. I wanted to touch him, to feel his warmth against my skin once more, however irrational that desire was. "When you purposely stayed mortal as long as you did... it wasn't for me, right?"

He sighed. "I was trying to stay off the radar. The war was approaching, and the Eternals would have no use for me if I was but a mortal."

"You found my mist horse," I said. "I could have never banished the Eternals without him. You still cared, even after Chronus summoned you."

"It took an enormous effort not to succumb to his dark will," he admitted. "Until the very end, I wasn't sure I was going to be able to resist."

"What about us?" I asked.

"Us?"

"Our attraction... Was any of it real? Or were you just hoping that sleeping with another mist rider might chase the darkness away? My mother suspected there was a black hole inside you feeding on morning magic."

He looked at me with weary eyes. "Were you not there with me? You can't fake that. I don't even know what that thing between us was, Luna. I've never experienced anything like it. That was not the plan. I lost control. I felt intoxicated. I fell in love. The rest did not matter."

His words did not have the effect he intended. The more he talked, the more the frustration and anger boiled up inside me.

Winter sensed my unrest and took my hand. A torrent of magic surged through the room, shimmering with ethereal colors, its sheer force shaking the apartment walls.

We exchanged a glance, both astonished by the intensity

of the power we had just unleashed simply by touching.

The realization struck me with the precision of a sharpened blade. Isadore's words echoed in my ears like a mantra: *Power is a beast that you can either tame or reject. Whatever path you choose, be certain it's one you can walk every day... Use it well, Aurora.*

"You stupid, stupid man. You don't even realize it."

"I'm not following."

"Maybe because you're stupid."

"Is this flirting? Because it's not great."

"No, you're really an idiot. The answer's been right there the whole time."

"What answer?"

"The one where our combined mist energies heal you."

He was the darkness I was supposed to defeat. I was Aurora, the light of dawn, vanquishing the night. My mist essence would purify him.

He shook his head. "Get that idea out of your mind. Move on with your life and never look back. You deserve peace."

Winter for you. Stubborn, dangerous, brooding, infuriating. I would drag his ass back to the light even if he kicked and screamed.

"Either I heal you or I kill you," I said. "I'm not about to leave a fucking night rider loosed upon the world. Not on my watch."

"Using your mist essence to purify mine, will weaken it, Luna. You'll never reach the full potential of mist riders. In fact, you'll lose much of the power you have now."

I sighed. "I understand. The Eternal threat has been thwarted. I trust Isadore to keep the timeline safe. And to be honest, nobody should have that much power, Winter. Not you and not me."

He said nothing.

I took *The Book of Night Rituals* off the shelves and started to prepare. I moved the rug out of the way and drew symbols on the floor inside a circle of salt and crushed gemstones. The air grew thick with the aroma of the cleansing candles known as Essence Embers in the Deep Down. Their pale, flickering flames cast eerie shadows on the walls.

Winter and I sat in the center of the circle, facing each other. Our eyes locked, and I felt our profound union as the light and the dark intertwined and resonated. With a deep breath, I began the incantation I found in the book, hoping the spell would come to life.

Please, please work! Save my shadow warrior.

Energy swirled around and enclosed us, a kaleidoscope of shade and flashing light. The room shook and the air buzzed.

I reached out. My hand touched his chest, right above his heart. My fingers dug into his shirt, my skin glowing with mist energy.

Winter closed his eyes. Pulsing dark energy radiated from his heart, spreading outwards like the spokes of a wheel.

With each breath we took, the energy grew stronger and brighter. His dark energy turned to white light, expanding to fill us with power and clarity, as if the great source was placing us anew in the clean wide world, fresh beings of the earth and of all living things.

The white light contracted and condensed, swirling straight back into the center of him like a vanishing whirlpool.

My mist essence flowed from my body into his, slowly washing away the transference of dark energy that had tainted his core.

The exchange brought a searing pain that threatened to consume us.

The candles went out with a sigh. We collapsed to the floor, gasping for breath.

"Are you okay?" he said. His hand crawled over to find mine.

"I'm not sure, I feel the same."

"Give it time. Our energies need to stabilize."

"Do you think it worked?"

He placed my hand on his heart. "I know it did."

Thank the gods. The choice isn't always between the light and the dark. The choice can be a mix of shades, a union of energies. The answers always lie in the gray spaces in between, in the memories of the then and now, in the distance of the here and there, in the struggle between us and them.

I want my life lived between his eyes and my heart.

Epilogue

THANKSGIVING

Lucia's Thanksgiving feast was a sight to behold. Her table was set with all the traditional trimmings, highlighted by a juicy herb-roasted turkey cooked to a golden hue. Aromas of roasted potatoes and biscuits filled the air, tempting our palates.

In the kitchen, Lucia, Gram, and Celia were hard at work, while Faion, Joey, Lily, Emmet, Winter, and I lounged in the living room, sneaking peeks at the delectable spread. I had invited my adoptive mother, Clara, but she felt weak still and preferred to stay in the Deep Down. Using my last potent mist magic to revive her was my best reason to be grateful this year.

For once, everyone was harmonious and getting along. The only disagreement arose between Lily and me.

"What the hell, Lil?" I protested. "You guys can't just

jet off to Europe for Christmas. It's full of Europeans, you know that, right? You guys should stay here with us. The West Coast chill, sis. Come on."

"Damn, Sophie, don't you have your own damn life to live? Leave those sickening lovesick puppies alone," Faion said, shooting me a warning glance. "And, please, I want to see you talk back to Lily like that when her mom's not around to scold her. One time. Please. Miss bossy's going to get scratched."

Joey hugged him.

Emmet laughed heartily. "That's true. Lily is not one to trifle with. Do not mess with her. Like ever," he said. "And she can swear like a sailor in two languages, three if you count the Urban Dictionary."

Lily shook her head. "Zip it, big guy. I'm classy and elegant. I really don't even know who you're talking about right now."

My smile nearly broke my face.

Emmet took her hand. "Sorry, babe. I was just playing."

"Watch it or I'll take away your favorite toy," Lily said.

A knock interrupted our banter. Sensing Chaos, I got up, still laughing, to answer the door.

Chaos did a sliding dance move when I opened the door, swiftly maneuvering past me into the apartment. He was always overloaded with hyper energy, but this was extra.

"Good timing," I said. "We were just about to dive in."

"Nah," he said. "I can't stay."

"What's got you so hyped?"

He licked his lips nervously, clearly preoccupied.

"You good?" I said. "Everything cool?"

"Yeah, I think so," he said. "I'm taking Chloe on a grand adventure. She hasn't seen much of this modern world. I mean to change that while..."

I nodded as I studied his uncertain expression. I grabbed his shoulder to calm him down. "Relax, she's just a woman, she won't bite."

He shook his head. "I'd feel more relaxed facing off with Genghis Khan and his Mongol Horde."

I chuckled. "You'll be fine. She's so nice. And she likes you."

He turned to go. "Don't forget about Isadore. She will need you."

"Don't worry. I'll visit. I've even invited her to meet my Gram and Clara."

He dashed down the stairs like a man possessed.

"Don't worry, brother," I called out to him. "You got this."

"I ain't got shit," he hollered back before becoming a blue puff of smoke.

We were all changing, adapting and discovering new ways to live. Chloe had struck a chord in Chaos; his desire to protect her was his life's purpose now.

Winter wrapped his arm around me when I took my seat at the table.

All my people were safe and thriving. The future looked bright and I couldn't wait to explore it.

"What was that about?" Winter said.

"Nothing," I told him. "Everything's good."

About the Author

Stella Fitzsimons was born in Athens, Greece, and lives in Southern California with her husband and two sons. After studying economics and language arts she went on to teach both Mathematics and English before launching *Stella's Literary Bistro*, a bilingual literary journal. Her works include: *Luna, Winter, Silver Dust, Shadow Fall, Moonlight Mist* and *The Last Rider.*